The Four Horsemen

Book 2 in the Light Series

Tara Brown

ISBN:-10: 1927866049
ISBN-13:: 978-1927866047

I dedicate this book to the fans.

Thank you to my family and friends for supporting me and believing in me. Thank you to my fans, you are the reason. Thank you to the team at Phatpuppy Design for this great cover. Thanks to my editor for taking this journey with me, love you Andrea Burns!! Special thanks to my kids and my amazing husband. In the short time this has all been going on, you have been very supportive, even when it all consumed me and you had to eat from the freezer. I am sorry about that. To the fans and the bloggers and reviewers, I bow before you.

Lastly, thank you to my Nators!!!!! Best Street team/friends ever!!!

Want to know a secret?

I am on team Constantine, I know I'm not supposed to pick, but there it is.

The White Horse

“I watched as the Lamb opened the first of the seven seals. Then I heard one of the four living creatures say in a voice like thunder, "Come and see!" I looked, and there before me was a white horse! Its rider held a bow, and he was given a crown, and he rode out as a conqueror bent on conquest."

Revelations

One

The sound of hooves beating against the ground startles me. I look around the room but no one moves, they don't hear it. A small, old woman with red eyes gives me an odd smile. Her face moves in a jerky motion, almost like a bird. She puts a gnarled old finger up to her lips. The finger rested upon her lips doesn't stop the smile that is satisfaction in its purest form. She winks slowly, as if she is being slowed down by something, and then she is gone and the beat of the hooves surrounds me again. In the darkness, I see the horses' feet but the dust they stir up in the room prevents me from seeing anything else.

A voice speaks out of the dust and finds me, "Free us, child. Free us so we may free them."

I sit up abruptly, crying out from the ripping as my wings shoot from my back and spread the dust farther. I spin and shoot up into the sky. The room is gone and I am alone with the night's sky, but there riding the cool breeze, I can hear the same whisper, "You will free us."

I glance about, trying to see the man who whispers to me, but there is nothing beyond the darkness of the night and the stars in the sky. I look up at the stars, swearing I hear them whisper too. They sound like the fire witch when they whisper one word.

"RUNNNNNN!"

I open one eye to see a white ceiling. I don't recall where I am for a second, and then as if my brain turns on or switches back from wherever the hell it went, I know I'm safe. I'm on the jet. We are flying from Rio. I have killed two devils and I am only five away from being free of the entire thing. It doesn't help that the last two are my parents, my real parents. There are places in my heart where I love them. Old places that sit in the dark and wait to be loved back. I'm afraid I'll die waiting.

I blink and lift my head to see the grin of a man that makes my heart skip a beat. He hands me a cup of tea, "How was your sleep, love?"

I sit up and clear my throat, "I don't know. I never do."

"How are the dead?"

I smile at him, "I guess they're dead and waiting for me to do something, angel-ish... Is that a word?"

"No." His dark eyes sparkle, "I wonder what magical thing they expect of you?"

I shake my head, taking the tea and sipping softly, "I don't know." Part of me wants to jump him and start something I have very naughty memories of, regardless of never doing it with him. The feelings of every one of my five lives living inside of me have become something of an issue. Sometimes we argue, sometimes we plot ways to get Constantine naked, and sometimes I just wish they would all shut the hell up.

I feel someone next to me move and look over to see Wyatt. My heart skips a beat for him, but then a wave of nausea hits and I smile. Feeling sick around him has become a bit of a trademark. The snarky comments in my brain make me smile. The five of us have a different opinion on the whisper of love residing in my heart. I try to block the other voices out. Personally, I want that Van Helsing, bad. The others want him too, but they don't want sex; they want to peel his skin off. I actually got a visual from Ellie, it was bad.

Wyatt gives me an odd look, "You okay?"

I nod and sip my tea. He takes the cup from my hands and drinks from it. When his fingers brush mine I get a jolt of pain and sickness. He sees me wince, “Wanna handfast again?”

I am about to nod when Constantine makes a noise in his throat. I glance back at him, “Where are we going?”

Mona walks from the back of the jet with a huge grin, “The Alps." She says it like we have discussed it a thousand times; we probably have. She looks giddy, "I have never spent a Christmas away from my mother before. I think this is going to be very interesting.”

Michelle rolls her eyes, “Your mother is probably enjoying her first Christmas without Dick. If I were her, I’d be sleeping with everything that moved and getting drunk. I wish that’s where I was right now. Except maybe not with your mom, Mona. No offense.” She laughs from the seat behind Constantine as she sits up, fixing her blonde hair.

I nod, “Sounds about right.”

Constantine gives me and then her a disturbed look, “Says the nun and the angel. Whatever is this world coming to?”

Michelle giggles, twirling her hair and smiling wickedly. She would jump his bones, dead or not, in a heartbeat. He doesn’t notice the way she stares at him. It makes me smile. She hasn’t stopped wanting him since the moment she met him. She probably never will.

My back feels funny, itchy. I reach behind and notice the new tear in my shirt. My back is scratching on the houndstooth seat. Wyatt slips his hand inside of it and starts to massage the spot where the great white wings shot from.

I look back, ignoring the twitching of Constantine’s lip and the searing of my skin where Wyatt makes contact, “Does it feel different? Is the skin bumpy or hard?”

Wyatt shakes his head and looks inside of my shirt, “There are two marks though.” He lifts my shirt, earning a growl from Constantine. I sigh and shoot him a look. His jaw is clenched and his eyes are dangerous.

Wyatt chuckles, "Easy Fangs, I'm just looking."

Mona sits next to Wyatt, "Oh my God, it's a flower. You have two tattoos, one on either side. A flower that has petals made from inverted hearts and a pyramid in the middle. The All-Seeing Eye is there in the pyramid, you know like in that Tom Hanks movie, *The Da Vinci Code*? I think you just joined the Illuminati, seriously." She looks at Constantine but it is Wyatt who speaks, "The harmony flower. It is a symbol of love, peace, and balance. A Buddhist symbol, if I am not mistaken."

Constantine stands and comes to inspect also, "This is the first time I have seen this. You never had this before, Ellie."

I glance at him, "Rayne." His lips toy with one of his grins. I sigh, "No, I don't recall tats before."

Michelle gets up and I feel like I am on display as they all see it.

"That is wicked. You have wings and insta-tats? Dang dude. I should have sold my soul for some of that shit."

I laugh bitterly but the other three look disgusted at her flippancy with the betrayal.

She blushes, "I just mean, well you know. This is awesome. Way awesome, compared to boobs."

"You love your vagina," I sigh and get up, "But instant tats is annoying. All of it is. I just want this to be over so I can start the term fresh and clean of it all."

When I get to the bathroom, I look in the mirror at the beautiful tattoos and nod, "At least they're pretty." They are. The flower petals are light purple and the pyramid is yellow. They are delicate, and if anything, they improve my back.

I look back out at the four of them and laugh, "You guys look weird." They do. Constantine looks like he might eat Wyatt, which would be a disaster for all of us. Wyatt looks like he might try to make out with me at any moment and Mona looks scared. Michelle looks jealous. She sort of always looks that way now. Everything is always about me and it drives her insane. Little does she know, I would trade with her in a second. I hate being the spotlight girl.

Mona gives everyone a glance, "I seriously can't help but wonder about this all. How did Lillith get pregnant, and how did the virgin end up with you, and then how did you end up in an orphanage? None of this makes sense, Rayne. It doesn't add up. You are an angel this time, and it feels like the first time to you? Why is that? Why didn't you have wings when Lillith and Lucifer were your parents the first time?"

I sit at the back of the plane and watch them, "I don't know. I guess because I never fought before. My father surprised me the first time. The second time he told me I had to die to save my mother. It was the only way. I believed him, but still I didn't want to die. The third and forth time, I was born of a virgin when the world got so sick that nothing else could help it. Both times I died before I could fight back. The fourth time was especially..." I meet Constantine's eyes, "Awful." He nods slowly. I look down, "This time it would seem that I am theirs, but why did my mother give me up? Why didn't she keep me in the garden and keep me safe?"

Constantine cocked a dark eyebrow, "Could it be that the elusive virgin who left you at the orphanage was your mother, and she never kept you in the garden because you have no soul? You couldn't stay there; only the pure may enter."

I open my mouth to answer, but it is impossible for me to know that. I close my eyes and try to remember her face. Dark hair and dark-grey eyes like mine. Her face was creamy and beautiful. She was a sight, delicate and stunning. It was no wonder my father loved her so. I nod, "She was young the last time I saw her, no more than twenty in looks."

When I open my eyes, Michelle looks confused, "Your father too. He was handsome and young. I didn't believe he was your dad. He was so beautiful."

I nod, remembering his face all to well. "They don't age then?"

Constantine snorts, “Do any of us?”

Wyatt snorts, “You look a little weathered.” Constantine fights something, maybe the urge to murder.

I laugh, "He's right. I think you are a little older."

Constantine's eyes flash hatred at Wyatt, but when they land on me, his lips toy with the grin that makes me squeeze my thighs together. “Well, I have only you to thank for my wrinkles and gray hair. Stress ages even the strongest of immortals.”

I laugh at him. He doesn’t look a day over thirty. He is handsome in a way that makes me want to undress. Michelle too. I can tell when she looks at him. Mona gets a little overly excited sometimes too, even she can't fight what he is.

Wyatt sighs, “Not that I am against spending our time on Constantine’s wrinkles, but maybe we should spend a little more on the possibility that your mother might be the same as mine.”

I scowl, “What?” Oh God, what does that even mean? Could we be related? No, I know his mother is Gretel.

Mona nods, “Yeah, that’s probably true. That actually makes sense.”

I scowl, “No, it doesn’t. I know his mother is Gretel and I know mine is not.”

Mona sighs, “Your mom might be bad like his mom, Rayne. She might have let Lucifer impregnate her. She might have a plan.”

Their words burn a little, making me scowl, “She was tricked by my father. The nixie trust her, so I do too. She wrote me the letter telling me to kill the devils and then come and kill her. She is willing to die for me.”

Wyatt gives me his smirk, “The sea witches are not the pillars of goodness you are assuming they are.”

Constantine points at him, “I can't believe I am going to say this, but the young whippersnapper has a point. I think we should tread lightly where both of your parents are concerned, my love.”

I sigh, "You said you know my mom. You are the one who said that she was good."

He nods, "Was, and I am a terrible judge of character. I have no soul. Your mother is a beautiful woman, that's about all it takes for me to believe her. And I don't know her currently. I knew her, past tense. I've not seen her in a long time. The communication I have with her now is through the fae only."

Wyatt folds his arms, "She isn't seeking you out either, Rayne. She is as much to blame for it all as your father is. I bet that's why she hides with the fae—protection from God."

Michelle frowns, "Why doesn't God just smite them both?"

Wyatt shakes his head, "He can't. He is impotent on this Earth. Why do you think he lets children starve and die? Why do think he lets sin happen? He is not almighty on this Earth, except in belief."

Michelle shakes her head, "And you say you're a Christian."

Wyatt laughs, "I'm not a Christian, my faith is much older than that. Much older than Christ or man-made churches where tithes pay for worship and forgiveness. A building does not hold my beliefs and my power is from God directly. He can help us or hinder us through his angels. He may not reign over our physical bodies, but he has absolute power over our immortal souls." Wyatt's tone drops off, like he is heeding a warning.

Michelle cocks a perfectly-plucked and penciled brow, "Hmph, that sounds alarming, like blasphemy, for reals."

Mona puts her hand up between them, "No, my God, stop. We don't want to talk about church. Have you never heard the expression, Jesus save me from your followers? Like damn. No one wants to be churched to death on a jet. Let's focus on the important stuff, like Rayne's mom being evil."

I feel injured by the mother I do not know, but I can't help the want to love her; she sent me to Willow. Willow was good. I clear my throat, "She tried to stop my father. She isn't to blame for this. She got tricked, the same way Michelle did. That is all. The nixie love her and trust her—they wouldn't help her if she was evil. She let Willow raise me. Willow was all goodness."

Mona opens her mouth but the captain speaks over her words, "Fasten your seat belts. We are about to land in Switzerland."

Constantine comes to me and sits next to me, placing his hand over mine. The feel of his skin against mine sparks memories. I think that is his goal, "I can't wait for you to see the chalet."

Something about the sentence is familiar. I look towards the window and close my eyes. His touch sends chills up and down my spine. His body writhing against mine as his lips press into my throat, grazing my skin. His hot breath and strong body cover me, every inch of me.

I exhale roughly and look at him with desire taking over my face. He smiles sweetly, "Bit of a daydream, love?"

I laugh, headily, "You are cheating, sir."

He growls, "I do like it when you call me sir."

I wink at him, "I remember."

He looks like he might ravish me any second but I shake my head, "We still have three devils and both my parents to kill. Don't go getting any funny ideas about you and me. I don't need the distraction."

He leans in, brushing his lips against my cheek, "All I'm asking for is one night." I see his eyes lower to the armrests and a slow smile creeps across his face, "You scared?"

I swallow hard, "Just stop, okay?" I shudder and prepare to land. As odd as it sounds, I don't like flying. Even though I have wings and a serious suspicion I can fly, I don't like it.

As we land, I have the strangest sensation, like I have something brewing inside of me.

We walk as a group, a herd, a family. A broken and strange family, and all I have left in the whole world, besides a father who would let me die horribly and a mother who neglected me.

Regardless of being her champion, I cannot forget that she left me. She always does.

The airport we land at is small and private. Being with Constantine has perks, avoiding customs is one of them. As we cross the small building, a woman in a stunning red dress meets us at the exit. She gives Constantine a smile that makes me nearly gag.

"Brother, you brought more guests than I anticipated."

He laughs, "Stella, this is Rayne. You, of course, recall her as my Ellie."

My jaw drops. Of course. She had black hair, not white-blonde, and she is tanned, not stark white, but the face is the same. The slim, strong body is identical. She beams at me, "Ellie, my precious sister. At last we have you back."

I leap at her, hugging her hard. "Stella!"

She wraps around me, "I have missed you, Ellie."

I could almost cry, I have missed her so badly and never even knew it.

When I let go of her, Wyatt steps closer to me. Her fangs drop and blue veins creep along the ashen skin under her bright eyes. She hisses, "You bring a present for me, Constantine?"

He laughs, "Oh how I wish I could leave him in your care, my fair sister, but alas the young Van Helsing is part of the cause this time."

Wyatt crosses his arms, "You couldn't take me and we both know it, mistress of Satan."

Constantine rolls his eyes, "Did I mention he is also very humble? All about the cause, this one."

Her blood-red nails grow into claws as she points at him, "What about Vlad? What about Mother and Father? What about Stephan? You would side with one of his kind and betray our blood again?"

I cock an eyebrow and glance at Mona. What does she mean again? Mona interrupts my thoughts as she stifles a laugh, "This is like dinner theatre."

I laugh aloud but none of them even crack a smile. Wyatt takes the great offense as seriously as they do.

Michelle sighs loudly, "Okay, look. You guys can play this out in the courtyard of whatever mansion we're going to. It'll be epic, but like... I'm tired. I have a hankering for some Swiss loving and a sandwich, maybe tuna. Can we go?"

Mona nods, "Not to sound like Michelle on this one, but yeah. This is a bit intense."

Constantine walks over to his sister, "Stella, let's away to the car. We can discuss it there."

Her eyes land on me like bright-blue daggers attacking, "Ellie, do you not recall the way they held you captive? Filling you with poison and pain? How can you allow this? How can you be near him? He is one of Gretel's, if my nose is not mistaken."

“He isn’t like them.” I shake my head, "I don’t know how else to explain it." My eyes are drawn to Wyatt's. I smile when I see his hardened and cocky face. "He isn’t the same as them."

Constantine sighs, almost exactly the way Michelle did, "He is half angel. He isn’t all Van Helsing. You will recall the indiscretion a certain someone had?"

Stella's mouth twitched, "That slut, I knew it. I knew it. I said it and everyone disagreed. He smells like her though, like old whore."

I snort, grabbing Wyatt's arm instantly. His muscles bulge under my hands as he nearly attacks. My hands burn and the nausea is awful, but holding him is better than letting the fight take place in a public place. I whisper, “Please, for me. Don’t do this.”

He growls, "Do not speak of my mother that way."

Stella looks down at her claws, menacingly, "I'll do as I wish, Van Helsing."

Mona grabs Wyatt's arm and drags him off to the side, "Let's go. This is ridiculous."

Constantine and his sister give each other glances. I know they're reading each other's thoughts, they always did. His whole family was able to do it. Now though, they are all that is left of the line.

I look at them both and turn to follow Mona, even though she has no idea where she is going. We both smile when we see the huge black Hummer out in front. She opens the door, "Come on, lover boy. We both know you have to calm down. Where better than the vamp Hummer, to find a nice place to sit and take a few breaths?"

Wyatt scowls at Mona, "You are so weird." Michelle rolls her eyes, "You don't even know the half of it."

Mona gives her a look. In it I see a thousand things, a thousand bad things. Mona is done with Michelle and her selfishness. I can't blame her, but I also can't be angry with Michelle. I have no ability to maintain a proper grudge—flaw in the system I suppose. Plus, I knew Michelle as Michael. I knew the lost boy who was always sad and alone. My heart broke every day for him, and now I have to celebrate her, even if she is overcompensating.

I close the door of the Hummer as I climb into the back with them. Wyatt sits next to me, nudging me, "You okay?"

I shake my head, "I have a bad feeling. It's been this way since I killed the first devil. It's like I'm expecting something bad."

Wyatt laughs sarcastically, "Of course. This whole thing is bad, everything is bad. Look where we are." He wrinkles his nose, "Speaking of which, what's that smell?"

I smell the air, "I don't smell anything. Leather seats?"

Mona shakes her head, "You smelling a devil? I don't smell anything."

Wyatt sniffs around us all, like a hound. I start to giggle, unable to stop myself. He moves around the Hummer until he leans over the backseat. He pulls back quickly, "Gross. What the hell? Why do they have to bring snacks everywhere they go?"

I lean over the seat, "Oh my God, is she dead?" A limp body lies in the massive trunk.

Wyatt shakes his head, "No, she's alive. They cannot eat dead blood. Stake to the heart won't kill them but dead blood, that's the ticket." He runs his hands through his hair, "Well that's the ticket for regular vampires that they make. I think dead blood only makes them sick, really sick."

I nodded, recalling that suddenly.

Mona shakes her head, "I'm not looking. I can't do this shit anymore. This is inhumane."

Constantine gets into the driver's seat. He starts the truck. I scowl, "Why is there a dying girl in the backseat?"

He looks at me in the rearview, "One of you is getting into the passenger seat. What do I look like—Morgan Freeman in Driving Miss Daisy?"

Michelle jumps at the chance. I can see Constantine's eyes narrow as he mumbles something. Wyatt's lips turn up into a grin, like he heard the muttering. He probably did. The guy is part hound, for sure.

Mona points at the backseat, "Dying girl? Let's focus."

Constantine sighs, "Mona, I have to eat. Stella brought me a snack, that's all. I won't kill her. I will reward her for the stealing of her blood."

Mona folds her arms, "I'm not riding in the car with her bleeding in the back. She has already been bitten."

His eyes twinkle, there is evil in them. I see a plan on his lips, but he doesn't speak of it. He doesn't need to. Wyatt looks back at the girl and then back at Constantine with an evil gaze, "You're turning her?"

Two

The chalet is a mansion. How many ways can one man say mansion? He's a psycho if he thinks this is a chalet.

He's a psycho anyway. I smell the air in the back, the girl doesn't smell evil at all.

Mona nudges me as we walk along the driveway to the house, "That was an awkward drive."

I nod, "Why is he making vampires, and why isn't he talking to us about it?"

Mona's eyes darken, "*Why* is all we ever have, Rayne. No one is telling us anything. Don't you think that's weird? They're doing this whole end-of-the-world shit and it's like by guess and by golly. Where is the science and research and planning? It feels a little half-assed, if you ask me."

I nod again, "I think it's all weird and half-assed. The witches and Fitz were the only ones who were actually making an effort to plan."

She gives me a look, "The other thing bugging me—we need to get rid of Michelle. I swear, she's going to sell us down the river again. I have a bad feeling about her."

I can't say I don't have the same feeling, but I've never been big on grudges. Even with Wyatt being an asshole to me, I have never been able to hate him for it. I notice, suddenly, my ability to hate has gotten weaker. With it, my ability to love has too. I don't love Wyatt or Constantine. I don't love anything or hate it, not even Gretel. I say I love things, but the depth is more like puddle deep, and the attachment is not there, not like it used to be. I shake my head, "Better to keep her close maybe."

Mona nods, looking like Blair off *Gossip Girl* more than ever. The scheming face is very Blair.

I force a smile across my face, "We'll have a good Christmas and leave it at that?"

She doesn't look convinced as we walk into the massive great room. The stone fireplace looks comforting. I sit down in front of it on the huge white shag carpet and sigh when the heat bears down on me. I shiver as my back tingles. Stella comes and sits next to me. I forgot about her, completely. I forgot how beautiful she is. I see Wyatt watching her, and I know it is the mesmerizing awe of her beauty. No one can help it.

She clicks a remote and the huge TV in the corner turns on. I give her a funny look, "What are you doing?"

She shrugs, "Just checking the news. I heard some people talking at the airport about a war."

I roll my eyes, "When isn't there a war?"

She puts the remote down when it's on the channel she wants, "Not a normal war." She leans against me; the smell of her is so familiar. It almost relaxes me. I remember being sick and she nursing me back to health. At first she was so angry that he had brought me to the castle, stolen from the Van Helsings. I was sick and dying and soon she saw that. She fed me broth and read to me. I remember her dark curls and beautiful face. I remember the way she always told me that one day we would be sisters for real.

And then I died.

The second time she was part of my life more. I grew to love her more and more.

Now she is like Mona to me, comfortable. Mona comes and sits with us, "Where is the war?"

Stella shrugs, "I didn't hear. My German is rusty and that's what they were speaking."

A journalist with a microphone and a grave look on his weary face, speaks slowly, "It is like nothing we have ever seen. The Palestinians, the Jews, and Christians have slaughtered each other in Jerusalem. For the third time in history, Jerusalem has been destroyed, wiped from the Earth. There is no winner, no clear winner. The UN has made a decision I feel many of us are mystified by. They have chosen not to interfere. Every country has pulled back, choosing to defend their borders only. Americans, British, Canadians, and everyone else have brought their military home. Bases around the world have closed. All military personnel have been flown home in what some are calling the most bizarre forty-eight hours ever lived on this Earth."

My jaw drops. Wyatt comes to the shag carpet, sitting next to me. Even he and Stella behave as we watch the broadcast.

"I have been instructed to be blunt and forthcoming with all details of the situation." The man's face has a look of uncertainty and disbelief. "We are seeing unprecedented movements and strategies by all countries. Everyone is stepping back from it. I have live reports coming in from our journalist in the field, Katherine Little."

The screen splits into a view of him and then a view of a woman standing on a hillside. There is smoke behind her, filling the sky. She pastes a forced smile on her lips but it's delayed almost from what the other journalist has said. "Hi Stan. Behind me is what is left of Jerusalem. The entire city is destroyed. This, two miles away, is the closest I am allowed to get. Reporters are not allowed closer than this, and the few living who have fled the city are being medevaced by private companies trying to help. Everyone here is stunned and disturbed by the choices made by the UN. No one here understands how the slaughter has been allowed." Tears fill her red-rimmed eyes as she stammers, "Th-th-there is a river of blood streaming through the city. Reports of the most bizarre nature have been our only information. I spoke to one witness as she was being strapped into a gurney." Her hand shakes as she lifts the charcoal-stained fingers to her face with a blackened piece of paper up so she can read it, "She said, there was a thundering of hooves on the street. The people stood in awe as a rider made his way through the streets. He had a crown and a bow and he was killing faster than anyone could hide. He killed alongside of things that couldn't be seen. There was fire and destruction everywhere. Again, it was like a war against things that could not be seen."

The screen cuts back to just Stan. He looks scared as he gazes off into the distance. He jerks, as if the studio has told him to talk again, "Thank you, Katherine. That is most disturbing. We have reports of something similar in the Vatican City but no eyewitness testimony. No video footage is coming from the city or Rome at all. We have been unable to reach our Rome correspondent for many hours." I can see tears slipping from his eyes as he pastes a fake smile on his lips, "We will try to keep you updated on the events as they occur. Please pray for the victims of this horrific event."

Stella turned the TV off, but it's not her that speaks, it's Wyatt. "Shit, Revelations, really?"

I frown, "What?"

Mona gives me a look, "Johnny Cash, the pale horse intro to *The Man Comes Around*. The rider is death or something, right?"

Wyatt scoffs, "Yeah well, before Johnny Cash sang about it, it was a bible verse. Jesus." Mona wrinkles her nose at him.

Stella looks lost, "I don't understand."

Constantine comes into the room, "That is because, dear sister, you never cared for scripture. But Uncle Vlad never let me get away with such complacency. I had to learn. The white horse is the first. As the seals in God's hand break, the riders come forth to bring about the end of days." He sips a glass of red wine before he continues, "The white horse is first. He brings with him a bow and wears a victor's crown. He is war, conquest and war."

I swallow hard, "What does that mean?"

Constantine shakes his head but I don't believe him. I don't trust him. I look at Wyatt. He shakes his head, "I don't know. You killing the devils and sending them to hell with the evil should stop the end of days." His phone rings as he speaks. He pulls it out and gets up, "Hello?" He leaves the room.

Constantine sighs, "I agree with young Wyatt, this shouldn't be the sequence of events as long as the devils take their evil with them."

Stella looks at me, "Do we continue to allow her to kill the devils or does she die to save the world?" Her face tells me which she would prefer, and I agree.

I look down, wondering the same thing over and over.

When I look up, Constantine is in front of me. He drops to his knees and tilts my chin up, "The world will end and it will find a way to save itself that doesn't involve your death. No matter what, I say we kill the last three devils, now. We leave now. Before the rest of the world falls apart; kill them before they come for you. Even if they are gone and the whole world dies, you and I will live on together."

I nod, it's selfish but I don't care. I don't want to die. I want to live. I want to feel again. I feel like I am renting my body, not fully experiencing it. The other versions of me are panicking inside of me too. I think it's why I can't feel everything I used to, we are spreading the emotions too thin amongst all five of us.

Stella wraps a slender arm around me, "We will help you, Ellie. No matter what, we want you to live. Let the world save itself."

I nod, "Okay."

Mona gives me a smile too, but I can see the fear in her eyes. Michelle texts on her phone on the couch, not really paying much attention to it all. I smile when I see her pose, "What are you doing?"

She gives me a look, "Snapchatting."

I don't know what that means but she poses again, duck lips this time. Mona rolls her eyes, "That is why the world is ending."

I laugh as Wyatt comes back in, "They want you to turn yourself in. The religious heads have teamed up and spoken to my parents, and they're blaming you." I wince and wait for him to switch sides. He looks at Constantine, "No doubt they were tracing the call—we should go."

Constantine nods, giving Mona a sad look, "Rain check?"

She smiles, "When the world ends and begins again, and no one cares who Rayne is, we will restart Christmas. Make new traditions. Or we will hide up here in the Alps and eat until the end comes for us too."

I feel sick. The other girls inside of me all agree, we feel sick.

Three

The plane lands in Ciudad Juarez. Again, we somehow get to land on some strip that looks like a dusty farm crop. The smell in the air is bad. I am hungry the minute we walk from the plane to the car that is waiting. Tom nods at me. I nod back. He shakes his head subtly. I realize he is nodding at the trunk. I pretend to fix my sock as everyone gets into the SUV. He pops the trunk and a man comes flying out. He looks like he might be Mexican and a little bigger than I am. He tries to run but I jump him, pinning him down. I see sore-like burns on his lips so I don't kiss him. I hover over him and suck his soul from him. He cries out into my mouth as he dies. I moan my exhale, "Wow."

Michelle watches me for a second before scrunching her nose up, "What was he guilty of?"

I shudder as the feelings and images wash over me, "Tom's favorite." He hates pedophiles. This one was also a serial killer. The images of his horrific crimes will sit in my mind, torturing me for the rest of the day. Michelle leans over his dead body, "Look, hash sores."

I frown, "What?"

She points, "He smokes hash. He has sores from the hot knives."

I get up and look down on him, "Ew." We walk to the car. Wyatt looks back out at me, "Really?"

I nod, "I was hungry and he was bad."

He sighs and closes the door. Tom drives and Wyatt does his weird smelling thing.

Stella laughs uncontrollably at it. I frown, "Laugh later, otherwise he won't do it."

Wyatt looks back, "There are a lot of bad people here. I can smell it everywhere. Witches and even a few vampires." He gives Constantine a look. I look at him but he avoids my eyes, "I thought you were the last."

He nods, "We are. Those are abominations."

I don't know what that means, and honestly, I have too much on my plate to worry about them.

We drive for what feels like an eternity. I almost close my eyes but Stella shoves me, "Stay awake, you know what you're like to wake up."

I smile, taking a deep breath and looking at the nasty surroundings. "This place is gross. I always thought Mexico was beautiful."

Mona nods, "This is not on the brochures. They keep this dirty little secret to themselves for sure."

Stella scoffs, "Most of it is. This place is a rat hole."

"STOP!"

Mona moans, "Finally."

Wyatt sniffs the air, ignoring us and our moaning. He points back the way we came from, "That way."

Tom swings the SUV around and slams on the gas

"STOP!"

I turn my head as the car slows to a halt. A warm breeze wafts through the window, carrying with it food, garbage, and pollution.

Mixed in with it there is something else. I'm over Michelle's lap and crawling for the door to the car. The smell has me by the nostrils. It drags me out.

I run, skipping steps and screaming as the wings shoot from my back. A child watches me as the huge white wings take up all the room in her eyes. I can see the reflection of them in her pupils as I run past.

I float up to a second-floor apartment, kicking the door in. A growl tears from my lips.

I don't even know who I am anymore. My eyes scan the place, like an animal's would. I move through the dirty carpet in the front room where the TV is still playing. I see a pot on the stove, boiling rice. The warm air hits me again just as a creak interrupts my thoughts. I look to see a door swinging back and forth as the breeze plays with it.

I'm out the door, leaping and floating through the laundry-filled alley to where I see him. He is running as hard as he can, but the ugly sweater is a beacon.

I get above him. He looks back, screaming as I land on him, taking him to the ground. My sword flies through the air at me from Constantine who is out of breath and standing across from me. I pull it as I catch it and spin. The devil's head rolls down the dirty concrete, still wide-mouthed and mid-scream when it combusts into the pile of black feathers.

It joins the debris and floats down the road, scattering with the warm wind.

I stand there, trying to get my breath too. Constantine gives me a look, "That was different."

I almost smile, but I'm scared of myself and the other girls inside of me are silent. All except the first me. She is excited.

The rest of us are silent.

Wyatt comes to me, pulling the blade from my trembling hand, "It's okay, Rayne. Take a breath."

I do it. I breathe and try to calm down. My heart beats in a way I don't think it ever has and my body vibrates. I can't taste any evil in the air.

Wyatt sniffs the wind, "Third time's a charm, babe. I don't even smell a little."

I nod, "I know. I can't taste any of it." I turn around to see Stella standing, watching me. She has a disturbed look on her face, "You move like them."

I frown, "Like what?"

"The angels."

I don't have a response for it. I don't know if it's a bad thing or not. Her eyes dart to Constantine. He shakes his head in twitches, "She is not like them. Her heart is human."

I almost tell him that with every one of them I kill, I feel my heart close off more, but I don't. It would be the honest thing to do, but I have a bad feeling about it. I feel like I should keep it to myself.

The car ride back is awkward again. I always make it awkward. Wyatt and Stella seem stunned and Constantine seems confused. Mona and Michelle ask about the kill, but I just shrug and say, "He's dead."

We get onto the plane, and when it takes off, I'm not afraid.

That makes me worried.

We land in Karachi, and for the first time, I feel like I'm invincible. There is almost no feeling at all except unwavering confidence.

"You're being quiet."

I look over at Mona and smile, "I feel a little weird. I'm scared." It is the truth; I know I should be scared, even if I can't reach the feeling."

She nods, "Me too."

The small airport smells like Indian food and spices. I like it. It makes me want to eat real food. I like it when I feel normal. Willow always cooked with tons of Indian spices. She was a huge fan of spices and herbs… obviously. Her name feels funny in my mind. She isn't important to the others. Only me. Willow. It's a name I haven't thought of for days. I don't know what to make of that. Am I forgetting her? Are they winning the battle for my mind and heart?

That gets added to the list of things that scare me, even if I don't feel scared.

We drive around in the car with Tom and Wyatt doing their thing. I can feel the heaviness of my eyes. I can't fight it. I hear them shouting at me as the dead take me.

The dream is a mess. Hooves beat the ground around me in a dark room. The dust dances in the dim light.

I don't move. I turtle as they ride around me in a circle, like a cowboy would. Their voices are creepy and crackle like they are smokers. "Free us, Rayne. Free us from the depths and let us fix it. Open the seven seals."

I shake my head and suddenly the dark is gone. I'm standing in the garden at the house inside of the picture where Willow secretly went to meet Wyatt's uncle. Willow is standing next to a bush, picking the flowers off of it. She looks up, smiling softly, "The petals make a calming tea. You can use it to help women get pregnant too."

I look around the garden, noting the clouds are actually painted. The flowers are like paint chips. Willow smiles, "We made a big mistake, Nene." She turns and blows the paint chip petals at me. I jump back and shoot awake. The room I'm in is dark, and I don't know if it's part of the dream or not. I look around, trying to get my bearings. No one else is in the room. I'm on a bed and it looks like a hotel, maybe. I can smell the Indian food and I'm sweating. I think it's real. I get up off the bed, wondering where the dead took me. I remember some of it. I remember Willow's picture.

"Wyatt?"

I hear rustling from the corner where I see someone sitting. It's Constantine, "Why his name first? Why not mine?"

I bite my lip, "I don't know. I just feel like I know him better."

He gets up and walks to me, pushing me back onto the bed. I sit up, "I don't want to do this. It doesn't feel right, I told you."

He climbs on top of me, biting down on my throat. I feel him pull blood from my veins. I scream but Stella is there suddenly. Her lips crush mine in a kiss that makes me uncomfortable. We have never kissed before. They hold me down, kissing and sucking and muffling my screams.

"RAYNE!"

I sit up, breathing heavily, lifting my hands to my throat, but there is no wetness. I have not been bitten, and I don't know why I think I might have. I assume it was the dream I don't remember. I look around at the room, shaking my head. It is a hotel room that I swear I have been in before, but that is impossible.

It's light out and when I look back to the left, Constantine stands over me, looking worried. I flinch when he reaches for me. He looks hurt, "What was that dream? You were screaming suddenly and then you were awake."

I shake my head, "I don't know."

It's true. I don't know. I never do. But I suspect that he hurt me in my dream. I still feel his fangs in my neck for some reason. I just don't want to tell him. I climb off the bed, "Where are we?" My stomach rumbles.

"Karachi, we never got to leave. We found him. Wyatt is there now, watching him. We need to go there." He holds a hand out for me, but I walk past him.

He grabs my arms, "What was the dream?" I shake my head. He shakes me a little, "Tell me."

"I don't know, but I think you bit me."

He shakes me again, "I would never do that to you. Why do you believe them? The dead lie, Rayne. They always have."

"I don't know." I have to assume this is an old fight. I can't find it in my memories, but he looks hurt like it's an old wound. The girls inside of me are silent.

Tom drives us to the place where Wyatt waits with Stella. "Where are Michelle and Mona?"

"The jet. This city is too dangerous for them. Mona was nearly assaulted."

I gasp, "What? How long was I sleeping?"

He gives me a confused look, "Three days. We thought you had slipped away, to the dreamland maybe."

"What about Mona?"

He shrugs, "Stella ate her attacker before he had a chance to get very far with it. Mona was very upset, naturally, and chose to stay on the jet. Once you have done away with our friend, we will be leaving too. The temples in India and Pakistan are under attack. We can't stay long. The world has erupted in religious wars, only the old countries though. America, Canada, and even Britain are safe. But China, Pakistan, India, Tibet, Italy, France, Iraq, Iran, Saudi Arabia, Egypt, Israel, and a bunch more are at war. War within their countries. It is not country versus country; it is within their borders. War against themselves and their beliefs."

My brow knits together, "I just don't understand."

He shakes his head, "None of us do. Even the Van Helsings are at a loss."

Tom parks the car and I smell it instantly. I can taste it in the air. I get out of the car, walking quickly to it, like Toucan Sam following the smell of the delicious cereal. I look around when I lose the smell. A black feather floats past me. I scowl as I see another. I break into a run to see Wyatt and Stella standing surrounded by feathers.

"What did you do?"

Wyatt looks at me from a dark scowl, "What I had to. He tried to flee. He got a phone call and fled."

I look at Constantine, "Does this change things?"

He shakes his head, "I don't know. Does it?"

Wyatt swallows hard, "I don't think so."

I bite my lip, "His evil leaked out a bit. I tasted it in the air."

Wyatt nods, not saying anything. I feel like screaming. What if the evil is back and I am responsible for it.

Constantine shrugs, "His kind are the ones who send you to the depths of hell each time; I would imagine he is able to send a devil there too."

Wyatt's eyes meet mine, "I'm sorry."

I nod. He rarely says sorry, unless it's about the incident but he hates talking about that. A smile finds its way onto my face, "It's not like the world is going to end from it."

Wyatt laughs, tossing my sword at me. I holster it, dripping blood and all, and turn and walk back to the car.

Four

The last devil is easy to find. They all were really. The witches had tracked them, Constantine and his team had located them to exact places, and Wyatt smelled them down like a hound. It is not the effort we assumed it would be. It is the only time it has ever been easy. The combination of earth witches, Constantine, technology, and a Van Helsing has never been used before though.

When we find him, the last devil reeks of destruction and evil. We chase him in an SUV. He doesn't realize we are the ones following him through the streets of Capetown. He's in the backseat of a car that is driving around Capetown. The men in the front seat are firing on crowds of people, with AK47's. When the car stops, the devil stays behind, like he is sucking the evil from the car before he gets out and walks down the alleyway.

Constantine wraps his arm around me to mask the smell of me. We follow the devil until the crowd thins. Then I sprint, jumping onto a barrel on the side of the road, unsheathing my sword at the same moment my wings tear from my back. He doesn't even get a chance to turn as the sword separates his head from his body. He crumples to the ground and becomes a pile of black feathers.

I turn to face Wyatt and Constantine but a wind comes up the alley before I can get a word out. My triumphant smile fades when I can't see past the dust blowing and mixing with the feathers. My feet slide along the cement from the wind pulling me to the funnel that has formed. I step back, trying to get out of the way as the feathers suck up into the air where they're released and become black raindrops.

My body is slammed into the building next to me. Wyatt shakes his head, "We gotta go now." I shudder from the pain and nausea, “We are getting handfasted again. This is bad.”

He smiles and turns, running down the alley. I jump, still holding his hand and lift us into the air with my wings. They flap like a bird's would. I don’t know how I feel about that, but as the black raindrops chase us, one lands on my wing. I wince as it burns. We land at the car. We don’t talk, we get in and Tom drives, fast. Stella, Mona, and Michelle are waiting for us on the jet; it's ready to go.

When we take off, I watch from the window as dark clouds cover the city.

"This is bad," Mona mutters.

I nod, "It doesn’t seem to be working, me killing the devils." My eyes seek out Constantine's. His face is stoic, but I can see the fears wandering about in his eyes. He offers me a smile but I shake my head and from somewhere hear Willow say the words, "We have made a big mistake, Nene." I don’t even miss her calling me Nene. That is a bad sign.

We fly to Britain, landing on a small airstrip outside of London. Constantine hurries to the car waiting for us that he called for. Tom jumps in the driver's seat. We all get in quickly. Tom speeds to the small castle that I recall the second we arrive. My heart skips a beat for the first time in days and Ellie softly weeps inside of my mind.

Stella looks at Constantine with her blue daggers, "You invited the Van Helsings to our home?"

Wyatt nods, "We need to talk to them. They don’t stand a chance against Rayne now. The devils are dead. None of this was the prophecy. They feel betrayed by God too."

Constantine keeps the stoic look going, ignoring both Wyatt and his sister.

I look out the window of the SUV as Tom parks the car.

Wyatt looks at the rain, “We need to stay out of this rain. Everyone hurry.”

We all run inside. I suddenly realize I have my sword in my hand and am face to face with Wyatt's evil mother Gretel and his ex-fiancé Sarah, in the foyer of the large estate. I don’t even recall pulling it.

Gretel laughs. I glare at her.

She shakes her head, "You think I can't hurt you, sin eater? You think I need the sin to weaken you? I can kill you just fine the way you are."

I flex my back, shooting my wings out of my back and ruining, yet again, another shirt. Her eyes widen, "No. It's not possible."

I point my sword at her, "Still feeling confident in your original statement?"

Her face is as pale as my shimmering wings. Sarah stares at them in awe, "So pretty."

Gretel looks at Wyatt, "What did you do to her? Why would you help her this way? How did she become an angel? The world is falling apart and you are to blame for betraying us and helping her."

I can almost feel his anger in the room. His body is completely tight and his voice is eerily soft when he speaks. "Want to tell me about my father, Mother?" He says her name like it is poisonous to his tongue.

Her lips tighten.

He laughs bitterly. I can almost feel the wounds inside of him. "I think not. Don’t you dare tell me any of this is mine or hers. This one is you, you and all the old ones. You people are disturbing. The length you have gone to live by the oaths we swore, and yet, you are nothing but a hypocrite."

She looks defeated. The mention of his father has pulled away her anger and made her small and weak looking. The others inside of me scoff at that notion and remind me not to be fooled by it. I still watch her, but lower my sword, pulling my wings back in, using the mental distraction and relaxation Wyatt taught me. I just wish he could touch me or kiss me without it burning and making me nauseated. I have a longing to soothe him; it's odd since I don't seem to feel anything else.

Stella walks in front of me, looking down on Gretel and Sarah. They both grow wide-eyed. Gretel tries to mask her fear of Stella with a smug smile, "How have you been?"

Stella nods, "Excellent. Seeing the sin eater destroy everything you have banked on has been delightful."

Gretel swallows hard. Constantine pushes his way between us all, "Ladies, ladies. Please. You are all welcome guests. We have matters far more important than this to attend to."

Gretel gives me a sneer. God, I want to feel my hate for her. I know it's in there. She drives me insane. Sarah can't stop looking at Wyatt and then me. Her eyes dart back and forth.

Wyatt steps in front of me completely, "We have something bigger than any war between our kinds. The black rains came, Mother."

Her eyes grow pained and shocked simultaneously as words leave her lips softly, "Then the Red Horse is also upon us."

The Red Horse

"When the Lamb opened the second seal, I heard the second living creature say, "Come and see!" Then another horse came out, a fiery red one. Its rider was given power to take peace from the earth and to make men slay each other. To him was given a large sword."

Revelations.

One

The fire is lit and we are huddled around it for heat. The castle is drafty, just as I recall it being. Maria won't stop hugging me, and crying. Regardless of being a vampire's servitor, she is very Catholic. Her desperation and despair at the loss of her religion weighs heavily on her. I wish I had a way of helping her, but I have nothing.

"You have wings now, Miss Ellie. You are the hand of God. You must give me last rights, in case I die. I cannot go to hell for being a servitor."

I kiss her forehead and hug her, "I don’t even know what the words are. I'm not Catholic."

She cries and shakes her head until Constantine comes to her. He tilts her face, so her eyes meet his, "You will not be afraid of the events that are taking place. You will be loyal and strong."

Maria releases me. She smiles, "Would anyone like tea?"

I frown but Michelle nods, "Can I have some liquor in mine?"

Wyatt nods, "Me too."

Mona raises a hand from the sofa, "Here as well."

I roll my eyes and look at Gretel, "I need you to explain it one more time."

She sighs, pacing in front of the massive hearth, "The four horsemen of the apocalypse have long been believed to be a lie. A rumor. A myth. Recent events have obviously proven that wrong. The first rider is conquest and strife. According to legend, he looks exactly as the witness claimed him to be in Jerusalem. Riding a white horse, wearing a crown and carrying a bow. The second rider brings war. Where the first caused nations to segregate themselves, the next horse brings war, nations against each other. The red horse is the destruction of civilization by fire. We are assuming that in modern times that would be bombs."

"What about the other two?" Mona asks.

Gretel shakes her head, "Let's cross that bridge when we get there. If we can find them, we can kill them and maybe the next two won't come. They come in order, and they wait for the horseman before them to finish his task before they come."

Wyatt points at her, "No 'we'. Don't 'we' us. We are not a 'we'. It is us and it is you. I am on the side of my family—this is my family. You lost that right when you tried to kill me, two weeks ago."

Gretel looks hurt, actually hurt. Her cold exterior looks melted. She pleads, with not only her words, but also her eyes, "Wyatt, we are your family. We love you. We made a mistake, asking you to choose between Rayne and us. I see now, we are all on the same side. I put duty before motherhood, and I have to ask you to forgive me."

"BULLSHIT! YOU THINK I WILL EASILY FORGET THE HATRED ON YOUR FACE AS YOU FOUGHT AGAINST US?"

Sarah opens her mouth but he points at her, "SHUT THAT NOW!" She closes her mouth. He turns back to his mother, "YOU STABBED ME, YOUR OWN SON!"

Gretel rolls up her sleeve, revealing a massive burn, "I never knew she could do this. She has never done it before. She has never had wings before. The dead fought for her. Rayne has released the first two of the four horsemen. She is the hand of God, and I believe you that we must help her end her parents. You know what Fitz saw her as, he always did. The churches are wrong, not you. She is the answer, not the problem. It took me nearly dying, nearly losing my son for my beliefs, and nearly plotting with the Catholic Church, to see it. This is the right way. This bizarre group of people you are part of is the answer. I think this strange combination is the answer. We have spent so many years fighting against the Dracula family that we have never considered we were all made for a purpose." She takes a step forward, “And you, my special son, you too were born for a reason.”

Her hateful eyes turn on me, she drops to her knee. I don’t know who looks more shocked, me or Sarah, but she bows her head, "I swear by my sword and my heart, I will die protecting you." I can hear her choking the words out. I almost choke and Mona snorts.

My eyes dart to Constantine. He twitches a no. I look at Wyatt, he does the same. I smile, the smile Willow taught me to use when I wanted to tell someone to eff off. "Thank you. I accept your help."

She rises, smiling. She looks at Sarah, "I cannot tell you what to choose, but what more proof do you and your family need?"

Sarah nods, "I agree. I will fight to help you, Rayne." Her, I actually believe. There is no production with her, and unlike Gretel, I see no demons in her eyes.

Constantine clasps his hands together, "Not that I don’t enjoy seeing you on your knees, Gretel, but let's see if the TV has any idea of the wars starting." Wyatt’s eyes dart open and Michelle and Stella burst out laughing. It takes me a second to realize what he has said.

When he realizes the comment he has made Constantine’s lips struggle with the sinister grin he wants so badly to let loose. Instead, he turns on the TV and instantly we see it. Massacres of tourists in every country, bombings and hate everywhere.

I walk to Mona and sit on the couch next to her. She looks tired and rests her head on my shoulder, "You smell."

I nod, "I need to take a shower, but I'm scared I might get murdered."

She scoffs, "You so will. His mom is gonna roast your ass, the minute she gets a chance."

"Can you believe this?"

Her dark eyes water and her glossy lips tremble when she whispers, "No, and I can't reach my dad or my mom. She isn't answering and his phone isn't even ringing."

I don't have anything for that. What do I say? I hug her to me, "I bet they're safe. They probably have places for people to go. The US is a strong country. We'll be fine."

Constantine comes over to us. He kneels in front of us, "If you reach her, tell her to go to Montana. I have a house there; I've sent you the text with the address."

I start to laugh, "How is it you are more savvy with technology than I am and you're old, like scary old?"

He sighs, "Technically, you're older." My mouth drops open, "Look at you and all the zingers tonight."

"Is the US getting bombed yet?" Mona asks.

He nodded, "There are bombings. She might be at the university. I know someone there; I will see if I can reach her."

Mona looks frozen, scared to move and feel. She sniffles back her tears, "Thanks."

He smiles, "We have to make a plan, Rayne. Your mother is in Ireland or Scotland, if the legends and the sea witches are to be believed. What shall we do?"

I shake my head, "I don't know. I'm more concerned about my father. Why didn't he try to help them?"

Constantine frowns, "Who?"

Gretel must have heard. She walks over, "Yes, why didn't Lucifer assist the devils as you slew them? One would think he almost wanted you to kill them."

I nod, not liking that I am agreeing with her. I still really want to stab her in the eye. I remember Wyatt's father, the angel John. He is always confused as the Book of John. People never realized he was an angel, not a man. The angel of truth and wisdom. I remember when Gretel betrayed him, letting him die. I remember this, and yet, Wyatt is so young. He does not look old enough to be the son of John, but I know he is.

Wyatt sits, "What if it is as the book says it will be? What if the seven seals have to be opened to make the world new and take the spirits of the penitent to God?"

Gretel scoffs, "That is a very inaccurate description of the end of world, firstly. Secondly, that would mean the antichrist and lamb have been born." Her eyes dart to me, "You must be the antichrist this time."

And there it is, his asshole mom calls me Satan. So much for being on my side. Bitch.

I sigh, "I'm not the antichrist, Gretel. I am born of angels, archangels."

She shakes her head, "You have opened the seals, killing the devils must have opened the first five, and we are slowly seeing the end of days. Tribulation is at hand."

I give Constantine a look. He makes a duck face, making Mona laugh, "She calls Rayne Satan and you make a duck face?"

He scowls, "I'm thinking. That's my thinking face. I made it before ducks existed. It should be called a Basarab face." He sighs, "She might be right."

Wyatt throws his hands up into the air, "I've heard enough." He grabs my hand, making me instantly sick and drags me through the massive castle. I pull my hand from his, gagging slightly. "Where are we going?"

He gives me that cocky grin, the one that started it all, "A bedroom."

I laugh, "I'll probably die if we have sex now."

He laughs, "I wish."

I gasp, "Ass."

He puts his hands up, "I wish we could have sex, not that you would die. Anyway, that was awkward. My mom and the whole speech—she's full of it. I need a shower and you need a shower, and I don't trust my mom. So, we shower together, for safety. You know safety in numbers."

I laugh, "You do wish. No. You can sit on the toilet with my sword while I shower."

He smiles wider, "Sounds good." He turns to walk, but I point the other way, "The bedrooms are over here."

He looks confused, "You remember this place?" A naughty smile plasters itself across my face, "I do, actually."

He winces, "Oh God, I don't want to know."

"I wasn't going to tell you."

He gives me a sideways glance as we round the corner to the guest quarters, "You like torturing me."

I smile, "I really do. I really, really do." We get into a room, one I don't recall. I strip down in the bathroom, "Okay, you can come in." I jump in the shower before he can see me, but then realize the doors are glass. Apparently, Constantine has done some updating. Why couldn't he update the drafty front room?

The steam and water make the glass hard to see through, but I can still see Wyatt watching me.

"Look the other way."

"No. Come out and make me."

I laugh, "I'm going to kill you, one of these days."

He laughs too, "Can it be during sex? Please."

I roll my eyes and savor the hot water, "Do you think I'm the antichrist?".

"No. I asked Fitz before he died and he thought you were the lamb; now I do too. He always did though."

His words spin in my head, the lamb. The equivalency to Jesus?

No way. I pour the lemon balm shampoo into my hand and try desperately to find the answers inside of myself. As I scrub it through my scalp, Willow's words run through my head.

"You'll always find your answers in your own heart."

"Nene, the world is a huge place and the only spot you can worry about is your own garden."

"There is no sense in worrying about things you don't truly want to change. If you did, you would have done it already."

"Eat live enzymes to keep your body's good bacteria healthy, and don't eat meat or have sex. They waste your chi."

I tilt my head back, rinsing it off and nodding. The whole sex thing might have been good advice. I hear the glass door close and I open my eyes. Wyatt is standing across from me, completely naked. I can see the thing I have always sort of been curious about in my peripheral, but I don't look below sea level.

"Why are you in my shower?"

He gives me the charming smile that normally feels like he is using it to undress me, only I'm naked already. Very naked. "I just thought, why not? You can't touch me and I can't touch you, not without you being very sick. So why not?" He steps a little closer across the tiles, smiling down on me. "Why not just take a good," he steps closer, "hard," and closer, "look at what we can't have?"

My body is trembling. I can feel something I didn't know I had in me. It's a fire, something fierce. I look down, finally letting myself look at him. The water pours down on us. It feels cool compared to my skin. I swear I can hear a subtle sizzle as each drop lands on my skin. I step back, pressing my back against the wall of tile. He steps into the water, closing his eyes and tilting his head back. I have a filthy want to drag my hands down his chest, feeling his muscles.

He runs his hands through his dark hair, and I can't take another second of it. I grab his face, fighting the instant wave of sickness and pain. My lips touch his desperately. His hands roughly grab me, pulling me up into him. His body against mine is too much. I cry out into his soft lips, backing away.

His eyes are dark and tormented and he false starts several times. My hands do the same but neither of us move or get closer.

"I want you, Rayne. I've wanted you since I saw you order that ridiculous root beer float. I've wanted you from the minute you blew me off and even when I realized what you were." He takes a step back and my throat gets thick. He looks down at my body, his face blushing even beyond the redness he has from the passion we are both fighting. He licks his lips, smiling at the thoughts he isn't saying.

I whisper my own confession, "I want you too."

He gives me a hurt look, "I should have been honest with you, from the start. Once I knew what you were, I should have been honest. I did really awful things to the guys you were with. It just made me so mad, ya know? They could be with you and I couldn't."

"We can't change anything."

He drops to his knee on the tiles and looks up at me. His eyes narrow from the water splashing from my body onto his face. "I should have asked you last time. I shouldn't have assumed it was the best thing for you." He stalls. I can see the hesitation on his face, but he still says what he is thinking. "I handfasted with you in hopes that it would be something else. I know you think it was so I could track you, and it was. But it was so I could keep you safe."

"Why did you get engaged?"

He looks hurt and sighs, "I was born engaged, Rayne. Born that way. I was born ages ago. It takes us centuries to mature, we age so slowly. They say it's the fae in our blood. I've been engaged for hundreds of years."

I nod slowly, "The other me remembers your mother and Jonathan together." I look down on him, "Why are you kneeling?"

"Handfast with me again, I bet there is a fire witch who is stronger than the other who can put it back."

I almost nod, but the memory of the other fire witch eating my broken handfast wax and the evil I ate from her, comes back. I shake my head.

His face pinches, "I said I was sorry and I meant it. How many times must I apologize?"

I want to cry, but instead I offer him a smile, "It will always be one more time."

He nods, "Then I will say it every day for the rest of our lives in hopes of catching up."

I can't help but grin at that. It's hopeful and ridiculous. When I open my mouth, words fall out. I don't mean for them to, but they do. "I love you, Wyatt."

He nods, I can see a fire behind his eyes, "I love you too."

I can't technically feel for him. That's locked away or lost in the multiple personalities inside of me, but I know I love him. It's my heart's truth.

He looks like he's won the lottery but he doesn't move, "When we fix this horsemen situation, do you promise to try again?"

I nod. He stands up again, looking down on me. Goddamned, he is sexy! The way his hair drips water down onto his face, and the way his eyes melt my soul, it's too much. I grab his face again, wincing as the instant pain and suffering is there. I fight it, brushing the softest kiss against his lips. I'm shaking in pain when he backs away. I can feel sweat forming on my brow. I lean into the water and close my eyes. When I open them, he's gone. I know I'm sad. Tears fill my eyes and I cry into the shower water, but I can't feel the heartbreak of not being able to have the thing I want.

I think the others cry at the thought of me loving him and not Constantine.

I whisper into the shower, "I won't choose, not yet."

It doesn’t satisfy them. They weep inside of my mind and I swear I am crazy.

Two

The images are intense. The black rain is being called acid rain from the bombs. It burns and even kills those caught out in it for too long. It only burns organic matter. It has no effect on buildings or umbrellas. It makes no sense. The man speaking on the TV has no idea what it is, and he confesses scientists are equally baffled.

Gretel paces in front of the massive stone fireplace. She and Constantine have worn a path in front of it.

I sigh, “We need to go back to the States.”

Constantine shakes his head, “No. We need to find Lillith.”

Gretel shakes her head as well, “NO. We need to kill the horsemen.”

We are at an impasse, have been for three days. Wyatt’s eyes watch me from the corner of the room. They have done so for three days also.

He speaks softly but everyone listens, “Rayne and I will go back to the States. Mona and Michelle and Gill, you stay here with Tom and Maria. Stella and Constantine, you go and find the garden. Mom and Sarah will locate and attempt to kill the horsemen. Call the other Van Helsings. They will come and help.”

It sounds reasonable to me.

His mom’s eyes dart at Sarah who looks pained, “My parents are siding with the Catholic Church. There is no one but us.”

Gretel nods, “Maggie is with your father at the ocean front estate. She needs to be kept safe.”

Wyatt nods slowly, taking it in. “You go and find the horsemen; when you find them, Stella and Constantine will come to you after they’ve found the garden.” He smirks at Constantine, “Can you still fly, Basarab, or is becoming a bat a young man’s game?”

Constantine chuckles. Stella narrows her gaze, “We could never trust them to fight with them. Gretel is not known for her loyalties.”

Gretel looks savage, “I feel exactly the same about you, corpse.” Stella stands from her chair, looking dramatic in the firelight with her red gown and long blonde hair, “I guess I could always ask Jonathan how loyal you are.”

Gretel snarls, leaping at her. She takes her to the ground. They get in hits, but it gets serious when Gretel bites into her own wrist and drips her blood onto Stella who screams. She kicks Gretel across the room, smashing her into the brick wall. She is up and gone, and then in a flash, right in front of Gretel. Her hand comes back but Wyatt and Constantine are up and grabbing their perspective family members. Stella’s face looks like she has met with the acid rain. It is blackened and burned. Her upper lip is missing.

Gretel is wheezing from whatever is broken in her back from the wall.

Mona looks at me, “That escalated quickly.”

Michelle snuggles in closer to me on the couch, “That was insane.”

They all look at us three on the couch. Wyatt and Gretel on one side of the fire and Constantine and Stella on the other. With the huge fire flickering behind them, they all look positively evil.

I get up, “I’m going to the States, alone.”

Constantine opens his mouth but I hold up a hand, “The nixie can get me there faster than anyone, and under the water, the black rain can't hurt me."

I look at Mona and Michelle, "Stay here, it's the safest place you can be."

Constantine puts his hands on his hips, "Why are you so desperate to be back there?"

There is something I can't tell them. I shake my head, "It's hard to explain, but I need to see someone."

Constantine sighs, "Let's sleep on it. We can decide tomorrow."

I smile, "Fine. I'd rather not swim the Atlantic in the dark anyway."

Gretel, Sarah, and Wyatt go to the wing they're sleeping in. It was Constantine's wing for human snacks the last time I was here. Stella's face is healing but she still looks like a zombie Barbie. She puts a hand out for Michelle, "Come on." Michelle wrinkles her nose, "Is that going to go away or are you going to be fugly all night?"

Mona laughs but Stella frowns, "What does fugly mean?"

It dawns on me at that moment that they are lovers. I don't even know what that makes Michelle. Is she a lesbian now? Maybe she was always flexible.

I suppose love is love—can she love without her soul?

Mona loops her arm into mine, "Night guys." We turn and walk the hallway to our room. She leans in, "If you leave, find my mom."

I nod, "I will."

Of course I lied. It's dark and quite frightening in the castle when the torches and lights are all out. Luckily my eyes do their thing, and I slip through the dark hall silently, not making a single sound. I don't want anyone to know I am leaving.

When I get to the cellar door, my heart is pounding, but I know I have to go. I wince as I pry the door open. It squeaks. I close it and run. I know he will have heard me.

The cellar has not seen an update. The stairs are long and

winding down into the earth. It's cold and dank and smells like things Ellie and the others remember quite well. At the bottom of the stairs, I recognize the old door I knew was there. I pull hard on the rusty handle and the door squeaks like it's the friggin' alarm system warning Constantine of my escape. I leave it open and run, trailing my finger along the cobweb-covered wall of bricks. I can see that the stairs have no railing and the fall is far. My eyes do their glowy thing making it light in the room, light enough to see how horrid it is.

A light at the top of the stairs announces his arrival, "Rayne, goddammit. Get back here."

I look back at Constantine and jump. The torch he holds lights up the massive cavern he once turned into an amazing escape. My wings burst from my back, and I float past the dimly-lit staircase and pitted wall. He jumps too, but the moment I touch ground, I'm running and leaping. My huge white wings fold in when I reach the tunnel to the sea. I can smell the spray of the ocean.

"RAYNE!"

I push my legs harder until I reach the cold wind in my face. I see dawn's light on the horizon and leap into it and the misty air of the bluffs. My wings tuck and I dive fast for the sea below.

I split the water with such force I cry out from the pain of it. But instantly they are there. They wrap around me, surrounding me in light. I can hear the nixie singing and moaning in the water, talking all at once.

Seven beautiful sea witches. I smile at the nixie. They look up and I see the frothing sea explode with more commotion. He has followed me into the ocean. The nixie will smell their dead on him and attack. I see jeans and scowl; it's not Constantine. It's Wyatt. He looks at the nixie pleadingly, "Please?"

He surfaces again. The nixie look at me. I sigh and nod.

We all surface. I see Constantine's evil face from the cave opening high above. I wave, "I'll be back in a couple days."

He flips me the bird.

“Wow, that was rude.”

He turns and stalks back into the cave.

I look at Wyatt, “You can’t come. You have to be able to cross the Atlantic with them.”

Wyatt ignores me and looks at the blonde with the hateful look for him. “I am the archangel Jonathan’s son. Please let me come. I promise to do whatever you say.” He sounds sweet and obliging. They look like they won’t be fooled, “Fine.”

A redhead grabs him and pulls him under. I scream, “He can’t breathe.”

The blonde laughs, “He is nephilim. They can all breathe underwater.” She grabs my hand and pulls me under with her. I grab her shoulders, like I’m swimming with a dolphin and we start the trip. The sun rises above, lighting up the entire ocean.

It is beautiful and strange to be swimming across the ocean. I can’t see Wyatt. There is a pit in my stomach that they just dragged him down and murdered him. He has killed nixie before.

I feel an overwhelming exhaustion suddenly. Before I can stop them, the dead take me.

I wake to pain, knowing I never dreamt. I scream out and look down. I am in a room I don’t know, and the source of my agony and sickness is the man sleeping next to me. He has sprawled across me. I snarl and shove him off the bed. He lands with a thump and continues to sleep. It makes me laugh.

I look around but I don’t know this place. It’s a simple bedroom, nothing fancy at all. I get up, nervous of what I will find. I no longer think it’ll be Van Helsings who want to kill me. I trust him now. My belly rumbles, and I know it’s not the kind of hunger a sandwich will fix. I haven’t eaten in days.

I leave the room, recognizing where I am when I enter the next room. The picture with the star makes me smile instantly. It is the reason I have come back to the States.

“Did you push me out of bed?” I jump and turn to see Wyatt rubbing his eyes. “That was mean.”

I laugh, “You were touching me. I woke screaming in pain.”

He grimaces, “So I accidentally hurt you and you purposefully push me out of bed? I woke screaming in pain too.”

I roll my eyes, “You did not.”

He cracks a grin, “Okay, but I'm not a baby like you.”

I laugh, “Screw you, Wyatt.”

“That's why we're here, isn't it?”

I shake my head and an idea hits. I grab his hand and drag him to the picture. I press the star and instantly we are there. He cries out like a baby then.

“What the hell?”

I turn, searching for her. She is in the garden in the corner. I run over, “Excuse me, ma'am.”

She turns to look at me, making my heart stop. She isn't the lady from the picture before. She is Willow. I drop to my knees, tears streaming my cheeks. I can't reach the agony inside of me, but I know it's there. My body's reaction is desperate and uncontrolled sobbing.

Wyatt comes running over, “Willow?”

She looks at us both, “What? How?”

I press my hands down into the earth, grabbing at the soil and crying. She is on me, instantly. “Nene, my precious Nene. You found me. I knew you would. I tried to leave you hints with the dead. I hoped they would tell you to come to me.”

Her warm softness surrounds me. She smells like patchouli and dirt. I cry harder, “Mom.”

She cries too, “My baby.”

"Wyatt, what are you doing here? Is that Rayne?" I hear Fitz, but I am so lost in my tears and the embrace of my mom that I can't look.

She strokes my hair and kisses my head. "You came. I can't believe you came."

Wyatt hugs Fitz, "You're alive?"

"No, son, I'm a ghost but I am held here by the magic of the earth witch I love."

Wyatt shakes his head, "I don't care. I'm just glad I can see you. I'm sorry I wasn't able to help you."

Fitz laughs, "You are doing your job, trust me."

"Uncle, we need to find the garden. I know you're the only person who will know where it is."

I look up at Willow, "Can you tell me if Mona's mom is dead or alive?"

She nods, "Give me a minute." She closes her eyes, and even I get a shiver from the thing she is doing. I can't see anything different, but I can feel the electricity in the air. She opens her eyes, "Mona is an orphan."

I wince, "Oh God."

"She is with God. She made peace before she left. Mona's father was worried and went to her when things got bad. They died together, holding each other." She smiles down on me, "You have killed the devils, haven't you?"

I nod. She winces, "Then it has started. Have the horsemen come?"

I nod again, "The world is in turmoil. People are dying everywhere and the horsemen are wrecking everything."

Wyatt scowls, "You guys knew they would come?"

Fitz sighs, "We suspected they would. They are the only way to start the end of days and pit the lamb against the usurper."

I shake my head, "What?"

Willow kisses my cheeks, "You have to kill the antichrist. The horsemen will tip the balance of good on the planet to a disastrous level so that he might be born. It is judgment day for the believers. God's children are going home, and only the worst of the worst and the non-believers will remain. The children of light, the fae, will stay also. They do not belong in heaven."

My stomach cramps. Willow looks at me, "Have you been eating properly? You look tired." She looks at Wyatt, "No sex right, Nene?"

I sigh, "No."

Wyatt shakes his head, "You guys are really open in this family."

Fitz looks down, "You have no idea."

I laugh, "Has she got you eating plant enzymes?"

He shakes his head, "The week she died it was colonics week, that was…fun."

Willow laughs, "I wanted you to live forever."

"Willow, my love. I was already going to live forever." He looks at me, "Being dead together forever is better. No colonics and no enzymes. If I imagine it, it's here and there are no repercussions to eating it. No gas and no colonics." Fitz sighs but focuses back to the business at hand, "Why are you here? Why have you wasted time coming here? The nixie know the way."

Wyatt shakes his head, "They won't tell her."

Willow gives me a look, "Tell them, Fitz."

Fitz points at the small cottage, "Come in for a tea." Willow helps me up and we walk arm in arm. I grip to her for dear life.

Inside of the cottage, I shake my head, "It looks just like our house did."

Willow gives Wyatt a hateful look. He sighs, "I didn't know you guys then."

She sneers and sits on the couch, pulling me with her. We snuggle as Fitz makes tea.

"The garden is the least of your worries. The antichrist is clearly born. He is most likely your brother. We found texts that essentially said Lucifer and Lillith would make both. He is unaware of his mission in life."

I swallow the lump in my throat, "He's my brother?"

Willow kisses the top of my head, "I'm so sorry, Nene. We discovered it recently. He is most likely your brother and until the devil rises in him, he will not know what he is. He may even be frozen in a state of unconsciousness while he waits for it."

I feel sick. "I have to kill him?"

She nods.

Wyatt shakes his head, "How do we find the garden?"

Fitz sits at the table, waiting for the kettle to boil, "It finds you."

"What?"

He nods, "The garden gate will be there, somewhere random. Only a person looking for the garden for a pure purpose will find it. No one has ever recorded going in. People search for it because they want the healing and immortality of it. They want something from it. They don't have a pure purpose. Only the purest of heart may enter too. I have heard of the gates opening for people but their feet are unable to cross into the garden. We sort of assume that being minus a soul you cannot enter."

"Shit."

Wyatt nods, "Double shit. How do we have a pure purpose when she wants to go there and kill Lillith?"

Fitz puts his hands out, "That's why we hoped the nixie would tell you. They come and go; the last of the witches are able to come and go. They know how to get in there."

I give Willow a skeptical look, "Why don't you ask them?"

She swallows hard, "They don't like me much. They think I was working with Lucifer. The week your father was to meet us at the house, I spelled it. I knew it was my best chance at keeping you safe. I had hidden you away at the school, the land is hallowed there. As long as you were on campus, Lucifer couldn't get to you. It's the only reason I even let you go. The devils couldn't fill you there either. School was the safest place you could have gone. When it was time, Lucifer contacted me and told me that I was to bring you to the house and let him take you to fulfill your destiny. But I spelled the house. Whether you had been at the school or the house, he never would have found you. I couldn't take you to the witches; they wouldn't let you stay once it had hit. Once you ate the evil in someone that was it—the end of you being welcome there for any length of time."

"How are the nixie and Lucifer tied together?"

She looks pained, like she is seeing something behind her eyes that she isn't sharing, "Lillith. We think she might not have been who we thought she was. She sent Lucifer to me, knowing I had you. She sent word to me in a dream that you had to die once and for all and that she was grateful I had cared for you. She was the only one who knew where you were. I told the nixie this and they called me a traitor against Lillith. I never even told the other witches until it was clear to everyone who met you who you were. It's why we lived separately. I told them I had a non-magical daughter with a mortal. You were an abomination to them."

"But the nixie don't seem to think I'm supposed to die."

Willow smiles, again like she sees something she doesn't share. "They don't think it. They told me they don't think it and that is why they will not tell you where the garden is. They want you to live. They want you to rid the world of Lucifer."

"But that will take Lillith with him."

Willow's smile turns wicked, "They have been led to believe Lillith will be safe from you so long as the antichrist and Lucifer have been killed."

Wyatt looks confused, “You have lied to them?”

She shakes her head, “Not me.”

He looks at Fitz, “You?”

He nods, “They will only help so long as they believe their precious Lillith will live.” He looks at me, “You must go to the air witches. They are the only ones who know how to kill the horsemen.”

I drop my head into my hands, “What about the friggin’ garden? How the hell do we get in there to get Lillith?”

He pours the tea, “The answer will come. God will not leave you helpless. The answer will come when it is time. God has not left you alone yet.”

I shudder, remembering being chained to the wall and tortured, “Well, let’s not get too overzealous. He hasn’t exactly been there for every step I’ve taken.”

Fitz looks like he might explode for a second, “He has carried you, Rayne. Make no mistake of that. Everything that is happening is meant to be. Find the air witches.” He passes me and Wyatt a tea. I sip and think. Willow hugs me, like it might be the last time. She whispers, “I know you can do this, Nene.”

I nod, “I’m glad you think so.”

Three

"I can't believe they're both dead." I mutter, passing him the painting from Fitz's that's wrapped in several garbage bags and sealed with his vacuum sealer for clothes.

He shakes his head, "They don't seem very dead. Did you always know about that photo?"

I nod, "No, the dead showed me once."

"Spooky, Rayne. I asked Fitz about the fire witch. He is certain there is one in Boston who is strong enough to redo a handfast."

I smile, "Excellent!"

We slip back into the water and let the nixie surround us with their warmth. They smile and flutter about the water. I point up, "How does one go about finding the air witches?"

They shake their heads and the redhead speaks softly, "One doesn't. Why would you want to see those pontificating winged devils?"

I laugh, feeling weird about the water in my face when I do it. "We need them. I have to kill the four horsemen, for Lillith."

I look around at all of them, so pretty in the water. Their movements are fluid and smooth. The memory of the nixie on the shores is traumatizing; the jerky movements and dresses that seem alive still haunt my daydreams.

The blonde nods once, “We will take you to the place.” She looks at Wyatt, “Does the evil one have to come?”

I smile at him, “He does.”

She makes a face, grabs his hand and drags him through the water like a child dragging a doll by its hand. My ride is much smoother. We come to the shores after a short swim, “Go to the old part of town, Salem. The fire witches will help you find the air devils.”

The redhead kisses me softly. The lights in her eyes make me nervous but the soft lips are calming. Wyatt sputters as we climb from the water. The black rains have stopped. The sky still brews as though a storm is coming, but at least there is no weather beyond the cold wind.

“We need to find dry clothes.”

I nod ahead, “I have an idea.” We cross the street in the dark. He looks at me funny, “Your eyes are doing that glowing thing.”

I nod, “It’s dark out. They always do it in the dark. The darker it is, the brighter they are.”

“Creepy.”

I stick my tongue out.

He laughs, “I love how mature you are about all of this.”

“Whatever.” I stalk across the dark street to a row of old houses. I do the thing I hate and walk to the one with no lights on and creep into the back yard. I can heed his dissatisfaction at the idea of what I’m about to do, but I don’t care. I open the back door quietly. Poking my head inside, “Hello, Uncle Stan?”

No one makes a sound or answers. I open it all the way, stripping my drenched clothing from my body. I almost leave my underwear on, but after the shower, I don’t bother.

“This started out wrong but I’m liking it more now.”

I look back at Wyatt, “Shhhh. Just strip.” I carry my clothes to the garbage and feel a small pit of remorse. I'm always losing clothes and throwing them away and ripping them with my wings. I never get to have nice stuff.

Wyatt scowls, "These are three hundred dollar jeans—you want me to put them in the trash?"

I smile when I see his naked body, "Yeah."

He smiles, shaking his head, "Eyes above sea level."

I laugh, "This is probably the worst experience ever."

He closes the cupboard to the garbage and looks down on me. I like the way he towers over me, casting a shadow so big I can't see past him.

"Your eyes are really glowing now, like a cat with a glimmer of light in them."

I nod, "I know. They're crazy."

"I want to touch you."

I smile, "This family could be home at any second. Trust me, hide and seek with glowing eyes is not easy." I turn and walk towards the stairs I know he can't see. "Besides, I don't want you to touch me."

I dash to the shower, jumping in and rinsing the sand and salt from my body. He gets in with me. When I'm clean, I jump out, "I've never been naked this much in front of anyone, except Willow. She's always naked. Huge fan of nakedness."

"I can see that." I can hear the smile in his voice even though I can't see him past the shower curtain. "I've always been around nakedness. Sports teams are brutal."

I wrap in the towel, "How old are you?"

He doesn't answer right away. "Old, hundreds of years old, I think. It's taken me ages to get to this age. Apparently, the angel blood will freeze it here. I'm fully grown, so I won't age anymore. Not like my mom and Fitz, who are older now, hundreds of years later. I did the majority of my growing recently. I was stuck in a ten-year olds body forever. Then I hit that puberty stage about a decade ago. I got to go to normal school. I guess it's common for my family. But mom said Maggie has stayed at the ten year old level for a shorter amount of time. Apparently she is about to bloom." He turns off the shower and pulls back the curtain, "We stay young for a long time, innocent. When we hit puberty, we age normally for a decade and then it slows down again. For me it's stopped."

I pass him a towel, fully staring at his naked body. He is like a sculpture, perfect and chiseled. His body is artwork. It makes me think things that are not quite pure. I have to turn away before I touch him, hurting myself.

I nod, "I've aged normally all five of my lives, I think if I was let to live, I would be like you. I would stop aging when I was done developing. I always die though."

It stings a little to say that.

I walk from the bathroom before he can try dosing me in pity. I don't want it. The house belongs to people a little older than us, by the clothes. I pull on two pairs of yoga pants, a Henley and a sweater, and thick wooly socks.

I pick him out a pair of thick jogging pants, a tee shirt, and a hoodie. He pulls it on and we head for the kitchen. I grab a yogurt cup from the fridge and pass it to him. He eats it fast. We raid their fridge for several minutes. Eating in silence and staring at the wall.

"Is this how you live when you're on the run?"

I nod.

"That's sad, Rayne."

I nod again.

He grabs my arm, turning me to face him, "Never run from me again, I'll take care of you."

I smile, pulling my arm from his grip to stop the sickness. "Don't smack me around, lie to me, or let your mom break my arms and we have a deal."

He looks serious, "How many times, Rayne?"

I smile, "One more."

He steps closer, smelling like cherry yogurt and orange juice. He runs a hand down my cheek, making me almost gag. "I have never been more sorry for anything in my life. I hate myself and who I am for ever hurting you or betraying you."

I smile up at him, "Nope, still gonna be one more."

He laughs, "You're a shit."

I nod, "I know it." I walk past him, stealing mail from the fridge.

"You steal their mail too?"

"And their car. I have to have a way to send them money." I open the shoe closet and pull on a pair of sneakers. I pass him a pair.

We shrug on coats and walk out into the cold winter air. He starts the car in the driveway and we leave for Salem. It is only a few miles from where we were.

He parks it and we walk in the dark. I notice suddenly, now that we're in a busy area, how bad things are. Windows are broken in stores, houses are burned out and charred, cars are smashed and looted.

"It's like hell on earth." I whisper.

He steps closer to me as we walk in the direction his nose is telling us to. We get into an alley between two old houses, and suddenly I feel something I can't explain. It's like being gutted or exploding from the inside. I double over in pain.

"Why are you here?"

Wyatt turns around towards the female voice but I can't. I am stuck in agony.

Wyatt's voice is angry, "We are looking for the fire witches; we need to find the air witches. The nixie told us to come here. Now stop or I'll kill you, and it won't matter why we're here."

My wings shoot from my back, uncontrollably. I cry out as they do it, but the pain she was inflicting upon me is gone.

"How?" She sounds stunned. I gag a little and turn to face her.

"You bitch, that hurt."

She shakes her head, "You are the sin eater. How is this possible?"

I step closer to her, seeing the resemblance to the fire witch I met before. I give her a hard look, "I will kill you if you don't answer my questions, do you understand me?"

She nods, completely baffled.

I swallow hard, still a little out of breath, "I need you to do two things."

She nods again, terrified or just completely confused.

I look back at him, "I need you to handfast us and I need you to take me to the air witches."

She is conflicted but she agrees with a single nod. She looks badass. Piercings in her nose and lips. Her hair is black with red streaks and her eye makeup is excessive. She is a Goth, a beautiful Goth.

"I'm Lila."

"Are you the head of the witches?"

She shakes her head, giving Wyatt a deadly look, "You sure you want to handfast with that?"

I laugh, "I am."

Her eyes glow like mine but brighter, "You know what he is, right?"

"Yeah. He's a Van Helsing. I know the stories."

She shakes her head, "He's an angel like you. You can't trust them, Rayne."

I scowl, “How do you know my name?”

She gives me a cocky grin, “I heard about what you did for my sister. You sucked the death from her. I just never knew you were an angel. She missed that part of the story.”

Wyatt steps closer, “Tell us how to find the air witches.”

I smile, “He means please. Please show us how to find the air witches.”

She laughs, “Let’s go to meet the others first.” She looks at our clothes, “You’re going to need to change. You can’t do a ceremony in that outfit. Not since it’s the second shot and, technically, it shouldn’t be able to be redone.”

She takes my hand and pulls me into the side door of the creepy old house. We go down into the basement and through an old tunnel. She looks around, like she can see like I can. “This was once the way out of the city. The witches who ran during the trials came through these tunnels. We learned after the European trials to build a way out, before we built houses. The American Witch Trials were nothing, compared to the European. Of course the trials never killed many real witches. Only healers, wet-nurses, mistresses of men who got caught, and women who were too beautiful. The churches assumed they were witches because they tempted the men. Of course if I am a married man and I want a woman more than my own wife, that makes her a witch. Heaven forbid any of them admitted to being weak. Men would rape women and call them temptress witches. It was sick. We fled Europe during that time, fled for the East Coast. I killed as many of the bad men as I could, but when they brought in the witch hunters, I had to leave. We all did.” She looks back at Wyatt, “None of us can fight off a Van Helsing, not unless we have a full coven. Back then, women weren’t practicing in covens, too easy to get caught.”

Wyatt cocks an eyebrow, “You do realize I wouldn’t have been born during that time. I can’t take blame for things in the 1500s and 1600s.”

She points a long black nail at him, "Changes nothing, Van Helsing. Nothing. You and your kind…"

I cut her off and step in front of her, "He is my kind. He isn't their kind, trust me."

Her dark, and yet glowing, eyes flicker between the two of us. She smirks, "You defend him?"

I nod, "He is mine to criticize and torment."

Wyatt leans over me, "That's right. Only she gets to make my life hell. Trust me, she's doing a bang-up job."

Lila cackles perfectly, though it doesn't suit her beautiful face.

She nods towards the end of the tunnel, "Let's go. They aren't going to be excited we brought him with us."

She opens the heavy steal door that I would have figured would be old wood but once we are beyond it, I understand perfectly. We are in a cellar under an old house, but it is a shop of sorts, a magical shop.

She claps her hands and the candles everywhere light up. The room is spooky and mystical. Willow would have dug it here.

I shudder from the feeling in the air.

"Show yourselves, sisters. He cannot harm you. He is guarded by his love of the sin eater and his angel bloodline."

Women start appearing out of nowhere. The room is full suddenly.

We all stand there, looking at each other but no one speaks. I feel the nausea in my stomach from him being too close. His chest and stomach are pressed against my back. He's gauging the room to fight our way out. I can almost smell it on him, not fear but fight.

I reach back, taking one for the team and hold his hands with my own, "He is mine."

They make faces and whisper amongst themselves.

"Does it not hurt, sin eater?"

I nod, "Near-death bad."

The older witch with the white hair in the corner nods at me, "You wish us to handfast, even though you just broke it?"

"We do."

"Why?" she asks and the others nod in agreement.

I shrug but Wyatt speaks, "I fasted our hands without her knowledge of what it meant. I forced it. This time I have asked as is your custom, on my knees."

They all look disgusted. A dark-haired one points at him, "Typical man. That's how many a witch was made a slave in the old days. A handfasted witch cannot use her magic on her husband, nor can her coven sisters." She gives us a sickening smile, "But it wasn't ever hard to find a sister somewhere to smite his ass like he deserved."

They all cackle. They are more like the witches I expected in the world. Not the sneaky faces of the earth witches or the deceptive beauty of the nixie. No, the fire witches are Gothic and slightly haggard in some cases. There is very little beauty to go round. Instantly, I remember something I once read. The beauty of a witch shows on the inside and the out. It was on the wall, somewhere? Willow's cottage, in the picture maybe. I can see the darkness of them.

One of the witches, a particularly pretty one, smiles at me, "My sister is the one who fasted you last time. You saved her life. For that we are grateful, and we will spell your wishes."

I look around at the older ones but they seem satisfied by her words, like she is in charge.

They step to the side, making a path for the door on the far side. "There are wedding clothes in the room there. Go and change. Lila will bring you up to the hallowed ground."

Lila leads the way to the door. She opens it and goes inside. I follow her, feeling Wyatt hesitate as we cross into the room.

The door closes. Lila smiles at him, “Nervous we won’t let you out?”

He gives her his sexy, confident smile. “You can’t hurt me. The dark-haired one spoke an oath, it’s spelled. I felt it on my skin.”

She cocks an eyebrow, “Did I mention that I just love that you’re half angel? I think that’s fantastic.”

He rolls his eyes, walking past her to the clothes. His are dark jeans and a black dress shirt. He scowls, “I’m going to freeze up there.”

She smiles, “Awwww muffin. I’m sure we can manage a nice fire to keep you warm.”

I laugh and he gives me a look, “What happened to he’s mine?”

I shrug, “That was funny. I have a sense of humor, you don’t. It’s no biggie.”

She passes me a long black skirt with layers like a dead bride’s dress and a black corset shirt. I give her the puppy-dog eyes, “I don’t want to be cold too. It’s not funny when it’s me suffering.”

She shakes her head, “The clothes have to be black. If your underwear aren’t black, you have to take them off.”

Wyatt gives her a cocky, asshole grin. “I don’t like wearing them anyway.”

She can’t fight the attraction to him. None of them can. I can’t either. It’s one thing that he’s stop-traffic hot—it’s completely another that he’s a Van Helsing, and all things like us are attracted to him. He pulls off the hoodie and slips on the dress shirt. She turns around as he drops his trousers, with no regard for either of us. He smells the jeans, “These are clean, right?”

“Of course. They’re magic.”

He chuckles, “Well, when was the last wedding?”

She turns back around as he zips the zipper, “Not too long ago, but he only kept them on for an hour or so.”

Wyatt's face goes still. She laughs. He shakes his head, "Not funny, witch."

She shrugs, "Like the sin eater says, you just don't have a sense of humor, do you?"

He steps forward, "I do, it just seems the things I think are funny offend everyone else."

She swallows hard. I turn around with the corset over my breasts, "Can someone do this up?"

Wyatt touches me, making me jump, "Her—can she do it?"

Lila comes and does the bra and corset over it up. She whispers in my ear, "The clothes are new. We manifest them for weddings."

I smile, "Thanks."

She nods, "Let him sweat it out though, huh?"

I nod.

She opens a different door on the other side of the room and leaves through it. We walk up the stairs to a garden. It is dark and dreary. I can feel the wrinkled nose and disgusted look. When I see the first headstone, I gag.

She laughs, "Fire witches don't normally need the help of the dead to seal something like this, but you two just broke one off. That leaves a stain. If we didn't have a full coven and all our ancestors buried beneath us, we wouldn't even be able to do it."

We walk to where a gathering of women wearing black dresses stand around an old headstone.

I have the funniest feeling like I'm not making the right choice. The dead are there, I can feel them for the first time in ages. The other girls inside of me, the other versions of me, are gone. They are silent, probably in protest, but I don't care. I want to touch him and kiss him and make love to him, like I never have but I know I can.

Constantine's name whispers through my mind, but that's the only place it is. He is not in my heart. He is not my choice, he is theirs. I do not believe in being able to love two people at once. I am hardly able to say I love Wyatt. I know I do, but my heart is broken, and I don't know why or how to fix it.

We walk to the women who look almost like a murder of crows instead of a group of women. They are all draped in black. Mist trails through the graves and circles the women.

Lila leads us to the headstone and holds her hand out, "In the middle."

She cuts a doorway in the circle of mist with her finger. We step through it. The dark-haired one smiles, "Hold both hands and look at each other."

Suddenly, I see they all have unlit black candles in their hands. I wince, remembering the pain. The dark-haired one holds her hands like she is holding an orb. She chants and whispers, and as the magic brews, the flames grow higher on the candles and a ball of flames grows between her hands. She holds it to the sky; the winds come, bringing clouds and more darkness. The clouds dance and rub against each other making a low rumble in the skies. Lightning shoots from the darkest part, touching the ball of light in her hands.

Wyatt looks nervous. I feel the dead in the air, sparkling around me, excitedly.

Her crazed chants and whispers become shouts as the wind picks up, blowing the hood of her black coat down and letting her hair flow free. In giant black locks, it swings about, around her pale face as she distorts slightly and slams the ball of light into our clasped hands. We scream simultaneously. She falls back, breathless and smiling.

"The God you love wants this. He has blessed your union himself."

I sniffle back the tears and emotions.

She reaches over, taking two daggers from the girls next to her. She hands me one and Wyatt one.

"Put your blood on the blade, then stab each other in the heart simultaneously."

I shake my head but Wyatt presses the blade to my chest. I give him a look. He rolls his eyes, "It isn't going to hurt more than the mighty God ball. We can't die, Rayne."

My hands tremble as I lift the sharp blade to his chest. "It's a magical blade, Rayne." She points, "You'll want to take the shirts off or it hurts twice as bad. It drags the fabric through, really awful."

I wince but he's already pulling his shirt off. I turn and let him remove the corset, leaving me in the huge black skirt and black bra. The wind blows, making me shiver. His warm touch no longer burns, and I no longer feel sick. I realize how badly it's been bugging me. I haven't felt right since we took it off.

"Do you have a ring?"

He shakes his head, "Didn't know we needed one."

She points, "Give me that one." She points at the ring everyone in his family has. He thinks for a second; I almost see a hesitation but he pulls it off and drops it into her hand. He looks nervous without it. She holds it in her hands, "Stab."

I look at him, pointing the blade at his bare chest. I shake my head, "This is a bad idea."

His blue eyes are dark and full of something I can't quite place. It might be arrogance, but it could also be trust. I think most of his expressions look the same on his face, they have something to do with being cocky and sexy. He stabs me slightly, pressing the blade. I wince. He smiles, "One movement, just a single hard push. You ready?"

I nod, "Okay." I take several short breaths. He nods his head, "On three. One." I am about to chicken out and run away but my feet won't move. "Two." I tense up, waiting for him to do it. I know I won't. I can't stab him. I can't do this. I can't. "Three." I cry out as he walks into my blade while pushing his into my heart. I cough blood. He does the same.

Tears drop from my eyes as the metal sits there, pressed against my still-beating heart and chest. We are close to one another, only separated by the hilt of the daggers.

Lila puts a hand on both our backs and pushes us the rest of the way. When we are chest to chest I feel something warm. It gets hotter and hotter until it's searing my heart, and I am screaming into his chest. His whole body is tensed over mine. Somehow he manages to move his arms, wrapping them around me. He kisses the top of my head. I can't even see him anymore through the tears flowing from my eyes. I gag again. Lila squeezes her hands in between us and pries us apart.

I am sobbing and nearly collapsing, but Wyatt looks strong. He is strong.

Over his heart my name carves itself, in handwriting. I cry out again, looking down at where his name is carving over my heart.

Tears drop from my eyes onto my breasts, trickling over his name. I look at the name, shaking my head. "H-h-how?"

"The metal of the blade is the tattoo, it fades unless it you want it to show."

I shudder as it finishes. I am about to leap into his arms and make him comfort me, but the dark-haired witch puts her hand between us, "Put these on."

There is a man's ring and a woman's ring in her palm. I grab the woman's but Wyatt snorts. He takes it and puts it on my wedding finger. I blush, taking gulps of air now that all the pain is gone.

The ring is silver and covered in vines. I pick up the fatter one and slide it on his finger. He smiles, "Worst wedding ever?"

I laugh, "I have zero doubt that you love me."

He nods, "Witchy weddings are not for the faint of heart."

When the ring is on his finger, he clasps my hand in his. His eyes bear down on me, "I will love you until I am no longer even a speck of dust on the wind."

My eyes tear up again. I nod, “Me too.”

He grins, “Always so good with words.”

I sniffle, “You know.”

He tilts my face upward and lowers his lips to mine, “I know.”

I realize then we are standing in a graveyard with only the bottom half of our clothes on and witches all around us. Is it wrong to kiss? Better question is, do I care? When his lips meet mine, I do not. It is sweet bliss. He kisses me once and then pulls away, “Is there somewhere I might take my bride?”

I think we all know he means that in more than one way, and I'm insulted by one of them. The witch laughs, “She is pure of heart now because we have blessed. You cannot take her.”

I blush, “Oh…uhm…no. This isn't my first time at the rodeo, if you get my point.” I laugh but she does not. The other witches are stuck in the flames of their candles. Only the four of us are able to move.

She rolls her eyes, “I know that. But since the nixie have cleansed you and we have just now cleansed you, have you committed an original sin?”

I scowl, “What is that?”

“Sex, sex without marriage or with a married person, murder without reason or defense, theft, arson, injury to a person for no reason.”

I shake my head, “I ate some pedophiles and murderers.”

She smiles, “You are clean. You may enter the gates of the garden. Eating sin is your job. It is not a sin. You actually have the right of the God you serve to judge people's lives and choose if they live or die.”

“Creepy.”

Wyatt shakes his head, “So she can't have sex, even though she is married?”

The witch smiles, "Sex is sex, Van Helsing."

"Doesn't the goddess control the garden? Why does she care about sin?"

I look at Wyatt, "We can do it after the garden." He looks desperate. I laugh, "Is that why you married me?"

He cocks his head, "Yes, I stabbed us both in the heart and suffered unending agony to have sex."

I shrug, "Sounds legit."

He sighs, "Well, this blows." He gives the witch a look, "You never answered the garden question."

She laughs, "I don't make the rules. I just know an original sin will keep her from the garden and those are the original sins. Sex removes purity of the soul. It makes us less committed to our goal; we transfer our energy when we have sex."

I look at Wyatt, "Willow never had sex."

He scowls, "Lillith had sex to have you. She's in the garden."

I give the witch a scowl. She shakes her head, "I don't know. I just know witches who don't have sex, go into the garden. Witches who do, can't get past the gate."

Wyatt points, "This is a double standard."

I grimace, "Not if the nixie cleanse her every time she goes back in."

The fire witch winces. "I would imagine that is how it is done."

Wyatt shrugs but I nudge him, "They are our sisters. We don't let them die for us."

The fire witch nods at Lila. She walks to me and takes my hand in hers. She pulls her wand again and draws on my palm. She uses fire of course, burning a map into my hand. "Follow this and it will take you to the air witches. If you are there, they will come for you." Lila opens the door with her finger again. She smiles at us, "Be safe."

I nod, "Thank you."

Wyatt takes my hand in his and we walk through the garden of the dead. We are more alive than we have ever been and more relaxed. The girls in my head are gone but the lack of emotion is there still, like I still can only feel my piece-of-the-pie worth of love. I wish it was the same for pain.

He hands me his shirt. I scowl, "You'll freeze."

He laughs, "Yeah, but not every dude is gonna be able to see my wife's boobs."

I laugh until it dawns on me that I am a wife. I am married. I am like the biggest idiot ever. I just married a guy I've known half a year. A guy who has tried to kill me. A guy whose family hates me. A guy who I can't even have sex with.

Awesome.

Four

I step into the water in my skirt, shivering instantly. Wyatt kisses the side of my head, “Did I mention, I love you?”

I look up at him, and no matter how hard I try, I cannot fight the smile I get. I know I love him too. I nod and push into the next kiss he plants on my forehead. We dive into the water and they are there. I hold my hand out to the brunette who has met us at the shore, “Can you take us there? We followed the map to here, but it’s over there somewhere. An island I think.”

She nods once, giving Wyatt a look. I sigh, “He’s mine. Like the baggage I take everywhere with me.”

She scowls and Wyatt chuckles.

They grab my hand but not his. I grab his as I’m pulled away. He laughs when we are under water again, “They won’t touch me—never touch another woman’s husband.”

I growl, “You might have said something.”

He laughs in the bubbly-weird laugh we have under water, “I forgot till now.”

The swim is short, like seconds short. We near a floating dock. It is in the middle of the ocean. They leave us there. I swim to the dock after Wyatt. He hops up and offers me his hand. I let him pull me up. We both shiver, huddling into each other for warmth.

We are surrounded by mist and the dark night. It is creepy, maybe not quite as creepy as the earth witches’ house, but still very creepy. I sense movement in the fog and tighten my grip on Wyatt.

He turns around, pushing me behind him, and holds me there.

The mist moves again, and I swear I hear a song on it. It's lovely.

Wyatt winces. The mist swirls and forms into a figure and then a face, and then it's gone again.

I hear the song again. I realize it's a voice. "Why do you seek us?"

I look at Wyatt. He frowns, "What?"

"You don't hear that?"

He shakes his head, "Air witches are telepathic. They hear your thoughts and send you theirs."

I sigh, "You have to tell me these things before we get to the dock."

He shrugs, "Didn't seem important."

I concentrate and think, "We need your help with the horsemen."

Something drops onto the dock. I scream and jump. A massive winged woman walks towards us. The dock trembles under her feet. She looks like a Viking woman. Strong, blonde, scary and a little too muscular for a girl."

She lowers her eyes on me, and I swear they see right through me with their brilliance. They are blue in the way the sky is in July on a cloudless day. They are tranquil and yet harsh.

"Why do you want to kill the horsemen?"

I look at her, "I am the sin eater."

She narrows her gaze, giving Wyatt a skeptical look. I exhale and my wings pop out. She smiles instantly and the blue of her eyes is pleasant. The stress is gone from her face. She nods, "You are the sin eater."

I nod, not sure why we are repeating things. She looks at him, "What is he?"

"Mine."

She shrugs, she doesn't care about him. She wants me. She nods upward, "We fly."

I wince, "I'm not great at the whole flying thing. I sort of have to be falling first."

She shakes her head, "You fly or you stay."

I give Wyatt a smile, "We fly."

He grimaces, "You got this?"

I nod and offer him my hand. I do a couple squats. The air witch gives me a confused look. She jumps from the dock, shaking it back and forth. I almost get seasick and leap up too. My wings try to flap but we fall back to the dock. Wyatt laughs, "Fly first and then come get me."

I let go of his hand, "Ok."

I jump up, almost getting it. He grabs my foot and tosses me high into the air. I flap upward to where she is and shout, "Be right back!"

She looks confused, I don't think she has many other faces.

I dive towards the dock, soaring down. "JUMP!"

He turns and leaps. I catch his arms but we drag down. He goes under water for a second, like I've dunked a tea biscuit in my tea. I flap hard, really focusing on the wings. We start to go up again. It takes me forever to get back up to where she is. She points and takes off. Wyatt is shouting at me but I shake my head, "Not looking down at you. Sorry. I can't do this. If I look down, we're dead."

He starts to climb my body like I am a tree. He climbs around the front of me. I shake my head, "Stop moving. I'm going to get sick."

He shouts back, "You get sick on me, and I'll pull that damned dagger out of your heart and put it back in."

I sneer, focusing on the flying angel witch in front of me. "God, she's so graceful and good at this."

I can see his grin in my peripheral, "She isn't lugging two hundred pounds with her."

I growl, "You need to go on a diet."

"No way, baby. I'm at seven-percent body fat, I like it there. I still have an ass in my jeans but not my old hockey-player ass."

I laugh and suddenly the flying feels easier. The better my mood and the less worrying, the easier it gets.

We fly through a huge, white fluffy cloud. I lose sight of her and then I realize Wyatt is walking, and sort of carrying me.

"Can you touch?"

He nods, "This cloud is a platform."

I shake my head, "Don't let go though, okay?" I look down at the map on my hand. We are right over the burning red ember at the end of the line. I look up and scream, seeing the blonde. She is with other blondes. It's like Hitler's angel army in a cloud city. Where the other witches all have women of all nations and races, the air witches do not. I swear one girl looks like she might have exotic features, but she has blue eyes and blonde hair. It's creepy to see so many of them.

Wyatt drags his feet. My wings suck in and he's holding me in the air. We are surrounded by a white city. It is like nothing I could have imagined.

I still can't look down. I'm scared it's like that tower we saw in geography with the glass-bottom floor.

The blonde points at me, "Sin eater, meet the white priestess."

The blonde next to her, in the white gown that almost looks like a toga, gives me a nod. I bow, not sure what else to do. Wyatt shakes his head, "Please excuse her, she doesn't know anything. She was raised as a mortal."

The white priestess makes a face, "With wings and raised as if you were a human?" She finds this distasteful, apparently.

"Yes, your majesty."

Wyatt laughs and leans in, "Stop. She isn't your queen. She is the queen of the air witches."

The beautiful, and yet stern-looking, priestess nods, "Your pet is correct. You owe me no fealty. We serve the same true king. What are you wearing?"

I look down at the massive black skirt and Wyatt's black shirt. "What?"

"You look like one of those depressing fire witches." Her eyes trail Wyatt's bare abs, "His outfit is much nicer."

I smile at her lecherous stare. He tilts his head, giving her the smile. Bam! There it is. Sweet God. I smile when I see her response. She has weak knees and she's doing the heavy mouth-breathing thing I always end up doing. He is like an addiction. She blushes and turns back to me.

I blank my thoughts, actively working at filtering the dumb thoughts and weird judgments I constantly have.

I point at her, "She looks like Nicole Kidman a bit, huh?" Okay, some things get through the filter.

Wyatt smiles, "Inside voice, not the outside one."

She ignores my idiotic comment and looks down at the cloud-covered floor, "Do you know how to kill the horsemen?"

I shake my head, "That's why I'm here."

A sly smile creeps across her perfect pink lips, "You don't?"

I shake my head, "No. I don't know how."

She shakes her head as if teasing me, "No. You don't kill the horsemen. They are the mighty king's men. They are God's horsemen. He has sent them to test his people—to see who will falter and not stay strong in their belief, in the face of pain, death, and suffering."

It doesn't feel right. I frown, "Are you sure? It seems like they are kind of evil."

She shouts for no reason at all, "YOU DON'T KNOW ANYTHING,

CHILD!"

I step back. Wyatt steps in front of me, "She knows her gut feeling. If she thinks it's wrong, it is. Who told you this was the way it would be?"

She paces in front of him, suddenly shaken or upset. I don't even understand why. No wonder the other witches think they're crazy.

Her eyes turn on me, "Those traitors think we are the crazy ones?"

Wyatt gives me a look. I wince, "Sorry. Weak mind."

He turns back to her, "If you ask me, the air witches are the best ones. You have stayed true to the angels who helped make you what you are. You serve God, as we do. You fight for the cause of God's people, like we do. Fire witches are selfish and don't even get me started on earth witches. Slutty space cadets. The nixie are creepy, very creepy. You guys are the only ones I trust because we both serve God. Now tell me, who told you the horsemen were his?"

She swallows hard, "The angels."

"Which ones?"

"Michael. Our father."

Wyatt bites his lip and takes a deep breath, "Michael is the angel of war. He wants war. He wants to get back to Earth and have a big old war. I'm not saying the horsemen aren't God's. I'm just saying their purpose is extinction. They're supposed to kill off the weak and save the truly penitent and suffer the evil. But they go about it in a dark sort of way."

"It is a dark deed that is being done."

Wyatt puts a hand up, "I agree, but we can't let them all loose. The third brings starvation. People starving and the scripture says the rich will be fine; it is the already impoverished and the middle class who will die from starvation and poverty."

She nods, her eyes burning with something. She knows something we do not. Her lips twist into a grin. "The black horse is upon the Earth now. They shall all be tested."

"Shit."

Wyatt nods, "Double shit."

"The horsemen will come for Lillith's blood." The priestess laughs as if we've told a joke. I feel like it might be on us though.

The Black Horse

"When the Lamb opened the third seal, I heard the third living creature say, "Come and see!" I looked, and there before me was a black horse! Its rider was holding a pair of scales in his hand. Then I heard what sounded like a voice among the four living creatures, saying, "A quart of wheat for a day's wages, and three quarts of barley for a day's wages, and do not damage the oil and the wine!"

Revelations

One

We crawl up the slippery, slime-coated rocks of the English coastline. I look back at the nixie. They have become lights in the ocean and nothing more. I'm soaked and frozen. I look at Wyatt, "I'll fly us up. I can't scale that wall."

He nods, shivering too. I jump into the air, bursting my wings from my back and fly upward. I flap, lowering, "Grab my foot."

He laughs, "I'm fucking cold, Rayne. My fingers are cramping."

I nod, "Mine too. Just grab on and we'll be in a hot shower in like five minutes."

I feel his strong grip attach to my ankle. I flap harder, pushing us up into the air.

I struggle against the cold wind and hateful English winter weather.

"Say something funny. Make me happy. Make me smile."

"I have a serious case of blue balls, and the entire swim this damned painting smacked me in the head."

I start to laugh and he becomes lighter. My exhaustion is insane and my feeble brain decides that his statement, about his balls, is the funniest thing I have ever heard. I drop him down into the courtyard of the castle and almost fall into his arms.

He gives me a pained expression, "You think it's funny that I'm suffering?"

I laugh harder, "I'm so-sor-sorry." I can actually imagine the painting hitting him in the head.

He carries me to the house. Marie opens the door, "Miss Ellie, you alright?"

I nod. "My skin is blue and I'm exhausted, but I'm all right. Just cold." When we get inside, I moan, "Drafty, stupid castle."

"RAYNE!"

My eyes pop open. I step back into Wyatt. He wraps his arms around me.

Stella comes stomping down the hallway. Her eyes are black and the blue veins she gets when she feeds are there. She points, "What did you do to Constantine?"

I shake my head, "Nothing? I had to leave, that's all."

She sneers, "You had to kill my brother?"

My jaw drops open, "What? Oh my God! Is he…?"

"He could be." She grabs my shoulders, "He went crazy when you left. What did you do?"

I swallow hard, taking a breath. "Oh my God. You scared me."

Her eyes narrow and she leans in, looking at my finger where the ring sits. She whispers, "Oh God, why? Why would you marry him? You have broken my brother's heart." She hovers and I'm scared of what she will do. I shake my head, "Stella, I had no choice. The dead wanted it, and it was the right choice, I don't know why."

She steps back, stumbling a little. Her face breaks my heart even more. Her voice is hollow and emotionless "You have to leave. Take that Mona with you. I can't have her here. I almost ate her earlier. You have to leave." Her eyes dart to Wyatt and the rage starts, "Take your family and get the FUCK OUT OF MY HOUSE!"

Her fangs are there and her eyes are black, almost red. Her screams echo and bring the wind with them. The dead sparkle around me, making a barrier.

She is trembling and laughing bitterly suddenly, "Would you threaten me with the dead, Ellie?"

I shake my head, "Never." I can feel them there, waiting for me to ask them to fight. I whisper, "I love you."

She rages, "YOU LOVE NO ONE! YOU ARE TRULY THE DAUGHTER OF LUCIFER AND LILLITH!"

Tears stream my cheeks. I know I'm heartbroken, but I can't feel it. I am close to losing my mind. I drop to my knees and grab the dagger I know Maria keeps on her ankle under her dress. She flinches when I pull it. Stella's eyes are wide. I grab the blade, looking Stella in the eyes and turn it. I close my eyes, tears slipping down my cheeks, and drive the blade into my stomach. I gag and buckle forward. I cannot scream. I thought it would bring a scream, but it has stolen my voice. The pain is intense. I sob but it sounds like a sheep. Maria cries out and I feel Wyatt tense behind me.

I drop to my knees. Stella is there instantly, at my side. "What are you doing?"

I shake my head and speak in my sheep voice, "I feel nothing. I have no heart anymore. I have to feel the betrayal that I have committed and blood is the only way." The words are not mine. They are Ellie's and the others. "I have no love in my heart."

With a trembling hand, she reaches for the blade, pulling it from my stomach. Blood seeps out, spilling onto the floor."

She sobs with me, "Why?"

I shake my head, "I think I am not meant to feel this time, sister. I think I am meant to die. In the end, I am still meant to die."

She shakes her head, "Don't leave me again."

I curl into her. She looks up at Wyatt who has not moved, not even a little. "You did this."

I shake my head, "It was me."

She holds me until the blood stops flowing. Wyatt drops down onto the floor behind me. His body is no longer cold. It is warm, hot even. He presses against me and I feel something wet. I reach behind me, touching his wet stomach. When I bring my hand forward I cry out. My hand is coated in blood.

He whispers into my neck, "What happens to you, happens to me."

I shake my head as more tears fall. "I'm sorry. I didn't know. I just needed to feel the pain I have caused."

Stella laughs, "You always were so dramatic." She hugs me to her, but I know she is looking at Wyatt when she says, "Someone just guaranteed his ass would always be saved."

Wyatt scoffs, "You know nothing about me, fanged devil."

Stella laughs, "I'm just relieved you don't have her sense of humor now." She gets up, lifting me with her. Maria is pressed against the wall of the hallway, stunned and scared. I smile at her, passing her back her dagger. She takes it, shaking her head and whispering a prayer.

As we hobble to the great room, I ask softly, "Where did he go?"

She shakes her head, "I can only assume after the horsemen. He wants this to end so he can be with you forever."

My eyes lift to meet her pained ones, "I don't have forever, Stella. I have until I finish."

She shakes her head, "How do you know?"

I shrug, "Just a feeling."

Wyatt looks back at me, "You're wrong." He wishes I were, but I know he can feel it too.

Mona comes running over when we get to the fire, "Where did you guys go?"

I shake my head, "Boston. Just quick."

Her eyes are hopeful. I close my eyes, "I'm sorry."

Her hands slip to her mouth, "Oh God." I wrap my arms around her, holding her to me. She sobs into my already-wet and stinking over-sized shirt. Wyatt gives me a look. I hate this. I hate everything. I can't feel the hate, and I can't be angry or sad for my friend. But I know I do. I know I hate it all.

Stella sits on the couch next to Michelle who looks up and takes her headphones off. "Hey guys! Where did you go?"

Wyatt speaks in the same tone he always uses for Michelle, "Boston."

She nods, "Cool." She looks at Stella, "Wanna go for a walk?"

Stella smiles at her, "No. Constantine told me you were never to leave the castle. No matter what." She tilts her head and plays with Michelle's blonde hair. Michelle frowns, "Why?"

Wyatt gives her a disgusted look, "Because you sold your soul to the devil and we don't want him tracking you. Constantine puts a guard on his houses. Can't you feel it in the air?"

She looks down instantly, "Oh."

Mona pulls away from me and leaves the room. I don't have what she needs. I don't have compassion. I don't have anything. I am a void, an empty void.

I hear the others inside of me, muttering and speaking in low tones. They are panicking. They sense him. I spin, seeing the most tragic thing I have ever seen, walking into the room. Constantine laughs bitterly, undoing his blue dress shirt. His eyes land on the ring on my finger. I see hatred burning on his face. His dark hair is wet from the rain and mist. He looks tragic and beautiful as he crosses the room to me. I see Wyatt's eyes on me. Constantine opens his shirt. There, on his chest is my other name; Ellie appears just like the witch said it would. It is exactly like Wyatt's.

My lips are open but nothing comes out. I don't recall it. Ellie is sobbing inside of me. She is trying to take control and run to him. But I stand there frozen. He turns his face to Wyatt, "Don't get too excited. She gets one of these every couple centuries. It's less of a big deal to her."

Ellie's pain becomes mine and I feel it. We share the agony. Me and Ellie and the others, we hurt the same for once.

I can't look at Wyatt. I turn and leave the room, following after Mona. I feel the shame and the hurt and the hatred of myself. I feel it, and though it burns, it is bittersweet. I am grateful for a feeling.

Mona is on the bed, curled up in a ball. She is dialing on her cellphone over and over, listening to her voicemail messages from her mother. Her mother wishing her merry Christmas and happy New Year. Her mother panicking that she hasn't heard from her. Her mother wondering if she has found somewhere safe to go.

Mona is a wreck, obviously.

She dials and presses speakerphone. Her mother's voice fills the room. "Oh, uhm hi, sweetie. I am so sorry for everything. I watched the news today, and with everything that's happening, I'm scared that you are dead. If you get this, please call me. I have prayed for forgiveness, in case we don't speak before one of us is gone. I love you. Stay safe."

I curl around Mona, but before I can help her, the dead take me.

The dream is instant. I swear my eyes have only just closed.

"Rayne, where are we?"

I turn to see Mona. Her eyes are puffy and her face is tired. She looks like she did on the bed. How is she here? Is she here? "My dream."

She nods, "Oh. Creepy."

I look around. We are in a blanket of mist. I take her hand in mine and start to walk. It feels like we are not moving, the mist is so thick.

"Do you think my mom knows I love her?"

I nod, "She knows. Willow said she is with God. She is safe."

"Good." She sighs, "I just realized, I need to find my dad."

My eyes dart at her. She starts to cry again, "Really? Both of them?"

I nod, "Your dad is with your mom. He went to her and they were together when they passed."

She smiles through her tears, "I guess that's something. At least they had each other and they weren't alone."

I wrap my arm around her, "And we have each other."

She sniffles and points, "Do you see that?"

I look and there before us is a huge gate. It is silver with a greenish hint to it. We walk up to it. It opens slowly, as if a ghost opened it.

Mona takes my hand and pulls me through. When we are inside, the gate closes again. I hear it click and the mist clears up. Before us is a massive forest. There are birds, butterflies, and flowers everywhere. I smile, "This is the garden."

She takes a deep breath of the warm air, "It's sweet."

I nod. It is like breathing honey-scented air. It is summer but lusher than any garden I've been in, in the summer.

There is a subtle path in the long green grass. It doesn't look like it's carved out but maybe walked a lot. We start down it, still holding hands.

"Your mother should be in here."

"Yup."

She looks back at me, "She might be a total bitch."

I nod, "Yup."

She makes a face. I can feel the dead around me though. They are there, sparkling. The grass tickles against me. This is the first time someone else has come into my dream, except my mother and Willow. I hope it doesn't mean Mona is going to die. My mom is and Willow is already dead. I can live without Michelle. It's a terrible thought, but I know it's a truth. I can live without Stella. I don't want to, but I know in my heart of hearts I can. I can't live without Mona. She is in my heart, and she has worked her way into the rest of the people inside of me. Mona is the real sister none of us have ever had. Stella would have turned me away, had I not demonstrated my love for her with the blade. Mona never would have abandoned me, no matter what I had done.

She is solid. Her being in the garden proves she is pure of heart and soul.

And sometimes I catch myself just staring at her glossy lips, not in a way that means I want to date her. It's not totally a lesbian stare; it's more like how we all agree Ryan Gosling is hot. Men and women alike agree, he is a sexy man. Mona's lips are like that. Men and women alike stare. I have seen them. Not just because she looks so much like Blair from *Gossip Girl* either.

We leave the grassy field and enter a forest that looks magical. I sort of assume it is. We're in a dreamland, in an enchanted forest or the garden of the fae. Either way, this is some magical shit.

When we get deep into the forest, a woman in a long white dress walks towards us. She has golden-blonde hair and a perfect face. Mona looks at me, "This is *Lord of the Rings*."

I nod, "I know. I was just thinking that."

"Is this still a dream?"

I shake my head, "No clue. The dead are here with me."

She makes a face, "Ewwww. That's doesn't make me feel better."

I watch the woman walk towards us, "It should. Never underestimate the dead."

The woman in the white dress walks right past us. She doesn't see us, nor notice us in any way. I scowl, "Uhm, miss, excuse me."

She walks on.

Mona scowls, "Snooty bitch or 'cause we're in a dream, they can't see us?"

"I hope the second." We continue on the trail that is more like a goat path between the trees. Houses come into view. They seem like small cottages. When we get closer, a small palace can be seen between the trees.

Mona smiles, "I'm going to assume your mother is in there."

I laugh, "I would bet my life on it."

We walk through the small village in the forest. No one looks at us. No one speaks to us. They wear long dresses and old-fashioned tunics. It's like *Masterpiece Theater*.

Mona shakes her head, "Dude, this is messed up. That guy is wearing deer-skin shoes."

I wave at him, "Hi!"

He walks past. Mona shakes her head, "They can't see us."

We walk by them to the cobblestone path where the palace starts. The houses are like the courtyard of the palace. It is an ivory palace with turrets and strange oval windows. It shimmers almost. I take Mona's hand again. We pass over a bridge that isn't really a bridge. It's shaped like one, but it's got no moat or water below. We enter the large doorway that is open. The dead stop. I feel it when the tingle in the air is gone. I stop too. Mona gives me a puzzled look, "What?"

"The dead have stopped. They aren't coming in with us."

She looks behind us, making me smile. "You can't see them." She blushes and turns and walks farther into the palace. Inside is like being in a historical movie. Stone walls and lavish tapestries. They all have forest scenes with creatures and nature on them. The furniture is made of wood but still rough and unprocessed. It's actually cool to see. It looks like the newest urban trend.

There is a massive set of stairs in front of us. We climb them slowly, our feet not making a sound. A man walks down the stairs. He has the tunic thing on. He looks like an idiot, to be completely honest. I hate tunics. The pants are another story. They are tight and the man walking towards us has been graced by God himself in the groin.

Mona gives me a look, "Michelle would love it here."

I laugh, "That guy should have been part of that thing she was petitioning about."

Mona frowns, "What thing?"

I roll my eyes, "The whole free the Hamm-aconda movement."

She snorts, "Jon Hamm's underwear situation?"

I nod, "That's the one."

"I would have signed that."

I laugh, "Wow. I never saw you as a petition sort of girl."

Mona blushes, "I may be a virgin, but I'm not that kind of virgin. I'm just picky. Have you seen the pics on Perez Hilton? Dude. Jon Hamm has a forearm in his pants."

"You sound like Michelle."

She glares. I put my hands up, laughing, "I like that we can talk about Jon Hamm's penis while dream walking through the garden of the fae. This is what I love about you. You keep it real."

She blows me a kiss with her glossy lips.

At the top of the stairs, there is a hallway to the right and the left. Mona starts right immediately so I follow her. We get to a series of rooms, like bedrooms. They are simple, not what you would expect to find in a palace. The furnishings are the same as downstairs, very rustic.

We turn around to go the other way, but a man with a tunic and an old face is standing behind us. He has white eyes. He smiles, "You have come, finally."

We both look behind us and realize the blind man can see us, somehow.

I bite my lip, nodding slowly.

"Sin eater, daughter of Lillith. We have waited this many years for you to come. She waits upstairs for you."

He points the other way, to the other hallway. I walk past him, pulling Mona with me. He stands there, not moving. We continue to walk away from him, not sure if he's coming or not. I am actually lost in this dream. In the other hallway, we find an open area with chairs and a fountain. There is another stairway. We climb it, still looking back for the man.

"I don't think he's coming."

I shake my head, "No. His eyes were weird. Really white."

"I'm going to have nightmares about this for the rest of my life."

I laugh, "You won't remember it. The dead never let me see where they took me."

We get to the top of the stairs and again there are two hallways. Mona walks right. "We went right last time, we should go left."

She pulls my hand, "No, right again." She pulls, and when we pass by several ladies in dresses, I have a feeling she is right. The room is a grand sitting room. There is a great throne made of the brightest white crystal I have ever seen. It's empty and looks like it's not really there, like it's a hologram.

There are people milling about the room. I catch a glimpse of one of them in the corner. Instantly, my eyes are drawn to him. He is not a man, and he is not a monster, but he is somewhere in the middle. He has dark-blue veins running his face and throat. He looks like he might have been a vampire who fed off dark-blue ink instead of blood.

He speaks to a woman in a pale-violet dress. I know who she is the moment my eyes land on her. My mother's hair glistens in the light, the way I remember it. Instantly, Ezara and Liana start to cry inside of me. They sob for our mother. Only Ezara, myself, and Liana know her. Maggie and Ellie could care less about her. They want her dead and they want this ended. Liana and Ezara weep as I walk to her. Mona pulls me back, "Is that her?"

I nod. Mona shakes her head, "What if she can see us? What if she kills you?"

"She won't. She wants to die for me."

Mona grabs my hands, "You are an idiot. She doesn't want to die for you. I am telling you. She doesn't. She wants to kill you and live out her life here. She wants the world to end, I bet you anything."

I pull Mona with me, dragging her against her will to where my mother stands. I see her back straighten. She knows I am here. She spins, looking at the air around me. Her face breaks my heart. I cringe as she looks around me.

She smiles but I see terror in her eyes that look like mine. She whispers, "You cannot see the truth here. You cannot see the chains. Bring a dagger next time, child."

She turns back to the man with the blue veins. He scowls, "What was that?"

She shakes her head, "I think a wisp has made it inside. Downstairs maybe. I can feel it." She smiles softly, placing a hand on his arm, "Where were we?"

He smiles, "We were discussing how my mother was just telling me that when the era of man is gone, and they are but a stain upon the Earth, the reign of the fae shall return."

My mother nods slowly, "Yes. What a wonderful notion that is, but what about the angels?"

A man next to the blue-veined one gives Lillith a fierce look, "The angels? You would dare to ask me about the very traitors who betrayed us from the start? You will always be one of them, Lillith."

Her mouth opens, but instead of hearing her words, we are sucked backwards. Mona holds my hand tightly as we are flung backwards. It is as if a vacuum pulls us down the stairs. When we get back to the door where the dead are, we wake.

I open my eyes, seeing Mona next to me on our bed. She smiles at me, "Did that just happen?"

I scowl, "What?"

She cocks an eyebrow, "Jon Hamm's penis and the crystal throne and your mother?"

My brow pulls together, "I don't remember. Did we see the penis? Did you come into my dream?"

She smiles, "I do remember, no we never saw the penis, and yes, I did join you in that bizarre dream walk."

She tells me a story and I don't recall anything. I pace the room, trying desperately to envision the dream the way she recalls it. "I just wish…" I stop myself, "Oh my God, I have an idea." I grab her hand and drag her off the bed. We run down the hallway to the room with the fire. I smile at Stella who is listening to music with Michelle on the couch.

"Stella, can you get the images from Mona's head and put them into mine?"

She cocks an eyebrow, "What?"

I nod.

She looks at Mona, smiling devilishly. "Of course." She gets up and saunters over to Mona who has a nervous look on her face. "Is this going to hurt?"

Stella shakes her head, "Only if you want it to."

Mona scowls, "I don't want it to, at all."

Stella puts her hands on Mona's head, "Stay very still."

Mona nods.

Stella lowers her lips on Mona's. Mona freezes for a second before returning the kiss to Stella. Stella bites down gently on her lower lip, sucking it. Mona moans into the kiss.

Constantine walks into the room, still looking wounded. He sees the kiss and I know he's jealous. He narrows his eyes, "What is this?"

Stella sucks a little more before pulling back. She takes my hand and looks into my eyes deeply, "You will read my mind and remember everything you see."

I nod, "I will." The sound of my voice is weak and trancelike.

Her pupils dilate and instantly the images flood my mind. My heart cracks a little at the sight of her face—my mother's face. She is unchanged, young, and exactly as I recall her.

Stella steps back, smiling at Mona again. Michelle stands up, looking confused, "What was that shit?"

I grin, "Jon Hamm's penis, a crystal throne, and my mother."

Michelle smiles, "I so need to see Jon Hamm's cock. He has a forearm in there, I swear it."

Me, Mona and Stella laugh.

Two

He doesn't meet my eyes as I retell the dream to him. Constantine paces in front of the fireplace, "So she is a captive? We are to believe that regardless of leaving several times, she is a captive?"

I shrug, "That's how it seemed."

He shakes his head but Gretel nods, "That makes perfect sense."

I scowl, "What?"

She nods, "It does. If the fae took her in with the hopes of using her to end the world, she wouldn't be able to escape. They are more powerful than anything. There is no way they will let you in with a dagger though. The garden doesn't allow sin in and it doesn't allow violence."

I scowl, "Holding her captive isn't a sin?"

Gretel shakes her head, "Not if they believe in their hearts they are doing it to save the Earth. That could be a legitimate thing for them."

Wyatt enters the room. He doesn't meet my eyes either. I know inside of me, my hearts—all five of them are breaking; Liana and Ezara for our mother, Maggie and Ellie for Constantine, me for Wyatt, Constantine, and my mother.

He sits on the couch next to Sarah, "What have I missed?"

I get up and leave the room. I don't want to be in there with them, retelling the story and living through all three things that are hurting me.

Mona runs after me, "Do you think you and I could find the garden?"

I look back at her, "We need to."

Mona scowls, "Where are you going?"

I grab the door to the cellar, "I'll be back in a bit." She folds her arms, "I saw on the news that pillaging has gotten so bad that they're doing food rationing and only allowing people to take so much per week."

"I don't know how to help them. The air witches said we don't kill the horsemen, but that feels wrong. I need to end my parents and be done with the devils so I can face the antichrist."

Her eyes glisten like she might lose it any second.

I nod, "I know how you feel. This has been a very bullshit year." I stomp down the dark hallway to the nixie.

When I get to the cliff, I can feel the dead. They're trying to tell me something, but they aren't using their words. The day is gray and cold. The ocean is covered in white caps and froth. I hold myself for a second, thinking about what I'm about to do.

"The queen, the sea queen. That's who you need." When I hear Wyatt's voice, my guts burn. I turn back to see him in the tunnel. He winces, "I don't care. I don't care what you did with him, before. When you were the other girls." His eyes burn like my stomach does. He steps towards me, "I love you. You. The person you are right now. I don't know those other girls; I don't even really care about them. I love you. I adore you. You scare me more than anything in the whole world, because like I told you before, I don't think I can live without you."

I walk to him, "I didn't know he and Ellie did that. I swear I didn't."

He nods, "I know. You were too scared to know. I could see that you didn't know."

I take his hands in mine, kissing the palms of them both, "I love you. I can't feel it right now. I can't even feel your words. My heart is splintered into the five pieces of my soulless soul. But I know I love you."

He smiles, "I'll take that. I'll take a fifth of the love you can give." He lowers his face, brushing his lips against mine. The feathery kiss is delicate and something we don't normally do. I like the smell of him, the feel of him, and the warmth of his body against mine. I wince into the kiss as my wings burst from my back. I grab onto him and leap. We soar up into the air, like a backwards swan dive. My wings pull in as we break the cold surface of the ocean.

The redhead from before is there. She smiles, "Have you seen your mother?"

I nod. Wyatt leans over me, "Take us to the queen, please."

She looks like she might say no, but she glances at me again and offers me a hand.

I take Wyatt's and suddenly we are pulled down. We go down for a long time. We pass an old, rusted shipwreck, fish, and weeds. Then we pass into darkness like I have never seen. Her eyes glow like mine. I can see, and yet, I cannot. It is dark and there is nothing to see. We pass through the darkness until it gets light again. There, in the water below, is a series of miniature palaces. When we get closer, I realize how far down they are; they're huge.

We soar towards them, gaining speed. I am ready to burst my wings like a parachute when she slows us and we float down. There is gravity. It is like a regular place. I could walk if I chose to. It's not the same as the ground above. I can float and swim, but I float down to the surface.

We pass sea life, rocks, and plants. It's like an aquarium. I don't even have words for it. Wyatt doesn't either. He is staring like me. She pulls us to the largest of the palaces. It is made of shells and sparkles in an unnatural way; the light is unnatural. It is blue and effervescent.

She looks back at me, “He doesn’t speak, no matter what.”

I nod. I don’t need to look at him. He knows this shit better than I do.

We get into the palace, and instantly I am regretting my decision to seek out the sea queen. She looks like a fairy, but she has sharp teeth and scales. She looks evil and cartoonish. Her features are sharp and tragically beautiful. Her glowing white eyes land on me, “Sin eater.”

I nod, “Your highness.” I bow again. I have to. She smiles, “You are exactly as I imagined you would be.” She holds her nose a little higher, “I saw you coming. I predicted it. I knew you would look this way and be this way.”

I don’t say a thing. She makes me nervous, that I can feel. I think all five of us are freaking out.

She does a swim-walk back to the shell throne. “You wish to know how to get into the garden?”

I nod, “Please.”

“The garden will come to you when you desire something pure of it. If you want a thing, it will never come. You must truly wish to lie at the feet of Lillith and worship, and gain nothing from it.” She is smug. She and Wyatt should talk, they would get on like a house on fire.

I offer her my hand, “My mother is a captive of the fae.”

She laughs instantly, “You are a fool if you believe them capable of evil. They are the keepers of this world.”

I nod, “They want the world back. They want the humans dead.”

She stops laughing and motions for me to come closer. I go closer, offering her my hand. I don’t know why I feel like I should, but the dead are urging me to do it. They are whispering that she will read me.

She snatches my hand, bringing it to her face. I don't expect the intense pain I receive and cry out. Her sharp teeth bite down hard on the palm of my hand. I stand there, tense and trembling until she lets go, "Who has planted this memory?"

I shake my head, "It is the memory of a dream walk in the garden. The dead took me."

She looks stunned, less smug for sure. She gets up, pacing back and forth. Her dress moves around her like a bunch of snakes or eels. She turns sharply, "You must take him with you. That is all I have for you. The best place to have the garden show itself to you is a stream in Ireland. She will take you there now. Leave and never come back."

She turns her back. I have shamed her or something, but either way, she is not going to help me again. She speaks without looking back at us, "Seven of our strongest will go with you. He must be cleansed before he can go. Take them to the shores of the riverbank."

Wyatt looks sickened. He opens his mouth, but the redhead gives him a look. She grabs my hand and I grab his. My hand is throbbing still where she bit me. The redhead pulls us up, fast. I swear my head feels like it's going to explode. When we break the surface, we are not on the cliffs near Constantine's, but Constantine is there. He offers me a smug smile. I crawl from the ocean to where the riverbank is, but Wyatt stays behind.

The first nixie offers her throat to him.

Constantine shakes his head, "Let me."

The nixie scowls, but he is gone in a puff of smoke and then behind her. He bites into her throat, pulling the essence into him. He screams as he swallows. There is a sizzle as the nixie essence goes in his mouth. The next one swims up. She holds her head to the side.

"Constantine stop, we need Wyatt to come into the garden with me. Stop!"

He smiles, "If I eat their essence from them, I can come instead."

Wyatt tries to grab at Constantine, but he is gone and the nixie are too. Wyatt slaps the water, "What the hell is he doing?"

I shake my head, scanning the water for them. Constantine is next to me on the shore, dripping wet and angry looking. He smiles, but I can see the pain in his eyes. "You can fill me in while we wait for the gate."

We walk up to the stream we are in front of. I am shivering and aching. Constantine gives me a look, "Hungry?"

I nod. He grabs my face, kissing me harshly. I suck instantly. His kiss is filled with the last of the bad things he has done. Wyatt grabs my hand, but I am pulled into the food. I can feel when it changes over, and I am no longer getting evil from him. He continues to kiss me. I push him back and land in Wyatt's embrace. Constantine's eyes dart from my face to Wyatt's. I wipe my lips, "Where is your unending supply of evil?"

He laughs, "I am clean as a whistle again. Nixie essence is truly a miracle drug. I saved you the last little bit, just in case you hadn't remembered to eat. I recall that about you. Always starving and then attacking." He walks up to the creek, "So, when does the garden gate come to us?"

"How did you know where we were?"

"The nixie. There was one at the shores when you dove in, a blonde who stayed behind. When I ate her, I could see everything. The nixie are linked. They speak to each other without speaking."

"Like you and Stella."

He nods, "And the air witches. The fae do it too. Only the earth and fire have lost that. Too mixed with the humans."

Wyatt gives him a sneer, "The gate probably won't come for you."

Constantine smiles, "You doubt my resolve in this, don't you?" he leans into Wyatt, "The thing you don't realize is that I have been on this path for hundreds of years, with her. Your six months and weird Van Helsing juju is nothing, compared to the undying love I have for her. I wish for nothing but her success, and I will die to see it happen."

Wyatt laughs, "You think I wouldn't?"

Constantine shrugs. They give each other the same arrogant and cocky expression. Constantine smiles, "I know this much, when push comes to shove, and I die for her, you better be ready to step into my boots, son. They're big boots to fill, and you have to be up to the task."

"Oh, don't you worry about me, old man. I got this."

Constantine gives him a smug smile, "We'll see, won't we?"

I grab them both, "Pretty sure arrogance isn't going to get us in the gate. You two shut the hell up and start wishing you could lie at my mother's feet for no other reason than to see her succeed."

We sit on a mossy stump. I'm shaking, cold, and tired. I'm tired of friggin' winter, cold water, swimming with the friggin' nixie, and the damned cold wind in England and Ireland. I need a vacation, somewhere warm. I need to sleep with the dead for a year.

Wyatt leans against me, "People are starving everywhere. The first horse has come and gone. The rich are fine, still eating what is left in the warehouses. The military is guarding them and delivering the food to the people who can afford it the most."

I shake my head, "That's sick. I do wish my mom could succeed in her goal. I wish the world was free of the bad things people do."

Constantine nods from beneath the tree across from me, "Yes. Humans have long lived a life of greed and selfishness. Lillith and the fae have the right idea."

I feel my eyes threatening to close, but I push the dead away. They sparkle around me, wanting me to follow them to sleep, but I can't. We have a goal.

The last thing I see is Constantine shouting at me. He disappears as I close my eyes.

When I wake, I am in my bed at Constantine's again. There is warmth next to me. I see Wyatt's face, not Mona's. I smile, "Why are we here?"

He laughs, "You passed out. We waited for two days and then we both got hungry and mean, and decided to come home. The nixie swam us back the castle."

Constantine comes into the room. His eyes are pained when he sees us on the bed. He sighs, "There is something unbelievable in the courtyard."

I get up, noticing the dead there. They're sparkling and twirling about me. Wyatt takes my hand, pulling me behind Constantine through the halls.

"What is it?"

He shakes his head, "I cannot even describe it. You need to see it to believe it."

I scowl, "Okay."

We walk out the front door and I stop instantly. There is a lineup of people. They are starved and ragged looking. They are weak and tired. They have sores, and in some cases, severe injuries. I don't even know what to say or do. I can smell and almost taste the evil in them. My stomach rumbles.

Constantine smiles, "I know, right?"

I give him a confused look, "Why are they here?"

Stella comes walking around the corner with a man in her arms and blood dripping from her lips, "They want to die. God told them to come to you for absolution."

I stumble down the stairs, "I can't help you. I'm sorry. God was wrong. I can't kill you all."

A man walks to me, "You are the sin eater; you must bless us and let us go to him. You are our redemption."

I look around as the crowd starts to come towards me, "Why are you giving up? Why don't you want to fight and save this place? Why not fight together to kill the horsemen and save the Earth from Lucifer?"

I look back at Wyatt. His jaw is set, I can see he is ready to fight. I shake my head, "We cannot sin."

He smiles, "Self defense is not a sin."

"Wyatt, I need the light of the world. I need it from my mother. I have to get into that garden."

He nods, offering me his hand. He pulls me to him. Constantine looks around and then at Stella, "End them, sister. No one wants a bunch of cowards on the Earth anyway."

Stella starts to laugh. I hurry back into the house with Constantine and Wyatt. My stomach is burning from hunger. I drop to my knees, pressing my hand against the door and leaning my exhausted head.

Constantine drops to his knees too, "We need to go now. We need to find that garden."

Mona walks over, "I'm coming. I have a feeling I'm supposed to."

I glance over at Michelle. She shakes her head, "No way. Not even for the road trip. I'm staying here. That's the freaking Z-Apoc out there. You guys go ahead." She has slowly become less of a human. I suppose not having a soul has ruined the person she used to be. The person I loved.

I look at Wyatt, "I'm taking Mona and him. When I ate from Constantine, you would have absorbed some of my evil; the taint will be on you. You're not the sin eater, you're just tainted."

He opens his mouth but his mother comes forward from the couch, "She is right. The sin eater has reason for eating sin, you do not." She smiles, "I need your help anyway."

He is about to argue, but she shakes her head, "I have found the horsemen. I need your help."

He looks back over at me and nods, "Okay." I don't like the look I see in his eyes. He looks at Constantine, “You keep her safe.”

He nods once.

I look at Mona, “I’ll fly you, and he can do his weird vanishing there.”

She smiles, “This is the right choice, trust me. I can feel it.”

Three

The gate comes when we least expect it. We have sat in the same spot by the stream for a day and a half. Mona has run out of her packed food, and Constantine has been eyeing her jugular up like it's nobody's business. I'm hungry in a way that can't be helped. I push away the desire to suck Mona of every last drop. When I am lost in a thought about ending this all by any means necessary, the gate materializes.

It looks the way it did in the dream. My feet walk before I'm actually ready. Mona grabs my hand, and I swear I'm in a fairytale. We get inside and look back as Constantine walks through. He closes his eyes and swallows hard as his feet cross the boundaries. He smiles wide, "Well, that's that then, isn't it?"

I laugh, "What?"

"A vampire has never entered the gates before." His eyes twinkle, he's always so cryptic. "We have too much sex, too much killing, and a general lack of a soul." He winks at me, "But I am not a regular vampire." He steps to me, "Let's hurry."

We cross the grassy field to the village. A woman in white walks towards us; the one from the dream walk. Her eyes lift and a fearful look crosses her face and we see her realize that we shouldn't be there. We are not fae. She stops dead in her tracks, "How?"

I smile, "I'm the daughter of Lillith. I need to see her. She has summoned me."

The woman looks around quickly, panicked. "You brought it right to them, after all these years and after all her hard work… You brought it right to them?"

I shake my head, "What?"

She sighs, "The weapon against the angels."

I look at Constantine. He looks pissed. "What weapon?"

"The light of the world."

He gives me a sideways look, "Where is it?"

Mona's jaw drops, "Oh God, is it inside of her?"

My jaw joins hers on the floor. I shake my head, "That can't be right. I have only death and badness in me. Not to mention, a bunch of other girls. There's no way."

The woman shakes her head, "You must leave now! Back to the gates before they see you."

Constantine steps towards her, "Why are you helping us?"

Her bright-blue eyes flash, "Not everyone wants the world put back the way it was before God changed everything. Not all of us believe in genocide."

Mona looks at me, "What do you want to do?"

My jaw sets in typical Rayne stubbornness, "I want to free her. She is expecting me. She wouldn't have called me here unless there was no other way."

The woman smiles, "You know she is captive here?"

I nod, "We suspected. That or she was in league with my father."

"She would never help him, not ever."

Constantine gives me another look, "We need to turn back. This could be a trap. I don't know enough about the light. I assumed…"

I snap at him, "We all did. My mom and Fitz both thought it.

Everyone thought it was in her—Lillith."

Constantine laughs, "And all this time, those Van Helsings have had you in their grasp, forever seeking the light for his holy pain in the ass." His laugh makes us all laugh. I've never seen him so free.

I scowl, "Don't talk about God like that." I don't even know why I'm defending him. The guy has never done me any favors.

Constantine scoffs, "Not God—Michael. God would have nothing to do with this." He starts to laugh harder. He bends forward, almost taking a knee.

The woman in white laughs, "The garden takes your cares. You are like a child again. The effect will wear off."

I shake my head, "I don't want it to. Look at him. He's free."

She speaks over Constantine's howling, "You have to flee, sin eater. They will kill you and steal your light. They will use it and send everything with a soul back to heaven. It's the reset button. The fae will take back the world, the fae and the witches and the creatures."

I shake my head, "I have to kill Lillith first. The gate may never show itself to me again. I have to use this chance. We only got through because the nixie helped us."

She bows subtly, "Please reconsider."

I squeeze Mona's hand, "Sorry." I look at Mona, "Can you take my friend back though? She's human."

Mona scowls, "I'm staying." She gives Constantine, who is still laughing, a look. "Maybe we should send him back though. He's a mess."

Constantine grabs my other hand, but doesn't stop snickering. "Let's go do this. I need to get out of here. I'm cramping up."

I smile at the woman, "Thank you."

She shakes her head, "Don't thank me, I should force you from the garden. But I too desire her free, I suppose. Go around the town. Avoid the people. Take the back steps and avoid eyes. Yours are obvious."

We walk to the village but stay on the outskirts. Constantine looks around as we sneak about the dense forest. "When I say fly, Rayne, you fly as hard as you can. You fly hard for the gates and kill your mother just outside of them. They cannot keep you here without a bargain. No matter what, do not deal with the fae." He's back to being crabby and serious. I'm actually relieved. His constant laughing was weird.

He whispers, "We will not have an argument about this. You will make me a promise on this now, or I will carry you like a child back to the gates."

I can't reach my fear of this place, but I know I'm terrified so I nod, "Okay."

He stops me, looking into my eyes, "Do you promise me that you will do whatever it takes to end Lillith outside of the gates?"

I nod, "I do. How do we kill her with no weapons in here? Can you bite the fae?"

He laughs, but it's his usual bitter one. "No." He looks around, "They must have weapons somewhere. We don't need to worry about killing the fae. They won't fight us. They'll use cunning. Besides, silver is the only thing that can kill them. We only need a knife to kill Lillith. You separate that head from the shoulders, just outside of the gate. That's the plan."

I look at Mona, "You should go to the gate or hide."

She shakes her head, "I have a bad feeling that I have to stay with you."

Constantine sighs, pulling us towards the castle. I look at the town below us when we get to the other side of the castle, "Why do they hate us?"

Constantine leans in, "They don't hate—they're perfect. They don't have negative emotions. They can be worried or cautious, but they don't hate or even dislike. They are not fighters. Why do you think they have never defeated the humans? They have never fought them. They would win in a heartbeat, but they do not resort to violence."

Mona narrows her gaze, "How is Lillith here then?"

He raises his eyebrows, "They're cunning as hell and evil as the day is long, as long as their purpose is noble. Noble to them means serves their purpose. They are not to be trifled with. At all. They are the only creature, beyond Lucifer and God himself, that can trade your soul in a bargain. I would bet Lillith bargained hers away to be protected from Lucifer."

We climb the steps to the crystal palace and my heart is in my throat. Mona leads us to the top floor. Constantine looks around uneasily, and Mona looks like she has tears in her eyes. I can't feel anything, but I am scared. I know I am. The girls inside of me are silent.

When we get into the large throne room, my mouth is dry and my heart is beating out of control. She is where she was the last time, speaking to the man, only he isn't himself. He is something else altogether. He is stunningly beautiful. The kind of beauty that makes me forget who I am. Lillith's back stiffens and she turns. The man's lips curl into a sexy smile. I moan a little. Mona grips me, "Who is that?"

I swallow hard, shaking my head, "I don't know. In the dream world, she was talking to a man who had the blue veins."

She wrinkles her nose, "He was hideous. I remember."

"That's him." Constantine says.

She shakes her head, "He is beautiful."

Constantine leans in, whispering so softly I can barely hear him. "Try to keep remembering him as the man from the dream. I have a bad feeling about him in particular."

I frown, "Why?"

He gives me a disturbed look, “When I saw him, I felt movement.”

I scowl, “What?”

He nods at his pants, “Movement, growth, attraction.”

I make a face, “What the hell? Why? Ewwww. Dude.”

Mona laughs nervously, “I think I misheard you.”

He shakes his head, “You did not. If I’m attracted to a bloke, we have an issue. That’s never really rung my bell, if you get my drift. He probably doesn’t even know he is the bait.”

The room isn’t silent but it’s quiet. The few scattered people talking in small clusters watch us but continue to speak to the people around them.

My mother smiles at me, “What a surprise.” I can see that it is not. She walks to us, desperate to look controlled, but I can see the panic in her eyes. I barely register her being there. The man next to her is all I see. His blue eyes meet mine and I am lost. He smiles, so I smile. He looks down, bashfully, so I do too. His smile turns to a lip bite, I bite mine. I bite so hard I blink as if leaving a trance. Constantine nudges me, “Easy tiger.”

Mona is a forgone conclusion on whether or not he can have her. She is entranced, fully. She looks up at him through her lashes, and I see him do something I don’t think he expected to do. He seems genuinely surprised at his reaction to her. He is stopped in his tracks. Instant jealousy fills me, but my mother catches my eyes again.

When I look at her, I feel nothing. I want so badly to run to her or kiss her or cry, but I am silent inside.

Her eyes fill with tears, “You misheard me, I suspect.” She glances at the beautiful man. I notice he doesn’t move or blink or do a single thing. He stares. It’s creepy. He is as lost in Mona as she is in him. I look at my mother and realize she has a sly smile creeping across her lips.

She ignores the man and looks back at me and Constantine, “You must go. Do it and go."

I shake my head, "I have one question."

She nods once. I look around the room at the people watching us. They don't speak. They stand there like a Jane Austen movie, watching us in gowns and jewels. If it weren't for the rustic furnishings and throne, I would swear we were in one of those rooms where you gossip and do a turn about the room.

"How did you get pregnant with me and where was I born?"

Her eyes sparkle, "I left the garden, met with Lucifer. I'm sure you, being a succubus of sorts, have figured out how babies are made. I came back here and gave birth to you. You were born in the garden, but you have a complicated soul. So I had to take you away. I took you to the orphanage and got the nixie to find the right witch."

I look about the room. Constantine whispers, "How does one lose their head in a place like this?"

Lillith laughs softly, "They do not. The sharpest thing here is the wit." She winks at Constantine, "I'm sure you know this already, but you brought your weapons with you."

The mention of weapons makes the others in the room nervous. They look shocked at Lillith's wording. Silence falls upon everyone as a woman comes from the back of the room, from an arched doorway. She is dressed over-the-top fancy, like Marie Antoinette but worse. Her blonde hair actually looks like a cake with pink flowers all through it. My mother's face draws in. She whispers, "Do it now."

I frown, "What?" What does she want? Does she think I'm psychic?

I see something dawn on Constantine's face, but the woman comes towards us with a soft smile. My mother points, "This is the high priestess, Faranelle."

She looks down her long, creamy nose at me. Her pale skin and sparkling blue eyes are an amazing contrast. The fae are so beautiful. I see what Constantine was talking about. I have only ever been attracted to guys—okay, and Mona's glossy lips, but this woman makes me feel something I have never felt before.

Constantine becomes something I have also never seen before. He drops to his knee, "Milady." He is humble suddenly.

She smiles at him, "You may rise, Lord Basarab. You owe me no fealty."

He shakes his head, "And yet, you inspire it in me."

She blushes and I see my mother is again confused at the behavior of the lady as she was the man. Mona and Constantine have an effect on them both, just as they do on Mona and Constantine. The four of them have a moment.

The lady tears her gaze from Constantine as he stands. Her eyes dart to me, "You must be Rayne."

I nod.

"You have come to aid us in our quest to end the angels reign over the world?"

I nod. I don't know why.

She smiles, "Excellent." She looks at Lillith, "You have kept your side of the agreement. Our covenant is fulfilled."

My mother smiles at me, "Thank you, milady."

I have a bad feeling. It's just there suddenly. Liana and Ezara flash an image into my mind. It is the face Lillith is making now. It was the same then. She is leaving me here. She has betrayed me, and I don't know how to stop her. I could jump at her and punch her in the face, but I don't have enough anger.

I look at Constantine. He is entranced in the lady still. That's just great. Perfect timing for him to become a smitten schoolboy. At least he's occupying the lady.

My mother smiles, "Rayne, do it now. Do what you have come here for."

I scowl, "You have to come with me, out of the gates." She nods towards the priestess. I shake my head, "What?" I look at the lady, "I need to take Lillith from the gates to end this."

The lady ignores me. She is lost in Constantine.

Suddenly, the man with no eyes from the dream, walks from the back of the room. He limps a bit, but I can see his eyes are white, as they were in the dream. He puts a finger to his lips, "They cannot see me, child. Just you."

I don't move. He whispers loudly, "The weapon is not what you think it is. The one who is your enemy is not the one you think it is. You must hurry."

I nod once and flash a look at my mother. She gives me an expectant nod toward the lady again. I have no idea how I'm supposed to know anything she is hinting at. The man with the white eyes smiles at me, "Love is a weapon; did you know that, Rayne? Sacrifice of love is the ultimate weapon."

I feel like we are frozen in time. The room is still. The eyes of everyone are upon me. The lady priestess is lost in Constantine, and Mona and the beautiful man are swooning at each other.

The man with the white eyes gives me a look, "Sacrifice your love and kill her."

I look at my mother, "Will you leave with me?"

She gives me a desperate look before shaking her head. "I have to find forgiveness, Rayne."

From my father? Of course. She has a plan. She looks at the priestess, "Will you excuse me, milady?"

The priestess nods once, still not taking her eyes from Constantine. Lillith looks at me; there is something in her eyes. She seems like she regrets her choice or the fact she never filled me in on the decision she is making. "Good luck, Rayne." She turns and leaves the room.

I'm confused and want to run after her, but I don't know what to do.

I grab Constantine's hand. He looks at me like he has come out of a trance. "What happened?"

I shake my head, "She left. We have to go."

The priestess looks confused, "She is free to go, of course. You must stay."

"I thought she was here, hiding from Lucifer."

She frowns, "Did no one tell you your role in all of this?"

I shake my head, "I eat the sin and save the world, it's pretty simple."

She laughs, "No child, you free the Earth from the humans who are trying to kill her. Lillith had the light but when she gave birth to you, the light left her. It went into you. We didn't know it would do that."

I sigh and look at Constantine. He shakes his head, "That's not possible."

The priestess smiles at him, "She is the weapon that was made. She was forged to save us, forged by God to help us from his mistake."

The man with the white eyes whispers again, "Pull the dagger, Rayne. Kill her."

I scowl at him, "I have no dagger." I wish he would shut up.

The priestess smiles, not realizing I am not talking to her. "Of course not, we will wait for the humans to suffer through the last horseman, and then we shall take you to the place you were birthed the first time."

The man with the white eyes shouts at me, making me jump. "PULL THE DAGGER, RAYNE!"

I look at Constantine and suddenly I see it. The dagger. Of course.

He looks at me, trying hard not to look at the lady. I bite my lip,

"Do you love me?"

Constantine nods, "More than anything."

"Pull your name from my heart."

He looks disgusted, "What?"

"Ellie, the dagger you put in Ellie."

The lady scowls, "What is an Ellie?"

I smile at her, trying to stay patient when I am ready to run after my mother. "I am an Ellie. Once upon a time, I was called Ellie. I loved a man with my whole heart and I gave it to him. Then I was born again, I fell in love with another man, and I gave him my whole heart, not knowing it belonged to another man from another life. To save the world, I had to give up the first man and sacrifice my love for him. Sacrifice is the only way to save the world."

She looks confused but Constantine looks devastated. He shakes his head, "No. Why, my love?"

I can feel the tears in my eyes, but my heart is empty of the pain. He tears open his own shirt and suddenly the word—the name Ellie—is there. It shines in the light of the crystal palace. He grabs my hands, "You take mine."

I can't. The tears blind me, but I feel him push my hand into his chest. I feel the hilt of the dagger in my hand. I cry out, "Please, no. Take mine."

His face is one of agonizing betrayal. He shakes his head, shoving me back. He screams as I am freed from his chest, me and the dagger.

I turn, holding the trembling blade in my hand. The priestess cries out, "You cannot have that in here! There are no weapons in the garden! How have you brought that here?"

I sniffle, "I cannot help you. I have to help my people."

Her blue eyes go wide, "We are your people. You were born here in the garden. We loved you first."

I shake my head, "I can't help you. What do I do? How do I stop her? How do I stop the horsemen?"

Her lip twists into a hateful look. So much for Constantine's theory on them being positive all the time.

"Swear you will stay here to be with us and help us, and I will tell your friends how to save the humans. But the light must stay here with us."

I shake my head, "What can you do with the light? What good is it if the whole world is burned and destroyed?"

She laughs and it's almost a cackle. She looks at the others like her. They laugh nervously, staring at my blade. "The angels stand no chance against it. It opens the heavens and takes everyone home."

I look at Constantine, "I'm going after her."

He nods. I look at Mona, "You coming?"

She doesn't move. She doesn't look at me. She and the man are lost in each other's stare.

The lady snarls, "You make that deal with me, or I will kill them both."

I shake my head, "No, you won't. You don't commit sins and they are innocent."

She steps closer to me, "You misunderstand. I believe my cause is just."

My hand flies, all on it's own. I don't have the strength or the care to stop myself. The white-eyed man laughs in an evil tone that sounds like a cackle. The priestess gags and chokes as the silver blade slides into her abdomen. I hear gasps and people crying out, but they do not move on me. The man next to Constantine, the beautiful man, turns his face from Mona finally. He smiles, "Goodbye, Mother." His bright-blue eyes flicker to me, "Thank you, savior. You will find your mother at the gate, if you hurry. Then we can both be free of the horrors they bring."

I look at Constantine; my heart is pounding. The lady drops to her knees and blue blood spills from her lips as if it were ink.

Constantine grabs my hand, “FLY NOW!”

I open my mouth to argue but my feet move back. I pull the dagger from her stomach as I back away.

I look down at my feet as they turn. A single tear drops from Constantine’s left eye. He offers me something that resembles a smile, “A deal made beyond the gate is a deal sealed. You promised you would fly.”

My feet drag me to the window. I cry out, “NOOOOOO!” My wings rip from my back. I scream, forcing them hurts even more. I fling myself from the window and instantly start to fly. I soar over the town until I see her. I lower in my flight as if on autopilot.

As I get on top of my fleeing mother, I kick my feet out hitting her in the shoulder. She lands hard to the ground. I can barely keep control of myself. Liana and Ezara are there in my mind.

Lillith stumbles as I land on my feet. I hold the dagger out, feeling the blue blood of the dying lady slither down the blade and hilt.

Lillith looks at the blood “You did it. I was trying to tell you, she is an evil queen. She wants the world for herself. Her motives are driven by her hatred of mankind and God. They tricked me, using the man you saw there. He was so beautiful, I believed he loved me…”

I hold the blade up, “SHUT UP! SHUT UP!” I feel like I am going crazy. Tears pour from my face, “You left me. You let him kill me, not once, not twice, not even three times, but four. You let them torture me, your own child. You let them hurt me over and over, and you never came for me.” I lower the blade, “You never came for me.”

She starts to cry, “He tricked me, Liana. He tricked me into believing we could save you. But it wasn’t true and my heart was broken. I loved you. I swear I did.”

“THEN YOU SHOULD HAVE DIED FOR ME!”

She shakes her head, “I could not. I had fallen—my soul was tarnished.”

“Oh bullshit! You could have sacrificed yourself and spared me! God would have forgiven you!”

She backs away from me, and in the bushes I can see the gate. She turns and runs for it, but I manage to grab her arm.

She turns, desperate, “We can still win this, you and me. You and me can still win this and be together, just like you always wanted.”

I shove her, “The difference between you and me, Lillith, is I already died four times for you. I already proved I have what it takes inside of me to sacrifice. I just sacrificed hundreds of years' worth of love and devotion. I just sacrificed a friendship worth more to me than you ever could be. I have given all I have to him and you and God and the people.” I step closer to her, seeing something on the shores of the riverbank that she does not. She lifts a hand to strike me, but the twitchy redhead upon the shore with the white dress grabs Lillith's arm first. She tilts Lillith's head to the side, and in her singsong voice she whispers, “She is ready to give herself to you, sister.”

I don't think. I don't let myself. I just swing once, hard. The blade that used to hold my name in someone's heart, slices the throat of the woman I only ever wanted to have love me.

I drop to my knees, sobbing and broken as something inside of me snaps. A great and powerful pain erupts. Me and the other four girls all feel the same loss. It cripples me. She looks at me from the puddle of blood and smiles, “I forgive you.” The nixie drag her from the gate. I pull my arm back and swing, separating her head from her shoulders. She becomes a pile of feathers, white feathers. I drop into them, like I am falling into a pile of leaves, and sob.

I close my eyes and beg God to just do the rest for me. I haven't got an ounce of whatever I need left in me.

Four

Fingers stroke my cheeks; they're hers. I would know the softness of them anywhere. Not to mention, the air around me smells like her. I smile into the stroke but suddenly the memory of slaying my mother comes back. On some level, I feel sick for calling Lillith my mother when I have Willow. I open my eyes, seeing her beautiful face and force a smile on my lips.

Willow shakes her head, "My Nene, you don't have to pretend with me. Cry, let it out."

Tears fill my eyes, "All I do is cry. I cry every day now."

She smiles softly, "It's a release, my love. It's a way for us to rid ourselves of the pain and sorrow we are stuck with. Let it out, it blocks your chi."

I snort, sniffling and wiping my tears away. She smiles, "She forgives you, Rayne. That's the important thing."

I feel anger claiming my face, "I don't care about her. I don't care if she forgives me. I don't want it. I've never done a thing to her."

Willow cocks a delicate eyebrow, "You killed her."

I scoff, venomously, "Then we are nearly even. I only owe her three more deaths and loads of torture."

Willow puts her hands up, "This isn't healthy. What abut the Rayne who never held a grudge?"

I sneer, "She's in here with the rest of us. It's quite the party."

"The others are there too?"

I nod.

She smiles, "Then the dead have claimed you. You sleep with your sisters, your past lives. The dead who wish to keep your soul for you. Embrace them, do not hate them. Do not hate Lillith. She was lost when she made her mistakes."

I stand up abruptly, ready to fight with cruel words and savage thoughts.

Instead, I am dropped from the ceiling onto my bed. I jolt upward, coming awake from my dream in a gasp.

Wyatt wraps his thick arms around me again, "It's okay, Rayne. It's okay."

I start to cry again, "Mona!"

He looks sick, "Where is she? She and Constantine never made it out. The nixie only had you. She told me she had a message for you and left you with me."

I shake my head, "I have to free them. I have to find them. I don't even know how. I doubt the garden will show itself to me." I turn to him, "What did the nixie say?"

"That the blood of Lillith will satisfy the devils or draw them."

I swallow hard, "What does that even mean?"

He shakes his head, "I got something cleaned up while you were gone. Want to go see them?" He gets up and grabs the picture that Willow and Fitz live in."

I hold his hand and touch the star.

We are there instantly.

Willow smiles at me, her eyes are filled with tears. "Are you okay?"

I shake my head, stumbling towards her, "I left them there. I can't get them back. Mona doesn't even know that I left her there. And Constantine cut my love from his heart to free me, so I could kill

Lillith. It's all a mess."

She shakes her head, kissing my hair, "It's okay, Nene. Lillith is dead. That's half the battle. We can get Mona and Constantine back. They're safe, the fae won't hurt them. They are nonviolent people."

I sigh, "I don't know what to do. The nixie said Lillith's blood would satisfy the horsemen. How do I end them with her blood?"

She looks at Fitz who smiles, "We don't know. You have to have Lillith's blood."

I scowl, "Why does everyone keep saying that? I didn't exactly collect a jar of it as she was bleeding out. She died and became feathers, nothing more than feathers."

Fitz looks shocked, "She became feathers?"

I nod.

"Did you keep any?"

I reach into my pants pocket and pull out a handful of feathers. He points at them, "They might work. Did you clean the knife?"

I look at Wyatt. He shakes his hands, "The nixie gave it to me. It was coated in their sea-water slime."

"That will seal the blood to the blade. The nixie know what they're doing."

I look at Willow, "What are they doing?"

She scowls, "Getting vengeance. They have long been the only witches to believe in Lillith. We tried to tell them, but they wouldn't listen to it. Lillith used them to gain access into the garden. She used them as her go-to people. She made them swear to always aid her. They have spent their lives watching over you, protecting you. They would do anything for you."

Wyatt gives me a look, "We have always documented them as part of the other versions of you."

Fitz nods, "The witches have never helped you before this though.

The nixie have, but none of the others, and they don't help each other. Not normally. They warred before, the witch wars, and that was it. They all went their separate ways, controlling their separate types of magic."

I sigh, "None of this is useful."

Fitz gives me a look, "I'm trying to help you understand hundreds, thousands of years of history."

I can see the disappointed look in Willow's eyes. I look down, "I just mean, how do I get the horsemen and how do I kill them? I'm tired, that's all."

Wyatt offers me his hand, "Let's go sleep."

I scowl, "I can't sleep until the dead take me, don't you see? I don't…just… just—just sleep. I never rest. I need the blood of Lillith? What does that even mean?" I can feel something building inside of me, "I don't ever get a minute's fucking peace from this mess! I just want to be done with it all! I want to go to school and become something other than a poor sin eater! But now I can't. The whole world is gone. It burned up. My college is probably ash. I'm tired of being homeless and owning nothing and having no one! I have no parents and no home, and my mom is a ghost in a goddamned painting and everyone wants to kill me. Do you have any idea the level of stress I am constantly being bombarded with?"

Wyatt gives me a grin. I scowl, "Fuck you, Wyatt." I press the star, the one that takes me back to Fitz's painting. I stand in the room, looking at the painting. The rage is still there, making my breaths laborious and my heart pound. I pull my dagger and stab into the painting, dragging the knife down it. A scream rips from my lips as I do it.

I feel my heart again, I have taken away the one way in which I might see them again. I have destroyed it.

Panic sets in. How will Wyatt get out?

"NO!" I grab the destroyed canvas, pulling the jagged edges

together. I slap it on the floor, pressing the edges together but they won't meet again. The canvas is too tight. I hold it with my trembling fingers, pressing the star.

I bend over the edges of the picture, lying on top of it. I don't even cry, even though I've trapped Wyatt in there. He will press the other star and end up in Boston on the side of the road and alone. On the side of the road in a, no doubt, destroyed city. I close my eyes and hold it. If I hold it maybe I can heal it. Maybe he can come back to me.

Michelle comes into the room, looking exhausted, "Hey, you're back."

I nod. She looks around, "Where's Wyatt and Mona and Mr. Sexy pants?"

I sigh, "Shit. Goddamned shit."

She flops onto the bed, "Don't panic. Just start at the beginning of shit and go from there."

I look down, "We went to the garden and there was a man. Mona got stuck staring at him and Constantine a lady. I murdered the lady and then went to my mom. I killed her with the nixie and they brought me here. Then Wyatt got stuck in that painting, and I ripped it so he's stuck in there, or he might be in Boston."

Michelle starts to laugh, "Okay, that sounds like a lot of shit. I don't even know what that means. What's the guy Mona found like?"

I shake my head blankly, pretty much dead inside or at least lost in the panic attack I'm having silently.

She nudges me. I lift my head, screaming at her, "I DON'T KNOW WHAT YOU ALL WANT FROM ME!"

She slaps me hard, and grabs me, "I'm so sorry, Rayne. That was an accident. I didn't mean to."

I burst into tears. "I killed my mom, I didn't even know her. I don't think she loved me and I killed her."

She wraps around me, pulling me into her, "No. Don't cry. You have Willow."

I cry harder, "Willow is dead too. Everyone is leaving me."

"Not me. I'm not leaving you."

I sniffle, "I don't know what to do next or where to go. I'm fucking tired."

She starts to laugh, "I know, babe. I'm tired too."

I pull her back, "You haven't done shit!"

She scoffs, "I've been reading with Stella every day and every night. I'm beat."

I laugh, rolling my eyes. "Death by orgasm doesn't count, ya ho."

She smiles, "Trust me, that's not all we do. We mostly research the old Van Helsing books. We got this, Rayne. You tell me what's next—we got this."

I wipe my face, "I have to find the horsemen. They will come for Lillith's blood. I don't know what that means."

She looks around the room, "Let's see if we can't get Stella and Wyatt's douche mom to see if they know."

I hold her to me, "No. I don't want to tell Stella that Constantine's gone; she'll murder me. They're the last of their family. And Wyatt's mom is the devil in heels."

Michelle looks confused. "Well, how should we get the horsemen to come to us?"

I nod to the window, "Go outside." It's the instinct I have. If we go outside, maybe they'll come for us.

She looks hesitant, "Maybe we should get help."

I shake my head, "Just come with me, please?"

She nods, "Okay."

We slip to the far side of the castle and leave. The weather is cold and dark.

“Have you noticed how dark it is all the time?”

I shake my head, looking about the vast gardens and grassy landscape.

“This place looks like Jane Austen movies, huh?”

I start ignoring her, looking around.

“What are we looking for?”

I almost shout at her, but I realize she is the last person with me. She is it. My oldest friend is my last friend. I’ve betrayed and abandoned everyone else.

I shake my head, “If I had to guess, I would say they are huge and smelly and undead sort of. I think of them as the ‘Ringwraiths’ from *Lord of the Rings*.”

She makes a face, “Great. You sure you don’t want to go get Constantine first?”

I sigh, “I want him to come, I just don’t think he will.”

I can’t tell her about the thing I asked him to do. It kills me inside. At least all the devastation has brought back my feelings.

I have to go to Boston. I have to find Wyatt. I look at Michelle, “Is your phone here?”

She gives me a look, “Where else would it be?” She pulls it from her boobs, of course. I take it and press Wyatt’s name. She has sent him messages in the last two days. They were in the house together texting while I was in the garden? I don’t know how to feel about that, it doesn’t even make sense. It can’t matter right now, and yet, it does. Instead of messaging him, I scroll up as she looks around the massive yard for the huge horsemen to arrive any second.

She has sent him random things.

Asking how he’s doing at 1 am or asking him if he gets lonely at 10 pm. He always responds. It’s out of character. He hates her, doesn’t he? He always acts like he does. She betrayed me.

God, focus, Rayne. Send him a message and see if he's okay. See if he's in Boston. See if he made it out. He is your husband for God's sake.

Instead, I press out of the message app. I dial his number quickly and hang up after the first ring. I pass her back the phone.

"No answer?"

I shake my head. I see her the way Mona does suddenly. Why would she text him? Him… the one person I love. Me, just me.

"What now?"

I swallow my hatred and anger, "You go on inside. I'm going to take a stroll and see if I can't stir up some dust."

She opens her mouth, but I shake my head before she can argue, "Trust me. Go back and keep Stella company. She is going to need it when she finds out her brother is in the garden."

She smiles, but I can see the pain in her eyes. She knows I don't trust her. "She knows already, Rayne. She knew he would never get out. She cried the first day you were gone, but she told me on the second day that she knew he was never coming back."

I turn away from her and walk out into the garden. The cold wind is intense, but I think I'm dying inside so it doesn't matter. I walk out to the cliffs, like I am Catherine Earnshaw on the moors. There is something especially tragic about cliffs in England. I don't know what it is, but I feel like I will never escape the feelings bogging me down.

I slump down onto the mossy cliff and look up. "Please help me. I don't know what to do. None of this is real. I don't even know if you are real, or if I am in one sick version of Alice in Wonderland or a coma in a hospital." The wind gets a bit stronger, and like a desperate psycho, I take that as a sign. I smile into the wind, "Just tell me what to do. Please."

The wind dies down, and I see that like the people Willow told me about, the ones who will always look for God when they are desperate, I too have seen a sign that is not there.

My smile fades, as if the wind washed it away.

I think I am supposed to feel the hands of God on me, holding me, carrying me the way he is supposed to when times get hard. But I have never felt more alone.

The Pale Horse

"When the Lamb opened the fourth seal, I heard the voice of the fourth living creature say, "Come and see!" I looked and there before me was a pale horse! Its rider was named Death, and Hell was following close behind him. They were given power over a fourth of the earth to kill by sword, famine, and plague, and by the wild beasts of the earth."

Revelations

One

"How the hell could you do that to me?"

I open my eyes, smiling when I see him. He doesn't look as happy to see me. Is it a dream? Do I ask that every time I dream?

Seeing Wyatt looking like he might strangle me, dripping on the carpet in the room and feeling nothing in my chest, makes me think it isn't a dream. I can smell the salt water on him.

His eyes are red and burning. "Why would you leave me there?"

I scowl, "Are you really here?"

His nostrils flare and I leap off of the bed. I whisper into his chest, "You're here?" I tackle him into the wall. He doesn't move. I grab him, climbing his body. My mouth is on his; he tastes like the sea.

My legs are wrapped around him, holding him tight to me, before he has a chance to run away. I drag his soaked shirt from his body, tossing it to the floor.

"Not now, Rayne. I need a shower." He walks, holding me in the air and carries me to the bathroom. His face seems wooden when I press my lips against his cool lips; mine are desperate and angry. He pulls back but I tear my shirt from my body as he holds me in the air. He is not responding the way I'd hoped. He's pissed. He puts me down and steps back but I step to him. I start to laugh nervously against his face as I plant kisses on his cheeks, but he growls.

"I got mad, I'm sorry." I pull back, there is fierceness in his face still. I run my hands down his cheeks, “I love you.”

He shakes his head, “You left me behind.”

I want to say that I didn’t, but I did.

His eyes burn down on me, “You keep leaving me. You are just never going to trust me, are you? I’ve backed way off on the controlling thing. I actively work at not bossing you around and dragging you all over. I let you call the shots, all of them. I let you bring me here, in some fucking stupid attempt at being with you and helping you with this.”

“You were texting Michelle? Why?”

His eyes narrow, “She texted me and I didn’t think it was a big deal. She’s your friend. I can’t believe you went through her phone.”

I can’t touch on any of it. I can’t. I’m guilty as hell of it. My face is red from the guilt of reading their texts, even if they were totally innocent. I shake my head to rattle my thoughts a bit. “How did you get here?”

He looks exasperated. He shoves me back a bit and turns the shower on. I can see more tattoos on his back. I scowl but he turns around, “I don’t know. Suddenly, I was in Boston. I was standing outside of some shitty old building; everything is burned out and ruined. Some guys chased me in a cop car, shooting at me. I ran for the sea and dove in. Nearly froze my balls off and begged the nixie to bring me back to you. They didn’t want to—some bullshit covenant that you don’t touch a claimed man.” His eyes are burning with rage, “But don’t worry, I let them know that was not the case. I had to prove it, but it worked. The nixie brought me back.”

“Is Willow pissed?”

He nods, “Yeah, Rayne. She can’t understand why you would be so hateful to her and Fitz and me. I explained that to her though, don’t worry about that.”

I can see myself in his eyes, in the hatred. It makes me hate myself.

He steps back again, “I can’t do this. I’ll shower in a different room.” He turns and leaves me there with his salt kiss still on my lips, in only my bra.

Stella comes running into the room, “Rayne, we have a major issue.”

I look at her, “Can it wait or is it major? ‘Cause I think my heart just fell into my stomach.”

She sticks her glossy red lip out, “I’m sorry, it can’t. Your father contacted Michelle. Constantine has been tracking her messages and she has a single one from Lucifer. She told him she thinks it’s him. It’s the same number as before when he was contacting her to betray you.”

“It’s so weird he uses a cell phone.”

“I know, that’s weird. Anyway, the last horseman is here, the pale rider. We have to find Lucifer, before he finds us. We think he used the message to her on her phone to track us down to the castle. Gretel has found the horsemen again, since they lost them the last time. She says that if you don’t end Lucifer before the last horseman does his ride, you cannot kill Lucifer. Whoever kills the horseman has the power.”

I sigh, letting my face fall into my hands, “Why does this have to be so hard? I seriously got excited when the devils were so easily killed.”

“Yeah well, apparently they were only the appetizers. You have to go get Constantine back.”

I nod, “I know.”

She takes my arms in her hands, “You have to dig around in there and find the girl I once knew. The one who didn’t let anyone tell her what she had to do.”

I look into her mesmerizing blue eyes, “I am so sorry about him getting stuck there.”

She shrugs, "It's probably not a bad place for him to be."

I wince, dreading the words I am about to say, but I have to. "I pulled the dagger from his chest."

She looks stunned. Her face starts to turn red, but she doesn't open her mouth. She points at me, pausing and pressing her lips together. I back up slowly. She shakes her head, closes her eyes and pounds her fist against her forehead. I turn and run for it.

"ELLIE!"

I don't wait for her to catch up. I leap out a window, smashing the glass, diving out into the air. My wings burst from my back but she has my foot. I fly into the air with her climbing me like a tree, dragging her claws into me.

"His humanity, he traded his humanity for your freedom?"

I lower us to the ground. She shoves me down, "YOU FIX THIS!"

I shout back, "I CAN'T! HE MADE ME DO IT!"

She snarls, there is a flash of white, and she's gone. I look up and Wyatt has her pinned to the ground. He snarls almost the same way she does.

She swings at him but he catches her arm and punches her. I wince, jumping up. "Don't hit her."

She hits me from behind when I get between them. He lashes at her again.

Somehow between the chaos of it all, I end up behind him with his arms around me. "She is MINE!"

Stella steps back at the noise he makes. She looks past him, "He has loved you, only you, for hundreds of years. I told him you weren't ever worth that kind of devotion, but he never believed me." She nods, almost bowing, "Thank you for proving me right."

She turns and she's gone.

I feel like I've been hit by a truck. My exhaustion is at a new level.

Wyatt turns to face me, "You okay?"

I shake my head, "I'm messing this all up. All of it. I'm the biggest mistake God ever made."

He laughs, "Let's go get you someone to eat."

I pull back, almost dizzy with hunger, "I have to go to the garden and free them. I can't eat first, it makes you sick. I can't risk the garden not letting me in if I do something bad."

He steps back from me, "Take me with you. I'll keep you safe."

I can see he isn't over the conversation in the room; he's going to be pissed for a while. I nod, "If the garden will let you in."

I hold him and fly. It isn't easy and I'm starving. When we get to the small stream, I stop mid-flight. "Look!" The gate is open and completely visible. I land us both on the bank of the stream. He walks towards it, "Is this it?"

I nod, scared.

He looks back at me, "What's the deal with finding it, if it's right here? Doesn't seem so secret."

I shake my head but hear the dead, whisper. It changes everything that they are the voices of my past. Not just the thoughts of the girls I once was, but the whispers of the actual people I was.

None of us like what we see. "Maybe we shouldn't go in there."

Wyatt laughs, "You really are the biggest chicken shit some times." My eyes narrow, "You really are the biggest jerk, all the time."

He nods, "I know."

He holds his hand out for me to take. I do it, even if he's annoying me. He's still the strongest thing I know. And his hand makes me feel safe and warm. We enter the gate, no issue. That's not right.

The field inside of the gates whispers, maybe announcing our arrival. I don't feel the sense of sanctuary I did the first time. I don't feel anything again. Great…

We enter the forest, and I pull him to the right, off of the path. He shakes his head, "Wait here. I'll be right back."

I grab him, "No. We stay together."

"No. I think I saw something. Wait here. I'll just be a second."

I try to argue but he just walks off. He disappears into the forest.

I sit on a log and wait for him. I don't understand why he wanted to leave. I don't understand why I feel such a terrible feeling here. It's different than last time.

The ground in front of me crunches. I brace myself but it's Wyatt. He puts a finger to his lips, "Something is wrong here." He offers me his hand again. I take it, jolting almost. I haven't felt that since we handfasted. He lets me lead, but he never takes his hand from mine.

Something is off, way off. I can feel it in the silence. The small village is motionless. Not a single person moves along the streets or buildings. We enter the palace from the back, like before. You could hear a pin drop and my skin is crawling.

We get up the stairs to the middle floor, and I see something in the corner of my eye. I turn to see a daisy float by. My stomach drops. I look back at Wyatt, but he doesn't seem to notice the flower, or care. When we get around the corner to the next set of stairs, I gag. Daisies are everywhere. They float by, filling the air with a sweet scent.

"Oh God."

Wyatt looks distant, "There is no way this place is this empty."

I swallow hard, "It's not."

He frowns, "Can you see people?" He looks like he doesn't trust me. I look past him to the archway where the man with the white eyes is standing. He shakes his head, "Don't come this way, child. Take the back stairs and run from here. Save yourself."

I cast a slight glimpse at Wyatt. He doesn't see the man. Only I can. I walk to him. He shakes his head, "You bring much trouble to my people."

I nod, looking down, "I'm sorry," I whisper.

He looks at Wyatt, "I see you have chosen your side, sin eater."

I look back at Wyatt. It's true. I have chosen his side. I pulled the dagger from Constantine, choosing. Even if I didn't know it at the time, I get it now.

"You betrayed us."

I look at the man, "I didn't."

Wyatt looks at me, "You say something?"

I open my mouth, but the man shakes his head, "Do not tell him I am here. His evil has done enough to this place. Get your friends and go. They are in the throne room."

I look back at Wyatt, "Wait here. I have to run up the stairs and grab them."

"No. I'm coming with you."

"You can't. You have to stay here; they're angry I brought you here."

His eyes flash, "What did they say?"

"Nothing, just that they didn't want you here."

He lashes at me, grabbing my hand harshly and shaking me, "WHAT DID THEY SAY?"

I shove him back, "STOP IT! I HATE THAT! YOU KNOW I DO!"

His jaw is set. I'm going to kick the shit out of him if he touches me, if I can. I will die stopping him. He's never going to get past his anger issues or the way he treats things like me.

My heart hurts. I've made the wrong choice, and the dead fill the air with their version of 'I told you so.'

Constantine never would have treated me that way. How did I

repay him for that loyalty and love? I broke his heart, and he has killed all of the fae for it. I turn and walk through a tumbleweed of daisies.

The stairs are littered with them.

Millions of daisies.

They all died here, in the throne room. When I get up to the top of the stairs, I make a noise. I don't shed the tears filling my eyes. I don't deserve to cry. I broke him and left him here.

He sits in the corner, looking out the window or staring at the corner, punishing himself.

Mona is alone in the room, kneeling over a pile of daisies. Her hands are filled with the flowers I assume were the beautiful man. She looks magnificent, dressed in a long white gown. She lifts her face when she hears my footsteps. The look she gives me confirms my fears.

I have killed them all and she will hate me forever. Her voice is soft, "You ever have that feeling when you meet someone, where you just know?"

I can't stop the tears.

She shakes her head slowly, "I know it's ridiculous. I'm not better than a Mary Sue in every YA romance novel this side of the Pecos River. But I knew it. I knew, the minute I saw him."

I look down, sniffling and wishing it had been me. Why isn't it ever me? Why does everyone else suffer?

She looks down at the flowers again, "I don't want an apology from you. I don't want anything from you."

Pressing my lips together, I walk past her to him. He doesn't move.

I drop to my knees behind him, heaving. I reach out for his shoulder, but when I touch him, the shape of him is lost. He crumbles, slowly into a pile of ash. I sob silently.

"DON'T YOU TOUCH HIM!" Mona screams. I'm flung to the side.

She stands over me, "DON'T YOU EVER TOUCH ANY OF THEM!" She starts swooshing the flowers to a pile separate of the ash. She uses her fingers and puts the ash into a small pile. She pulls her sleeve of her dress off and collects it in there. She looks distraught and obsessed.

Her hands shake, and as her tears mix with the ash, they make black stains on her. She tries to wipe it off but can't. She cries harder, putting her hands to her face. "How could you? How could you do it?"

I look down, "I'm so sorry."

"DON'T YOU APOLOGIZE TO ME! EVER! YOU NEVER SPEAK TO ME AGAIN!"

"What happened?" Wyatt's voice is like salt on the wound in the room, where choosing him unleashed death on everyone. I didn't even realize what I had done.

Mona looks up, screaming at Wyatt. She screams and cowers. He gives me a look, "She's gone mad."

Mona cradles the flowers and the sleeve of ash. She gives me a pleading look. I don't understand what's happening.

The palace starts to shake. Wyatt walks to Mona, "Give me the ash."

She screams again, shaking. I jump up, standing between them. "What are you doing? Did you do this? Is this where you went when you left me in the woods?"

He gives me a look. It's smug, but it's not his normal one. He starts to laugh.

I feel sick, "You murdered them all? You murdered him?"

He laughs harder.

Mona cries. I start to shake, I can't stop it. My hands shoot up, making a hellfire circle around Mona and me.

I can see his flickering eyes in the firelight. He stops laughing, “You really are a weak little chicken shit.”

I drop to my knees, “Kill him for me, please.”

The dead scream for me, but they don’t move against him. Black wings rip from his back, and he turns and runs for the window.

I drop into child’s pose, feeling the cold floor against my cheeks. My eyes are burning from the heat. I almost hope the flames reach me. I almost wish they’d burn me up. But I don’t. I would never get my revenge against him.

Mona sees the look on my face, “You didn’t know?”

I cry into the floor, “I didn’t know.” She starts to cry again. I smile, “I know that feeling you had. I had that once too, but I’m a fucking idiot who can’t get anything right. Not even the one simple thing I’m supposed to do.”

She shakes her head, “I’m sorry.”

I close my eyes, “Not as sorry as I am.”

Two

We land in the yard of the castle. Stella comes running, "WHAT IS IT?"

Mona hands her the sleeve of ash. Stella sighs relief. She grabs Mona's head, "You smart girl." She looks at her, "Got anyone else you brought that you want back?"

I scowl.

Mona pulls open the top of her dress. It's filled with daisies.

Stella laughs and looks at me, "I'm sorry, for before."

I shake my head, "Don't be. I deserve your hatred. All of you." I walk past them to the house. The whole thing is beyond what I am capable of feeling. His name is still in my heart. I realize it when I get inside of my room and collapse onto the bed. The heaviness of my heart weighs more than if the moon landed on my chest.

The dead take me.

I am in a garden, not the magical one but an English garden.

There is a girl who looks like me. She has dark hair and grey eyes. They light up when she sees me. She looks more like our mother. "Liana." she says.

I smile. Another girl comes walking up looking almost the same, almost identical. She nods, "Ezara."

I sit under the tree I am next to. They come and sit with me, and then a thin girl, who doesn't look anything like us, comes up. She smiles, "Maggie."

Lastly, the one who I remember the clearest, Ellie. She looks similar to me and the other two. I narrow my gaze, "You are my true sister in some way."

She grins like a Cheshire Cat, all the while curtseying like a lady. "Ellie."

We five stare at each other.

Liana sighs, "What a way to finally meet. The time of the fae has ended. Father has killed them all off and now he will kill the horsemen and take the power."

I am such a failure. I look at their faces, "I'm sorry."

They all smile the same, except Maggie. Her smile is sweeter than ours. She shakes her head, reaching for my chin, "Why are you sorry? You think each of us hasn't lived this fate? You think for a second we bested him, any better than you? He used the love in your heart against you."

"How are we able to meet now?"

"It is getting closer to your birthday. Your time is almost up. We will all be free soon."

I frown, "You have all been waiting for this to end, instead of going to heaven?"

They giggle. Ellie gives me a cocky look, "You don't know, do you?"

"What?"

Liana nods, "We won't ever make it to heaven. We may choose our form. I want to be a willow tree, near a river."

Maggie laughs, "A willow tree?"

Liana sighs again, "The thing I miss the most is the wind."

Ezara looks up, "I want to be a speck of dust, floating on the breeze always, exploring everywhere."

Maggie shakes her head, "I want to be water. I want to be part of the rivers and oceans and see what the nixie see."

Ellie gives me a hard look to take, "I want to be ash with my love."

I look at my shoes, "I want to be alone, where no one can ever get hurt by me."

Ellie takes my hand in hers. It sparkles like their voices on the wind. She squeezes, "That is one thing we will never be, sister. We will never be alone."

I stare at my shoes and listen to them. They don't plan or offer me advice. They expect I will not win this war. They don't care either way, not any more. They have all suffered so long and hard. I love that they laugh and smile and poke fun at each other. We are the truest sisters ever. They know the pain in my heart and the toll it has had on my soul. They know. Where no one else does, they do.

Ellie gives me an odd look, "How is he alive?"

I scowl, "Who?" Dear God, don't let it be someone bad. I'm so tired and so hungry, and not in the mood for another disappointment.

"Go back, see if it's true."

I look at the others to see if they know what she is talking about, "Go back where?"

She blows in my face. The others see her doing it and they join in. Suddenly, I am awake.

He is there. He is alive. He smiles at me, "Didn't think you would be rid of me that easily, did you?"

I leap at him, "Constantine!" He hugs me. I pinch him.

"Ow. What was that for?"

I shake my head, "Just checking. I couldn't be sure."

He hugs me tightly, "I'm sorry I made you pull the dagger. I thought you would bring it with you, and we would be no different than we had been. I didn't know you wouldn't come back to the palace."

I grip to him, relief isn't a strong enough word. I look up at the ceiling, mouthing, "Thank you!"

"Don't thank him, it was the magic of the curse upon my soul. There is only one way to kill a direct member of my family." I look up at him, he laughs, "I'm not telling you."

I nod, "That's probably not a bad idea. I tend to betray everyone at some point."

He kisses my hands, "I made you do it. I tricked you with the bargain. The fae don't tolerate dishonesty. All bargains made in the garden are firm. I made you have my dagger. I couldn't bear the thought of not being in your heart."

I look at him, "The dagger!" I slump, "Shit, I think Wyatt might have left it in Willow's picture."

He sighs, "We will find another way."

He pulls back, "At least your heart has my dagger in it."

I shake my head, "But Wyatt's is in there too and he's a bastard. He betrayed us."

Constantine laughs, "You don't think that was Wyatt still, do you?"

"What?"

"Oh Rayne, it was Lucifer. That was your father. That wasn't Wyatt. He has some witches on his side. They do magic for him."

My mouth drops opens, "That's how he knew I went through Michelle's phone. He must have put the texts in there, with magic maybe. To make me doubt Wyatt or cause issues." I have images of wrapping my legs around him and kissing his cheeks and neck. "No." I almost gag.

Constantine laughs, "Did you kiss him?"

I make a face, "I don't want to talk about it. That was Wyatt."

He shakes his head, "My love, let me tell you. Van Helsings are strong and willing to do anything to win, but they will not kill a fae. They are pure people. That was the devil himself."

I drop my head, "Oh shit. What do we do? How did he know so much?"

"He more than likely has young Wyatt prisoner. He used him to glean information." He smiles, but I can still see the pain in his eyes, "This isn't his first time at the rodeo, as you Americans say."

"What can we do?"

He leans forward, kissing my cheek, "Get the dagger from the picture, trace Wyatt's steps to where Lucifer has him, and kill Lucifer."

"He contacted Michelle. He could be here to kill me any minute. I don't even know why he didn't kill me before we went to the garden."

"He needed you to get him inside. He must have done a spell where you masked what he was. If he's already been here once, he will likely come again. We can't worry about him right now. We have other matters." Constantine's eyes glisten, "My humanity is slipping away. No love, no heart. That's sort of how things are for my family members."

"What if he never took it into the painting? I don't recall it in there, only him talking about it."

He looks around the room, "Where would he put it?"

I look around the room, getting up and spinning slowly. I smile and walk to the bed. I drop to my knees and fish it out.

"How did you know?"

I shrug, "I know him." I don't say that he would have been desperate to get to me. He would have carried it to my bedside and rushed to put the dagger somewhere.

It is still coated in Lillith's blood and the nasty nixie slime. I hold a hand out, "Handkerchief."

He fishes in his jacket and pulls one out, "How did you know I would have one?" I look at him, "I know you too."

I wipe the blade with the handkerchief and fold it carefully. When the blade is clean, I have the strangest instinct. I slice the blade along my arm, making Constantine hiss at me like a cat. I ignore him and rub my blood all over it. It sizzles, turns black, burns off, and then glimmers again.

He looks confused, "Was there poison on that?"

I shake my head, "I don't know. I just had a feeling like I should do that." I look at my arm and see a black line like a vein. Then there are a bunch of them. I nod, "Okay, it was probably poisoned."

"Oh come on, what the hell was Van Helsing thinking?"

I grin, "That I might be able to put the blade back, and he wanted to make sure you suffered."

He takes my arm and licks the wound, wincing when the blackened skin touches his tongue. I can see something behind his eyes, a thought process. He looks like he's just realized who the murderer is in a thriller. He looks at me, "Lillith's blood."

"What?"

He nods, I can almost see the apple hitting him on the head. He has a major 'aha moment', but keeps it to himself.

"What?"

He swallows hard, "Put it back."

I look at the dagger, "Under the bed?"

He sighs, like I'm a child who is annoying him, "Don't be obtuse. In my chest."

I scowl, "Obtuse, like fat?"

"Yes—like fat in the head! Put the dagger in."

My right eye twitches as I jab it into his chest, pressing hard. He laughs, "You were far more loving last time."

I roll my eyes, "You were probably a charming gentleman last time." We are chest to chest and alone in the room. He growls, lowering his face to mine, "Let's seal it with a kiss." His lips meet mine tenderly. Each feathery stroke against them is subtle and teasing.

I can feel his smile against my lips, "You still want me, Rayne."

I nod. I don't know if it's me or Ellie, but we nod. I have a momentary lapse in judgment. It isn't that I forget I am married: it is that I am not strong enough to fight him on this.

He pushes me back, "We have to go find lover boy."

My lips are still moving, "No. Kiss me once more."

He is against me in an instant, hands roaming my back, pressing me into him. His lips crash onto mine, his tongue invading my mouth. The kiss is sexual and tense. I moan into the kiss. His hands scoop me up while my hands roam his thick hair. Our desperate kiss is ruined by a voice I have never heard before. "Oh, I'm sorry."

Constantine growls, "The room you are seeking is the next one over, young prince."

I look past Constantine's face, inhaling sharply. The beautiful man is there. He smiles at me, "Hi."

I swallow, "Hi."

"You're the angel."

I nod.

He smiles wider and I think I moan again. Constantine does his impatient sigh again, "You need to eat."

I make a sound; it's like a goat bleating or something insane anyway. I can't tear my gaze from the beautiful man.

"I'm Prince Gillan, everyone calls me Gill."

"Like a fish, like a beautiful fish."

He blushes and looks down. I make the goat noise again, "What are you?"

He looks up through his lashes, "Husband to your friend, Mona."

Lucky bitch. I almost can't wait to see the look on Michelle's face. I nod in the direction of the front room, "You meet Michelle yet?"

He shakes his head, "I had a shower. It was wonderful."

I laugh. Constantine gives me a hateful look, "Really?"

I laugh again, it sounds like the goat bleat. I walk past Constantine and offer my hand to Gill, "Come with me." His hand is warm and soft. He smells like musky vanilla, and I want to lick him and suck his soul dry. It's a bad thought to have, but there is no stopping it when it hits. I want him, in the worst way possible.

Mona is the only thing that gets me through it. I know she will kill me if I eat him, and hate me forever. That's a long time when you NEVER DIE!

We get to the front room and, instantly, Michelle turns her head from the massive book she's reading, "Hey." She sees Gill and looks back down at the book, "Who's your friend?"

"Mona's husband, Gill."

Michelle looks up again, "What?"

"Yeah, she got married."

"To a gay guy?"

I start to laugh, "What?"

Michelle cocks an eyebrow, "He's gay." She puts down the book and saunters over, "You like to have sex with dudes, right?"

Gill looks at me, "What is he talking about?"

I look at Michelle, "That's a girl."

He cocks an eyebrow, "That is a man, a boy actually."

Michelle stops dead in her tracks, “I’m a girl.”

He looks confused. Constantine comes in behind us doing his know-it-all chuckle, “The glamour can’t hide you. The magic of Lucifer and his evil ways can’t hide what you truly are, what you were born as, from the fae. They can see past it.”

Gill slaps his hand on Constantine’s back, “Like my brother here, surely you see him as well.”

Constantine shakes his head, “I do not. I see a beautiful girl.”

I am lost. I give Michelle a look, “You don’t think Gill is sexy?”

She shakes her head, “He’s gay. Gay guys don’t really do it for me.”

I look up at the ceiling for a second, “Since when?”

“Since I turned into a girl, regardless of what twinkle toes here says.”

Gill looks even more confused, “Am I twinkle toes?”

Michelle leans in, “You are very twinkle toes. My ‘gaydar’ never lies. I could smell a gay guy in a herd of lumberjacks from a mile, through a whore house and a strip club.”

We have lost Gill. He is stuck in all those fancy slang words he has never heard before. Mona comes up behind us, “He isn’t gay.”

Michelle points at him, “You married me, but with a dick still. He is just like me.”

Mona crosses her arms, “He isn’t gay.”

Michelle crosses her arms, “Did he screw you yet? ’Cause I’m pretty sure I can guess how it went.”

Mona leaps. Gill catches her, holding her back. I look at Michelle, “Mean and off side, hard core. Say sorry.”

She makes a stubborn face as Constantine drags her back. When his eyes meet Mona’s, they soften, “Sorry.”

Mona shakes her head, “Screw you, Michelle. I miss Michelle who had a soul, let me tell you. That girl was my friend. You are nothing to me." She takes Gill's hand and stalks back to her room.

Constantine gives me a look and then turns to Michelle, "You are going to finish your research for the Van Helsings, and then you are going to go to bed. No more talking for you today."

Michelle smiles and walks back to the couch. I don't love it when he does his mind juju thingy, but it works to stop the bullshit.

Just when I think things can't get any worse, Sarah and Gretel enter from the other wing, "We found them. It's without a shadow of a doubt. The fourth horseman is killing with the other three. The reports are of plagues, violence, starvation, and a general breakdown of all society." She looks around, "Where is Wyatt?"

I swallow my fear, "Lucifer has him prisoner somewhere."

Her look turns cold. She is instantly the Gretel I remember from before. "We have to get him back."

It's not the thing I expected her to say. She's always so awful about that stuff. I put a hand up, "Why did he call you brother? Why is he here? How were you brought back? I need those answers first."

He sighs, "Gretel, tell our fair Rayne what I am. What I truly am."

Her eyes narrow, "His family were the first to betray the fae. The Dracula and Basarab family were kings among men. They wanted for nothing and took everything, including fae women. They discovered the way to enslave the fae women. Back then, humans were permitted beyond the walls of the garden, infrequently of course, but it happened. His family made bargains with the most beautiful of the fae women, enslaving them and bringing them home to be their wives. They mated with them, forcing them to bear their children. Constantine's mother was one of them. When each woman bore her husband a son, Lucifer made a deal with Vlad and his brothers, that he would make them immortal like their children, if he could have their babies. He took some of his blood and created the first vampire, Vlad Dracula. The immortal children made by the union were one thing, but the immortal children made after the men were turned to vampires, was another. Constantine, his siblings and cousins were not only abominations; they were impossible to kill. One thing killed them—fae blood on a sword injected into the heart. But the fae had locked themselves behind the garden gate, never opening it. And Lucifer lived off of the blood of the fae and mortal babies. I imagine he still keeps them around as never-ending blood bags. The blood makes him stronger than anything and feeds his magic."

Constantine smiles, "What happens in the garden is not permanent. You may die there and live again out here. That is why I forced you to kill your mother outside of the gate. That is a sacred place, second only to heaven. Mona brought my ashes and Gill's daisies. Any witch could bring us back from that."

I cock my head, "Why is he here?"

"He and Mona fell in love the moment they met. That's how fae do it. The love is instant—just a look is needed. They married instantly. You were gone. The ceremony was lovely, until Wyatt showed up and murdered everyone."

"How did he get the weapon beyond the gate?" Is it wrong I'm more upset my friend is married, and I never got to see the service?

Constantine shakes his head, "He pulled it from his chest. I don't know anything else."

I look at Gretel, "Okay, let's do this."

Three

Mona looks down, "I don't know what happened. His eyes met mine and my heart felt like it exploded." She smiles and twitches her head a bit. "It's silly." She looks up, "We haven't even had sex yet."

I scowl, "Why not?"

She swallows hard, "Wrong time of the month to get married. Came yesterday when we got here. Stella found me some old rags. I'm wearing them and basically blocking it out."

"Wow."

Her face twists up, "Even worse, he didn't care. He still wanted to you know, and I was like uhhhh, what? No. Hell no. He actually said, 'if it's your first time, you will bleed anyway.' I was stunned, I think I still am. Boys are gross, even fae boys."

It makes me laugh. She laughs with me. My chest aches, "I'm so sorry I missed it."

She shrugs, "Rayne, the fact I managed to fall in love quickly, while hell is breaking loose and the world is falling apart, is a miracle. My parents are dead. Your parents are evil. You have dueling daggers in your heart, fighting for the chance to be the most important man to you. Michelle is a skeezy bitch who has screwed us over. And we're in England at a castle, with no proper female hygiene products, and the world is ending."

I shudder, making her laugh again. “The world is ending, Rayne. Sneak out there and pick a guy and love him for all the time that's left.”

I nod. If only she knew how hard that actually was. Childish and immature Rayne wants to pick Wyatt. She wants to be in that young, freshman love that is so passionate, it blinds everything around it. Romantic Rayne wants to love Count Dracula and be his and let him consume her entire being with his ancient love.

I wish it were the same as it is for her. I wish I just saw one and knew.

She takes my hand in hers, “Now go and kill everything you can. Me, Gill, and Michelle are going to stay here with Stella and start scavenging for food and stuff. We have to actually build a life here, I'm afraid.”

My eyes lower, “I think it's finally hitting me. The future we wanted and worked for, it's gone, isn't it?”

She nods, “School doesn't matter. The world is on fire and no one is going to survive it. Not even you and not even me. You need to fix the things you can and forget the rest. Save Wyatt, kill your dad, and come back here to us. We will plot the antichrist thingy together.”

“Okay.”

She smiles again, “He isn't gay, right?”

I laugh, “He isn't gay. Just like Michelle isn't a guy, not really. He's fae, they're different. Maybe they're like flexible and think sex is sex, like prisoners. Not like prisoners, I mean uhm. Well, he met Constantine and never batted an eyelash at him. I think he's just a nice guy who the evil fae queen used to lure my mom and other women to the fae land and bargain their lives away.”

She frowns, “Like prisoners? What the hell was that? No. And Michelle is a bitch.”

I laugh, “Michelle is angry. Her soul is tarnished, and I don't know if we will ever get her back.”

She hugs me, "Be safe, okay?"

"Okay."

I get up abruptly and leave the room. If I hugged her any longer, I would stay there. My chicken-shit tendencies, as my father called them, are starting to act up. For whatever reason, I have made him bigger than Lillith in my mind.

Constantine is boarding his helicopter when I get to the yard, "We will fly to my jet; the pilot is waiting there for us now. He says the tarmac is alright, for now."

I climb into the helicopter next to Gretel because there is a lack of seating. She scowls at me, "We've spent so much time researching. We can't figure out where he would have taken him, but we know the horsemen are in Asia. They have been moving east. The only place the last one has to visit is America. From the sounds of things, one quarter of the world will be gone. That's over two billion people dead."

I can feel that number rolling around inside of me. "What can I do against them? How am I strong enough to fight them?"

"You have the light."

"What?"

Her eyes glow; I can see something lurking in them that she doesn't want me to see. "You have the light of the world, Rayne. I know you do. You killed Lillith, you have it. The light can kill the dark."

I roll my eyes, "Great. That explains so much. Lucky thing you researched a ton."

Constantine scoffs, "Stop being petulant. We have to end this the way it started. It started with the light."

"Whatever."

The ride is bumpy and the landscape is terrifying. Burned-out houses and destroyed farms. When we get to the city, I am stunned. London is on fire. Cars line the freeways, trying to leave, but they are not moving. People are walking, carrying everything they have left in the world. For most, it is children in their arms.

The roads are burned and bombed. The buildings are in ruin. One day the people in the future who survive this will look back and hate us for what we have done. We wrecked everything. For what? So my father could rule the world? It doesn't even make sense. Why did God even build the world? What is the point?

I am taken by the dead on the jet. My sisters claim me. I wake in a room somewhere. It's cold and there is no power. I am alone. The room is dirty and gross, like a seedy motel. When I leave, I realize that's exactly what it is. I am standing in a parking lot of a deserted motel. The sign is laying on the ground. It's cold and damp.

"Constantine?" I don't shout. I'm scared of what is in the grey air around me.

He's there instantly, "My love. We have to go. They found a trail."

I shake my head, "How long was I out?"

"Five days."

I close my eyes, "Why do they take me when you need me?"

He winks at me, "You aren't eating, Rayne. You need rest."

I look at him, "Let's go. I'm sure I can find food along the way." He smiles, "They are this way." We walk a block, and I find the thing I need. I follow it, the smell. It cramps my stomach. I've been too many weeks without food.

When I find the source of the smell, I am surprised. He's young. He smiles at me, and I can see the evil in his eyes.

"What are you looking at?" he asks with serious attitude. He is alone on the side of the road, outside of a destroyed gas station.

I smile back at him, "Have you been bad?"

He shakes his head, "I don't know what you're talking about. Get lost."

"I only come to those who have been evil, but you're what—

fifteen?"

He laughs but doesn't answer me. He pulls a knife, "Let me show you just how old I am."

I grab him by the collar. He sinks his knife into my side. I grab his face, planting my lips on his and sucking greedily. The taste is divine. It's coconut cream pie and fries and gravy. It's food I snuck, all the while pretending to love the roasted seaweed Willow made me eat. He tastes like a cheat day. When he drops, I pull the dirty blade from my side and drop it to the ground, next to his dead body. I need more.

Constantine calls me, "You can eat more later, come on."

I shake my head, "I'm starving."

"I know. Let's go. Wyatt is waiting."

I stumble after him, not happy about not eating more. It's addictive. Once I start eating again, I can't stop. Constantine mutters at me, "You always do this. You go long periods without food and then you eat everyone in sight."

"No, I don't."

"Yes, you do. You did it as Ellie all the time. I would find you face deep in the embrace of dead people after you had starved yourself for months."

I bite my lip. I know he's right. I can vaguely recall it.

"Where are we going?"

He points at the hotel district we are heading for, "Wyatt was down here. They caught his scent, his real scent." He looks at me, "You should be able to feel him when we get close enough."

I nod, "It worked that way last time. He could track me, and I could sense him tracking me."

He smirks, "Lucky you got handfasted again."

I sigh, "The dead wanted me to do it so I could bring the dagger into the garden, I know it. They wanted me to sacrifice his love in the garden and kill Lillith. They never wanted it to be you."

He gives me a sideways look, "Yeah, but you did."

"I didn't know I had to pull a dagger from your heart to kill my mom."

He doesn't say anything for a minute. I don't know what to say. I feel awful about loving two men. Awful!

He gives me a pained glance, "But you were happy it was me and not him."

I can't lie to him. I nod, "I don't know that I love him more than you, but I know I love him differently. I know I love you and him. I wish I could change that."

"You wish you could just love him?" The tone in his voice stabs at my heart.

I shake my head, "No. I wish I could love you both as friends. I wish I didn't love anyone romantically. It will make it easier in the end."

"The end of what?"

I feel sick, "Me." He doesn't get a chance to respond. I feel it instantly, "He's here."

"Here?"

I nod, walking to the right, away from Gretel and Sarah. I point to the building at the end of the road, "There."

We pass by people, homeless-looking people. They look exhausted and scared. They clutch to their loved ones and walk, maybe aimlessly or maybe to leave the city. I would if I were them. The country seems less impacted by the horsemen.

I can feel him. He is pulling me.

We turn again and I gasp—it's the church. The one Michelle went to, the one with the escape tunnel. I shudder, thinking about it and the spider webs. I break into a run before I can chicken out. Constantine does his weird smoke thing and opens the door ahead of me.

When we get inside of the side door, we are instantly bombarded with people. The church is full. Bostonians are there, praying for their souls as the world ends in fire, like we always guessed it would.

I squeeze my way through the masses of people standing and praying because the sitting room is gone.

When I get to the office that I feel like this whole thing started out in, I am stunned. The office has been ransacked but it is empty.

I point to the stairs, "That way."

Constantine takes my hand in his, pulling me through the crowd. We get to the top of the stairs, and I feel it stronger. He is here. I think I can even feel pain.

I run down the hallway to the door I took last time. I open it, uncertain, and yet, completely confident he is there. What kind of coincidence is this?

I open the door and run down the stairs. My eyes do their thing. I can see perfectly. Across the dark room, I see him. I finally can breathe again. He is unconscious, tied to the wall. His arms are above his head, and I can smell his filth in the air.

I run to him, wrapping my arms around him and whispering, "Wyatt. Can you hear me?"

Constantine bites his wrist and shoves it in Wyatt's mouth. I almost argue, but I untie him instead.

"That assaults the senses."

I laugh nervously, "He's going to be okay, right?"

He nods, "I think so. Depends on what Lucifer has done to him."

"This is hallowed ground, how could he come here?"

He shakes his head. Gretel speaks softly, "He can't. He can't come here. Someone else took Wyatt and brought him here."

I look back at her, "Did you do this?"

She laughs bitterly, "I know I haven't been mother of the year, but I would never do this to my own child."

I scoff, "No, but you would do it to me, wouldn't you?"

She nods, "In a heartbeat. I would save the world with your blood if I thought it would help. I hate that he loves you, and I hate that you love them both. You are naturally evil and selfish, and it has cost my son dearly. Can you not smell the taint upon him?" She takes a step towards us and I can see from her look that her heart is breaking. She shakes her head, "Just tell me if he will recover—I can't see down here like you. I can only sense him." She whispers, "I wish he never met you!"

I don't fight her on this. I don't need to. I know what a mess this is and how much of it is my fault. I never should have loved him, him or Constantine. I have no right to love, not anyone. Not even Mona. I'm a freak. I look at Constantine, who nods, "He will be fine. I am giving him something to help him.

"NO! NOT YOUR BLOOD, BASARAB!"

Constantine ignores her and continues until Wyatt starts to move. When I finish untying him, Wyatt grabs onto Constantine who lifts him up and carries him towards the stairs.

"This way." I point towards the door I know leads to the edge of the church grounds.

The smell of his filth and the feeling of his clammy, cold skin is disturbing. Constantine throws him over his shoulder, "You owe me for this."

I can't imagine having his sense of smell and being that close to Wyatt's filthy pants.

I go to the metal door, prying it open. The dank and stinky air greets me, just like last time.

I can hear Sarah, she is scared when we slip into the tunnel. I look back, "I can see, it's not scary down here. It's just an old tunnel."

She shakes her head, "I'm claustrophobic."

I wince, "I'll hurry." I break into a jog and run for the gate. I swear it takes longer than last time. When I finally make it to the gate, I smile at the subtle hint of lip gloss still shining on the hinge.

I pull it in, shouting back at them, "This way."

The grey day has not changed while we were inside.

We leave from the mound of earth that still looks like a hobbit hole and run for the woods. When we get to the walking trail to the water, I look at Constantine, "I'll take him with me to the ocean; the nixie will help us."

Gretel scowls, "Wyatt is coming with me."

Constantine shakes his head, "He isn't riding on my jet, smelling like that. No. I don't care if it is the apocalypse, he stinks. He will be awake soon, and he won't appreciate the smell of himself either. We will meet you at the castle. We need to go to the place where the Garden of Eden once was. That's where the horsemen will go."

I look at Gretel, but she doesn't say anything else. "Won't the horsemen come here?"

He shakes his head, "They don't need much time, Rayne. They move with deadly speed. Stella has Michelle working round the clock. They just discovered the horsemen will meet the antichrist where life began."

I sigh, "Of course. It can't be California or Montana; it has to be somewhere in the Middle East where God first created life!"

He walks towards the sea. The nixie meet him at the shore. They growl. There is no love lost between them and him.

I wave at the redhead, "I'm sorry. I need you to bring me back to Constantine's castle. Is that okay?"

She jerks up the shore. Sarah screams but Gretel cups her hand over her mouth. The nixie make sounds I'm sure I have never heard them make when they see Gretel. I look back at her, "You are popular everywhere we go."

She scoffs, "The nixie will not help Wyatt."

I ignore her, "Can you carry him? I give you my permission to touch him."

The redhead holds her arms out for Wyatt.

"He will drown, this is a terrible idea."

The jerky movements of the nixie are horrifying on their own, but the look they give Gretel will haunt me the rest of my days. The redhead scowls, "He is one of us, not one of you." She takes him, and just for show and to prove her point, she vanishes below the water.

Gretel gasps. I look at Constantine, "Hurry."

He nods, "You'll need the extra time to clean him up."

I laugh nervously and dip into the freezing-cold ocean. The nixie are there, a hundred lights below the water. The redhead holds Wyatt but a blonde hovers over him. She looks back at me, "They have filled him with evil."

I open my mouth, but I remember I ate. I shouldn't have. I shake my head "It was me. I ate and we are handfasted."

She gives me a disapproving look. They swim hard, dragging me through the ocean. I can sense the disappointment in the way they treat me.

Four

“He smells like shit, like actual shit.”

I scowl at Michelle, “Just help me get him up the stairs. He’s sick with the evil I ate.”

He moans, “Sarah, I’m sorry.”

Michelle gives me a look, “Did he just say…?”

I nod. She grimaces, “And yet, it’s you dragging his poop-covered ass up these stairs.”

“Of course it is, God hates me.” It’s my penance for kissing Constantine.

She nods, “I actually think he does. I swear dude, Hitler had better juju than you.”

She drops him in the shower, “This is where I end my duties as a friend.” She turns and leaves. I laugh, “You used to be a guy. You can’t help me?”

“No, hell no.”

I look down at him. His eyes flutter. I undo his pants and drag them down with his underwear. I don’t look, I can’t. This is beyond the things you are supposed to do for anyone.

I drag his shirt off, noticing suddenly the cuts and old blood in the back of it. I feel sick as I start the hot water flowing and take the clothes to the garbage in the kitchen. I tie the bag off and go back to the shower. He looks up at me as I round the corner of the huge shower.

“Rayne, how did you…?”

I help him stand, “You need to scrub with this soap everywhere and then we can talk.” I swear I am never going to get that smell out of my nose.

He nods, “Okay.” He takes the soap and starts the lather. I look the other way for the first time. I can’t imagine how humiliated he is.

“How did you get me?”

“Constantine. He brought us to Boston and your mom caught your scent. When I got close enough to you, I could feel you, like the handfast thing.”

“What happened?”

I shake my head, “My father must have gotten you. He took you to the church where you chased me and Mona that day and we got away. He tortured you or had someone else do it. We found you and brought you here.”

“I feel like hell.”

“I ate. I’m sorry. I know it makes you a bit sick from the evil you take on too.”

He sighs, “No, that hasn’t ever really affected me much. I feel like death. Something else.”

I look back, “Constantine gave you blood.”

He grimaces, “That would be it. We can’t take in vampire blood.”

He looks like himself again. Clean and strong. His body is battered though. He has bruises everywhere. He passes me the soap, “So I crapped my pants, literally?”

I take the soap as he turns. My laugh stops. His back is whipped like he was on the cross. My mouth won’t close. I am stunned still. He looks back, “What?”

My eyes are filled with tears, “They whipped you, almost to death.”

He nods, “I know, that’s the last thing I remember. The whip. It was barbed I think.”

My jaw trembles, “Oh my God. Who would do this?”

He steps to me, smelling like soap. “Hey, I’m okay. It’s healing.”

I shake my head, “It’s so bad, Wyatt. It’s so bad.”

He pulls me into him. I close my eyes and wish it had been me. Why isn’t it ever me? Why does everyone else have to hurt?

He kisses the top of my head, “It’s not bad, it’ll heal. I heal fast and Constantine’s filth in my veins will make it heal even faster.”

I just let him hold me, not moving or speaking. We just stand there as the water pours down on us. I don’t even know what to do with it all. There is too much, too much pain and sin and knowledge. I am lost in my own life, which makes sense. It’s technically fives lives. Five lives of five women who barely made it past childhood.

I kiss his chest and leave the shower. I have to change and we have to go. I don’t want him coming. I want him to stay here with Stella, Michelle, and Mona.

I change and leave the room fast. He probably isn’t even out of the shower when I board the helicopter.

We lift off and I force myself not to look at the castle. Constantine smiles, “I’ll give you three guesses who is tired of flying.”

I laugh, “It’s hard traveling by jet, compared to being dragged about the ocean by the nixie.” I give him a blank stare, “I know you suffer every time you have to do it.”

He cocks an eyebrow, “How is he?”

“Good. He’ll be fine. Lucifer whipped him, tore the skin from his back. It’s ragged and bloody and looks like chunks were torn out.”

Constantine grimaces. I nod, “It’s bad.”

“As long as he’s up and about, he’ll be fine.”

I sigh as we land at a farm. I glance around, “Why are we here?”

He looks annoyed, “The bastards destroyed the private strip I always use.”

“Great. Nothing is going to be left, is it?”

“They are bent on wrecking it all. I seriously don’t understand God’s plan with this one.”

I shake my head, “I don’t think there is one.” I climb off of the plane. Gretel meets me on the dusty grass of the field the plane landed in, “Is he all right?”

I nod, “He’ll be fine.” I use Constantine’s words. I don’t know how he will. I will never forget being tortured. Ever.

She closes her eyes and takes a breath, like it’s her first in hours, “Oh, thank you God.”

I feel sick seeing her devotion, “You’re thanking him—it was me and Constantine that saved him.”

She opens her eyes, “You are his angel, you will learn to love him.”

I shake my head, “Don’t count on that.”

She gives me an evil glare, “I am counting on it. You will need that in the end.”

I walk past her, boarding the plane. Sarah runs to me, “Is he okay? The cell phones are down now. Nothing is working.”

I smile at her, “He’s going to be fine.”

She sighs, “Thank God.”

That’s going to get old fast.

I force my smile to stay on my lips, “Yes, isn’t he wonderful?” I take my seat. Constantine jumps aboard and runs to the pilot’s cabin. The door closes and we start off. He comes back and sits next to me. He relaxes into the seat, “The pilot just refueled, so we have a direct flight to Iran.”

I scowl, "What?"

He nods, "This is going to be interesting, let me tell you."

"Can we fly into Iran?"

Gretel gives me a look, "If it exists still. The whole world is on fire." She says it like I don't know that.

I drum my fingers against the seat, "Anyone else think this is a particularly bad idea?"

Sarah raises her hand, "I don't think it's a very good idea."

Constantine sighs, "You are immortal; at least her being wimpy about it makes sense, she's almost human. She can actually die."

I scowl, "My head can get separated from my body. I can die."

His lip twitches but he doesn't say anything else. He pulls a huge book out from the bag next to him, "We have five hours. I suggest you ask the dead to take you."

I frown, "I can't just ask."

He gives me a look, "Since when?"

I close my eyes and I am gone.

I don't know if I dream or not. I don't know how long I am floating in the empty air with them, but suddenly I am awake. I sit up, gasping. The plane isn't flying. I am alone on it. Why do they always leave me wherever we end up?

I unbuckle and get off. I see smoke as far as my eyes will go.

Constantine is standing and looking out at a desert strip of land. I see a burning farmhouse in the distance. He looks back and waves. I walk to him, "Where's Gretel and Sarah?"

The heat and dust in the air are intense. I can't help but squint when I look around. I shield my face. He smiles like he's friggin' Indiana Jones or some shit. "The Garden of Eden would have been here, in Menykh."

I glance around, "Yeah, of course it was. Of course God would have the least lush place in the world called the Garden of Eden. Why not? He's a funny guy. He's ironic."

Constantine sighs, "You don't even believe in God."

I shake my head, "I do not, no."

He squints through the warm, dusty air and smoke, "They should be here any minute, really."

"Where is Gretel?"

He nods, "Had to be difficult. She is off checking with her little facts to make sure the rivers are correct in placement, compared to the ancient biblical texts of Genesis. Some crap about four rivers."

"Why did you let her come?"

He looks back at me, "I don't know if you or she has to kill Lucifer. Her family has one purpose on this Earth, killing things like you and me. She brought a serious amount of weaponry; it's in the jet. What did you bring? I brought that book. We aren't killing him with a book, and I sure as hell am not drinking his blood."

I look down at my chest, "We have weapons."

He scowls, "The blades are not meant to come out."

I know he thinks that, but I have a feeling the white-eyed man was on to something. To kill Lucifer and the four horsemen, I have to sacrifice. Love is all I have to kill off. What do I care, at this point, if I die?

God killed his son for the people. I will be forced to do the same, even though I am not God, and I will have no rewards. I stagger out into the sand, tired and weak. I am going to die, I have a feeling. 'Course I always have that feeling lately.

I sit down on a small dune and wait for them all to come and kill me. I make that decision instantly. When Constantine asked what I brought, I realized all I have is my life to forfeit.

Ellie is furious with my choice, but I don't want to pull a sword from my chest.

I would rather die than choose, it is that simple. The world is screwed whether I live or die. So what if I would rather die than choose? Who will know? What will be left? Some dust and some ash and some starving people who will forget the minute I am gone and their own survival becomes more important.

“You ever think that maybe the prophecies were all right, and 2013 was going to be an unlucky year?”

I look back as Sarah stumbles over to me. She slumps into the sand next to me.

I nod, “Yup. I think they saw this and went ‘Damn, 13 is the worst number ever.’”

She laughs, “We are going to die and they don’t care.”

“I know. But think about it, we die here in Iran. Our friends don’t have to know. We are alone, four near strangers, in a desert. No one will be broken over it.”

She nudges me, “Wyatt will feel your death, all the way back in London. He will die inside the moment you do. You have to stop that from happening. You have a purpose.”

I look at her, “You think that?”

She nods, “He loves you. It’s stupid, you hardly know each other, but he does. I think in some weird, twisted way, he always has. I swear he knew about you when we were kids. The girl with the dark-brown hair and the grey eyes. I remember him talking about you like he knew you.”

I frown, “What?”

She smiles, “He’s a freak. We should have known he was half angel, always has been the over-the-top show off. Strongest, fastest, bravest, wittiest, smartest, most loved.”

“What about his sister?”

She shakes her head, “She’s Gretel’s pet. But the rest of the family always loved Wyatt best. Even my family loved him best. They were so excited we were supposed to marry."

"You didn't want to?"

She scowls, "No. I could never be you."

I don't have an answer to that. Constantine comes over so we change the subject. She asks, "What about Mona and that hot guy?"

"Gill, he's a fae prince."

"Was."

I scowl, "What?"

She nods, "He can't be fae now that he's out. He'll just be a regular immortal now. No more fae. Only fae are in the gates. 'Course now that the gates are broken, who knows. Right?"

I nod, "It is odd they were just open like that. They never appeared—they were just there."

She looks confused, "That's odd. I don't think I have ever heard of them just being open. How strange. I wonder why?"

I run the sand through my fingers, "I don't know. It was odd. The whole thing. Wyatt turned out to be Lucifer, that's how we knew Lucifer had him."

She nods, "Peculiar."

Constantine walks over, "Gretel isn't back yet?"

Sarah shakes her head, "No."

He gives me a look, "Well, the horsemen aren't here either, obviously. I wonder if we have it wrong, and Gretel has it right somewhere else and she's fighting them."

I look at Sarah, "Where did you leave her?"

She points, "Back at a river bank."

I get up and dust myself off. We walk towards the riverbank. Sarah says, "You know she was walking. She wasn't just at a spot. She was moving and muttering."

I sigh, "Can't we just phone her?"

"The only time you ever mention using a cell phone and we can't. They are all dead. No cell service."

I laugh.

We all stand there for a minute. Something dawns on me, "I need to use the bathroom." I turn and walk back to the jet. My stomach slowly sinks. Oh God, why her too?

I can't believe I was so blind.

I get into the jet and close and lock the door. I rush to where Gretel has the weapons stored and grab my sword from the bag. Constantine must have told her to bring it. I stick daggers in their holders in my pants and grab a grenade. Gretel is clearly badass.

I find a bottle labeled holy water. I tap my chipped nail against it, is it possible?

I pull the label off and carry it to the door of the jet. I unlock it and open it.

Constantine is standing at the bottom of the stairs, "Why'd you lock it?"

I nod inside, "The dust."

He rolls his eyes, "You are such a princess."

We walk over to Sarah. She is looking around. I pull the top off of the water bottle and take a drink. The water tastes like mildew. I almost gag but I choke it down, knowing full well I will have diarrhea from this. I pour it on my face, moaning into it, "Oh, that feels good." It doesn't. It feels a little slimy 'cause it's been in here since Constantine was in short pants and had a heartbeat.

Sarah looks around impatiently. I wipe my face, "God, that felt nice." I give her a look, "You want a little splash?"

She nods. I cap it and toss it at her. She pours it on her face. I see the steam instantly. She cries out.

"It's holy water."

Constantine moans, "Jesus. Why do these Van Helsings make it so easy on him?"

I pull my sword as Sarah starts to laugh. She shakes her red, burned face at me, "You are so easy, Rayne. Such a disappointment."

I pull my sword, "I figured you out."

She nods, "I knew it. The minute I made the gate comment, I knew you would wonder."

I point the sword at her. She laughs, "What training have you had, child?"

I shake my head, "I don't need training to kill you, that's my job."

She laughs harder, "You think you will just know how to use a sword? I am not your mother. She was always soft. I learned how to fight."

I motion for her to come to me, "Then come and show me what you know, Father."

It feels a little too 'Luke Skywalker', but I do it anyway. She walks to me, I fake feeble and let her grab my hand. When she tries to pull my sword, I let Ellie take over. She pushes her hand at Sarah, smacking her fist into her nose and kicks her feet out from under her. She goes down hard, not realizing I have more than my fair share of strengths. It is actually way more than my fair share though. I have five people in me.

Sarah kicks her leg out to trip me and I jump to the side. She is back up instantly and ready.

"You're more limber than I imagined you would be."

Constantine sighs, "Kill him or I will."

She laughs, "Please, Basarab. We both know you don't stand a chance against me."

I charge her, she spins, grabbing my shirt and pulling me back.

She grabs my sword and stabs it into Constantine. He moans, dropping to his knee. She elbows me in the face. I let her get extra close and pull a dagger from my pants. She smashes me in the face again, and I stab her in the heart. She coughs as I pull a second dagger and slit her throat. Her warm blood spills out onto my hands. She sounds like herself again as she dies.

Constantine gags and pulls the blade from his abdomen, "Possession, wow. He really has become the devil he was labeled." He coughs and tosses the blade at me.

"We are in the wrong place, aren't we?"

He nods, "It was she that convinced Gretel that the four rivers met here. Fuck!" He stalks into the desert, bleeding. I kneel at Sarah's side, brushing my hand on her forehead. She blinks, staring at me and then her eyes look to the side. It is done. She is dead. I killed her.

I feel like adding her to a list of people I didn't mean to kill. There are far more of them than I am comfortable with.

I get up and walk after Constantine, putting my blades back into my pants.

He is cussing up a storm when I get to the river where he is. I see her on the ground, looking off to the right just like Sarah was.

I don't need to ask, I know she is dead.

He drops to his knees, "I always imagined it would be me." He looks at me and I see a single tear rolling down his cheeks, "Or you. One of us deserved the right of killing her. Not Lucifer disguised as Sarah. That is not an honorable death."

I scowl, "Are you crying 'cause we never got to kill her?"

He sniffs, "I don't cry and no." He sighs, "I hate that she didn't get the death she had earned."

I raise my eyebrows, "You are getting weirder by the minute."

He nods, "Let's go. The pilot is probably dead."

I realize I never even checked on him. When we get back to the plane, he is indeed alive and feisty. "We can't fly with no radar. We could end up getting hit by something a lot bigger."

Constantine leans in, "You will fly us to Northern Africa or I will kill you."

The pilot sighs, "You asked me to never listen to you when you get like this. I'm trying to keep you safe."

I look at him, "I hate flying, but I know that if we don't fly there, we will probably die along with the rest of the world."

He stares at me for a minute, "Fine." He turns back to the cabin and slams the door.

Constantine closes the doors, "I really never expected to have so much respect for a human."

I laugh, "You don't use your juju on him?"

He shakes his head, "I did. I used it to make sure he would never let me use it on him again. I have a bad habit of being impatient and feisty."

I laugh harder, "Maybe if you stopped jujuing everyone with your magical eyes, you would respect more people."

He points at me, "You always were a smart ass." His grin fades. He looks at me deeply, "You have chosen him, you need to let me go, when this is over."

I shake my head, "I can't choose."

He laughs bitterly, "You never could."

I scowl, "Did Wyatt and I know each other before?"

He swallows hard, "It wasn't like it is this time. He was a boy. You met him as Ellie when he was a boy."

I feel like I should remember that, "But…"

His eyes glisten and I know. He nods, "I should really cut back on the number of people I compel."

I feel sick, "Oh God. You made me forget him?"

"He was a child, Ellie. A boy. You didn't feel the way you thought you did about him. It was impossible to love him."

A tear slips down my cheek, "But you knew I would. You knew I would love him one day."

He clenches his jaw, "I am truly sorry."

I don't speak. He looks down, "I am truly sorry that I was never the right man for you."

"He loved me, didn't he? Even as a kid? He knew?" I shake my head, "How did you make him forget?"

Constantine smiles, "I didn't."

I look down, "You lied to me. You made me love you."

"No. You loved me on your own. You just loved me less and less, the more you thought about him."

I scowl, "He was a kid. How is that competition?"

"He would have become competition. He was a freak of nature. I knew it. Well, I suspected. Stella and I. He stayed young for so long. He never matured until you did."

"What?"

"When you were born again, they noticed he started aging again."

I am stunned, "You knew this all along?"

He nods. "Gretel and I have always been the worst of enemies, but we had one thing in common."

I sneer, "Keeping me and Wyatt apart?"

He nods.

I feel sick. I don't even know how to respond. I knew I hated her for a good reason.

I turn and watch out the window, desperate to be off of the plane and back in London.

"I am sorry. I just love you so much."

I nod, "I know." And it's true. I know he loves me. He is just such a monster that he has a hard time being normal with showing it.

He takes my hand in his and kisses it. It makes me feel worse. All this time. All this time, Wyatt and I knew each other from before.

I lay back and wish the dead would take me, but they don't. We land in Northern Africa, and I walk off the plane to something I never expected to see, peace. There is no smoke, riots, fire, or death. There is silence, sand, and wind. We are the only people here. The sun is setting but the air is still warm.

I look around, feeling the history and the heartache instantly. Liana and Ezara know this place. I look back at Constantine, "This is the place."

He knits his eyebrows together. I point at my heart, "Liana and Ezara."

He nods, "Like a beacon?"

I nod. I go left but it fades so I turn right. I walk for a while until I come to a riverbank. It's muddy and sandy. I fly across. Constantine jumps it. I smile, "I thought you couldn't cross moving water?"

He rolls his eyes, "That's witches and it's not even true." He takes my hand in his and pulls me along. I veer us right again. We don't need a marker for where to go. The scariest thing I have ever seen is there on the horizon. I know then, we are in the right place.

The dust of the sand kicks up as the hooves beat against the soft ground, coming towards us. They almost shake the ground, they are so large. A white horse, a black horse, a fiery-red horse, and a pale-grey horse all ride to us. The riders do look like the cast of Dementors from Harry Potter, evil and grim-reaper like.

They carry swords, axes, and hammers. I gulp, "What now?"

He squeezes tight, "Pull that sword and give me the dagger down your pants."

I pull it out and pass it to him. I hold my sword steady, "Come on, Ellie." I feel her fill me up, but even she is trembling at the dark skies behind the horsemen. They barrel down on us.

I am shaking when they finally get to us. They ride in a circle around us. It is so familiar, I swear I have dreamt of it. I drop to my knees, bowing my head to them.

I hear a scream in the air. It is a man's, "Come to me horsemen. See that I do not fear you. I am worthy of the gifts you have to give. Not like her—I would face you in battle and earn rewards!"

I don't lift my head, but I can't help but wonder why the man behind me is such an idiot, or am I a coward? No he's a moron. He can't win against them.

A horse stops and the rider drops to the ground. He walks to me in his huge metal boots.

"Rise!" His voice is like the nixie, but completely opposite and evil. I stand, not lifting my head to look upon him. I have a bad feeling.

"You would not look upon me?"

I shake my head, "You are death."

"I am conquest. I am the first rider."

"I would look upon you. I would look upon you and kill you." I hear a man's voice over the wind and the horses. I see Constantine's feet near me. He isn't moving. He must be doing the same as me. The man behind me has to be Lucifer.

"You would face me?"

The man screams in pain, and I feel like maybe for once, I have made the right choice.

The second horse stops and the rider dismounts. He walks to me in all his state, "Would you face me?"

I shake my head, "No, my lord."

He walks past me. The man screams in agony again. He says words but they are muffled and make my skin crawl. I wish he would die. I hate that I wish that, but I cannot listen a second longer. The third horseman jumps down and stomps to me, "Will you face me?"

I shake my head again, tears rolling down my cheeks. The rider walks past me, making the man scream again. I don't know what is happening around me, but I suspect I shouldn't look.

I am too scared to look.

Finally, the fourth rider stops circling us. He dismounts. But he pauses. He walks, not like the others but softly, towards me. He stops in front of me and then takes a step closer. He leans in, I can smell rot and decay, and yet, it is appealing.

He whispers on my neck with his hot breath, "Would you look upon me and let me do my worst?"

I twitch, shaking my head. I don't know why, but he bothers me the most. He gets too close and makes it too personal, like he knows me. He lingers, smelling me.

He pulls back, "Not even a slight glance?"

I shake my head again.

He walks past me and the man behind me begs. He pleads for his life. I don't know what he says because he sounds weird, like his tongue is missing. But I can get the gist of it.

The sand starts up as if they are riding their horses again. The man screams and slowly the riders start to walk back to me. They drop to their knees in front of me, one at a time. I don't look up. I don't know what to do, but I know I need to be humble in front of them. Or cowardly, however you want to say it.

When the final horseman is kneeling in front of me, I look up. They are black knights kneeling in the desert against the fading light of the sun. I turn, gasping when I see the man. He is frozen and twisted. He is not my father, not in his regular body, but that doesn't mean he couldn't be my father; he very well could be.

He has sores, a gaping mouth, stab wounds that leak dark blood and broken bones. He kneels, as if frozen in that position.

Constantine looks at me, wide-eyed and confused. I shake my head. He looks at the horsemen, “What does she do now?”

“Free us, blood of Lillith.” They all say it in unison and it rumbles through the earth to me. I almost nod; finally the whole blood of Lillith thing makes sense. I am the blood of Lillith. I will draw the horsemen to me. I look up at the sky for a second, “You knew all along didn’t you? You’ve always had this planned.”

I swallow hard, pulling my sword and looking at Constantine again. He shrugs, biting his lip. He does a motion, like he’s swinging the sword. I look back at the riders.

I lift the sword over my head, take a deep breath, and lower it like I’m friggin’ Ned Stark. The sword hits and the horseman’s cloak crumples to the ground. Something black like smoke rises from his body. I look at the next three and shudder. This is weird.

“Sorry about that.” I lift the sword again and again and again, until all four cloaks are lying in the sand, and I am surrounded by black smoke.

Constantine starts breathing again, “Oh my God, not even a little bit kidding. I thought we were dead.”

I drop the sword to the ground, “What happened?”

He shakes his head, “I have no idea.”

I point at the frozen man, “Who is that?”

He shrugs, “I have no idea.”

“Is that the antichrist?”

He gives me a look, “Rayne, we were at the same party. I have no idea.”

I sigh, “Where is my father?”

“Who cares? I feel like I’m having a stroke, and I don’t think that’s even possible.” Constantine offers me his hand, “Let’s go home.”

I nod, “Okay.”

We turn to go back to the plane, but Lucifer is standing there, with the full moon rising behind him. He is beautiful, ominous, and awful all at once.

“I can’t believe that you did it.”

I scowl, “What?”

He nods, “You lived. I have to give that one to you. I assumed they wanted you to face them, and of course, God wanted you on your knees. How pious of you.”

My lip trembles but I start to laugh. He looks affronted by my laugh, but it makes me laugh harder. Constantine laughs with me, “What is it?”

I snort, “I thought about the whole Indiana Jones thing.” I drop to my knee, “When he gets the Nazis to open the Holy Grail and they shouldn’t look.”

Constantine laughs harder, “Indiana Jones saved your life.”

Lucifer looks confused, “Who is he?”

I snort again.

Lucifer shouts, “STOP LAUGHING!”

Of course, like I’m seven years old, I laugh harder.

He pulls a gun from his hip and shoots me in the arm. I stop laughing as the bullet stings and blood trails down my arm. Constantine stops too. He walks to me, cautiously.

Lucifer sighs, “Give me the power.”

I look at Constantine, “What power?”

“The horsemen, what did they give you?”

I shake my head, “Nausea.”

He leans forward and screams at me, “WHAT DID THEY GIVE YOU?”

I flinch, "I-I-I-I don't know. Nothing."

He storms across the sand to me, grabbing me by the arm he has just shot. He presses his thumb into the wound, "The prophecy is that you will gain power from their death and be able to kill the antichrist and save the world. Now tell me what you felt."

I shake my head, "I swear, nothing. I swear, I feel exactly the same. A little freer knowing they're dead."

He squeezes harder, making me scream. Constantine tackles him into the sand. His fangs are out and his eyes are black. He drags his nails across Lucifer's neck. Black blood spills out. I grab one of my daggers from my pants and jump, stabbing it into his heart. He knocks Constantine off and pulls the dagger from his heart, snapping the blade. He tosses me back, I leap for the sword but he jumps up, stomping on my leg. He grabs my sword and swings around, stabbing Constantine in the chest with it. He gags. Lucifer turns and looks at me. Black blood drips from his face. "You know, when you were a baby, you used to sleep in my lap. I would twirl your hair and sing to you. You could sleep like I have never seen, for days. You have always been the most amazing child."

"You always tell me what a failure I am."

He shakes his head, "You are now. Look at you—we made you perfect and you waste it on him." He points upward. He laughs, mocking me. "You could own the whole world and make them all bow before you. But you refuse to acknowledge your greatness."

"What is great about making people bow before you?"

He smiles, it's a wicked grin. "You sound like him." His face turns fierce, "I hate him." He launches at me again, taking me to the ground. My back slams into the sand. His fists hit me. My face jolts and jerks with each hit.

He gets up and I cry out when his boots hit my side. I feel my ribs crack. Lucifer kicks again, but suddenly a broken sword sticks out of his stomach. He turns, swinging his arm and knocking Constantine back into the sand.

I spit blood onto the sand, "Why are you hurting me—just kill me. Leave him alone."

He laughs, "I don't want to kill you; I want to take the light from you. Now use it, show it to me."

I shake my head, "I don't know how."

He kicks again but the boot hits my chin. I'm knocked back. I swear my jaw is broken. He gets on top of me again, "Use the light, Rayne. Show it to me."

I start to cry. He mocks me, "Crying isn't the light, use the light. Do it for Daddy, Liana."

His voice grates on my last nerve. I backhand him. He falls back. I look at Constantine. I rub my hand over my chest, feeling the spot where my heart is. I close my eyes, remembering the moment Wyatt put it there, the dagger with his love on it. I reach into my chest, pulling it from there. I scream as the dagger comes out. Lucifer gives me a look as he wipes the black blood from his face. I look at him, hatred and pain filling me with every detail I see. I point the dagger at him, "Who is the antichrist?"

He laughs. I scream, forcing my wings from my body, "WHO IS HE?"

He staggers back, stunned by the wings. "They are so beautiful."

I look at him, seeing it suddenly. The power I gained from the horsemen. I smile at him, "You never could have gotten the power from them."

He scowls, "Where is it?"

"You know why you couldn't have it? Because it is something you cannot grasp. The thing I gained from them is belief. I believe. I know God is there. I bowed my head before the horsemen, and I was humble and pious. Not on purpose but by instinct. I believe. I never did before this moment. But they knelt before me and sacrificed themselves, because they knew I was the hand of God. I don't want to be. I don't need to be. I wish I weren't. And that is why I am."

He laughs harder, "You think belief will get you anywhere, Rayne? You are an idiot."

I hold the sword up, "I believe I can beat you because he believes in me."

He nods, "Then come at me."

I look up at the night sky, smiling at the stars above me, "I don't need to."

Light shoots from my wings and hands, blasting from me in all directions. It buzzes from me, blinding him. I can see it, like I am looking through the light. I walk slowly to him, holding the dagger of the man I love. I grab Lucifer's head, jerking it back. He cries out, but my blade slides across his throat and he falls. When he drops to his knees, I bring my arm back and swing, beheading him in one fell swoop.

I drop to my knees and tears pour from my face. The girls inside of me are sobbing. I hold him to me as the light dies away. Constantine gives me a stunned stare. I close my eyes, feeling the change of his dead body to feathers. I grip them and cry. Because even though he is dead, he was my father. He sang to me and twirled my hair.

The End of Days

Love

His lips against mine taste like cigarette smoke but his evil is like a s'more. He drops down into the deathly-silent city street. Constantine scowls, "Have you had your fill?"

I shake my head. "There is a good one here, I can smell him." I wander the streets, but it's like he's evading me. He makes me hungry in an unnatural way. I feel like a drug addict roaming the streets looking for that dealer I know is there.

Constantine grabs my arm. His eyes dart about the dusty city, "We need to go now."

I nod, "Okay." The walk back to the plane is quiet. He knows I am confused and exhausted.

Finally he asks, "So belief? That was it?"

I nod, "That was it. I am the blood of Lillith so the horsemen were drawn to me. Only the blood of Lillith could actually take them down. Lucifer never could have killed them. It had to be a mercy killing, a sacrifice. He wanted something from them. I wanted to free them. It's like the garden—if you want it, you can't find it. But if your desire for it is pure enough and you want nothing from the garden, it will find you. I have only ever gone there to kill my mother and free the fae from her, and to free Mona and you."

He smiles, "None of that was quite what it seemed, though was it?"

I laugh, "Not quite. My mother was a captive of the fae. I still don't get that one. And you were dead and Mona wasn't being held there. She was staying for Gill. It's all crazy. I can't even think about it, it makes my head hurt."

He laughs, "You make my head hurt."

I look down, "And your heart."

He shakes his head, "You pulled Wyatt's blade. Why?"

Giving him the most honest face I can, I say, "Because I don't need it. I know who he is to me."

He winces, "And who I am to you as well?"

"Yes."

"Who am I?"

I look back at the desert, "You are my dear friend. My very dear friend." I can feel him vibrating with anger but he controls it.

"I deserve that, don't I?"

I shake my head, "You deserve love, like the rest of us."

He shakes his head, "I don't. My family has always been evil. We have never been anything but." He takes my hand in his, "But in my defense, I am a heartless beast."

I grip his hand, "You are not heartless. You are anything but."

I look at his heart, "When I told you it was Lillith's blood on the knife, why did you look so interested?"

He smiles, "A man must keep some secrets, Rayne."

I narrow my gaze, "You aren't plotting, are you?"

He laughs, "Always." He points, "The plane."

I smile, "Thanks for not asking me to fly us. I hate flying."

He laughs harder, "I don't expect you to carry me, love. I never have."

The pilot is pissed about fuel and a bunch of other things. The road we have landed on is not great for takeoffs, and he thinks we might die.

I close my eyes when I get into my seat and they take me instantly.

“Nene?”

I hate the feeling in my heart, “Willow.” I run to her. We are in the painting but it looks different, less somehow.

She brushes my hair from my face, “Are you okay?”

I shake my head, “No.”

She kisses my cheek, “I am sorry you had to do all of that.”

I slump down on the grassy hill we are on, “When I killed him, I saw things. I saw his face smiling at me, kissing my wounds and telling me he loved me. It was awful and amazing.”

She sits next to me, “But you have killed him. You have killed the seven devils. You are free of them, and the horsemen too.”

I look at her, “Then why does it feel like it is the calm before the storm?”

Her eyes glisten, “It is. End of days starts now. You must kill the antichrist as he rises up, before he succeeds in taking the throne. You must kill him and then the world will reset, and there will be peace.”

I sigh. “End of days starts now? What about the shit show out there already?”

She cocks an eyebrow, “No cussing. It pollutes your aura.”

“Seriously though, end of days starts now? How am I even going to know this antichrist?”

She laughs, “He will be the false prophet who promises to save the world.”

I look down at my feet, my shoes are almost worn through, my pants are torn and filthy, and my hands are covered in cuts and bloodstains. “I don’t think I have any more fight left in me.”

"Then this is the time you must count on God."

I give her a sideways look, "You always said that religious people were nuts."

She laughs, "They are. The people who look to statues and buildings to find God are nuts. Where is God in a piece of wood or a mortal man's voice? God is a personal experience for all. God is in your heart. No one can tell you how to love him or where to find him. He is there for you and each person who believes in him, gets the same thing. The gift of light."

I smile, "It was so simple. We all complicated it."

She laughs, "We all did. Fitz was watching over you. He laughed aloud when he realized the power was belief. No one could tell you that. No one could teach you that. You had to look to the heavens and see it for yourself. You're the hand of God, Nene. Now go and do his bidding."

I wake, gasping for air.

Wyatt stares at me from the corner of the room. He looks evil. If I hadn't murdered my father, I would assume Wyatt has become him again.

My chest is heaving and my jaw is trembling.

He looks at me with disdain pasted across his face, "Really? You sneak off when I'm in the shower?"

I don't know what to say. I wonder if he has heard anything. I bite my lip as he rants, "You sneak off with Basarab, you don't let me come and protect you, and then in the middle of the night, a stabbing pain tries to kill me as you rip my heart out?"

I plead, "It wasn't what you think."

"What do I think?"

I shake my head, "I don't know. I'm so sorry about your mom and Sarah."

His face drops, "That's the news he refused to tell me?"

I close my eyes, "He never told you?"

When I open them, he is gone. I jump up and run down the hall. He has Constantine against the wall in the study when I get there.

"You let her die?"

Constantine looks at me, "Care to explain or shall I?"

I walk to Wyatt, touching his arm with my hand. "I'll explain." He shoves Constantine once more before releasing him and backing away.

He looks at me with hatred in his eyes, "You killed her, didn't you?"

I shake my head, "It was Sarah."

"BULLSHIT!"

I plead, "It was. She was possessed by Lucifer. We didn't know. She had murdered your mother on the riverbank while we waited at the jet. We thought we were at the right spot for the horsemen, but we were wrong. We were off and Sarah knew it. She was there to distract us while the horsemen came for the guy Lucifer sent there to gather the power for him. I think he wanted the guy to take the power of the horsemen, and then he would take it from the guy."

Constantine gives me a look, "That man was one of the sons of Dracula. He was my cousin."

I scowl, "Okay, well that's weird. Anyway, Sarah killed your mom and we didn't even know. By the time we figured it out, your mom was dead. We killed Sarah, forcing Lucifer from her body."

Wyatt looks back and forth between us. His nostrils are flared. "Why did you pull my dagger from your heart?"

I press my lips together as Constantine speaks softly, "You never needed it."

He looks down and leaves the study. Wyatt looks at me, "What is that supposed to mean?"

I don't know why, but I am terrified to tell him, "You know how you never aged for a long time, and you thought it was because you were a Van Helsing?"

He nods.

"It was because I was dead. Your aging slowed when I died and picked up again when I was born."

"What does that mean?"

I step towards him, "We knew each other once, a long time ago. You were a child but we knew. We knew one day we would be together. Like it was meant to be."

He scowls, "I don't remember you."

"But it happened. They took it from us, your mother and Constantine. Even the me from before doesn't remember it. They took it away."

He sits in the chair, "They stole our memories? Why would they do that? That doesn't even make sense."

I shake my head, "Constantine did it because he wanted me to love him and not you. I have no idea why your mother did it. She's dead now so that's not very helpful."

He cocks an eyebrow, "I bet Fitz knows, but wait. You ruined the picture so the only way in is that painting in that chick's house in Boston. The locked house."

I sigh, "We can go there."

He shakes his head, "I'm tired of traveling back and forth. I'm tired of all the nixie travel and flying, and all the bullshit. This is exhausting. Loving you is exhausting and everyone dies because of you in some small way. Loving you is like slowly being tortured." He holds his hand over his chest and closes his eyes. He puts his hand under his shirt and pulls the sword from his chest. Blinding pain is there instantly. It never felt that way when I pulled Constantine's from his chest. Wyatt's is like ten seconds of death and then nothing. He drops the sword to the floor and gets up, leaving me alone in the room with the blade.

He doesn't want to love me. I finally choose, and he doesn't want to love me. I look at the window and run at it. I break the glass and jump as my wings shoot from my back. I fly to the spot where the gates sit open still. I land and walk into the garden. A deer passes by me. I walk to the village but it is silent.

There is no one there, no one has lived. How is that possible? In the ten minutes he left me in the garden, how did he kill them all? How did he hurt everyone? I never heard a sound, not a single scream. I enter the palace through the front doors and walk to the throne room. The daisies are still littering the halls and stairs.

I walk to the throne, running my hands over it. The pure light of the crystal is stunning. It reflects the light filtering into the room. I sit down, resting my weary legs.

"You sit at the throne of the fae?"

I look up to the see the white-eyed man and jump up, "Sorry. I meant no disrespect."

He laughs, "Sit, it is your right. You have conquered the land."

I shake my head, "What?"

"You killed the queen. These were all your subjects." He holds his hand out at the flowers scattered about the floor.

"I never meant to kill her. I don't know what came over me."

His white eyes glisten in the light of the room, "You wanted to save your mother and yourself. You came to free the fae of the evil inside of Lillith. It had corrupted the queen. Lillith had her convinced she could take back the Earth. Lillith brought you here to kill her."

"Why do the fae hate God and humans?"

He smiles, "If you can find that answer, you can solve all the problems in all the world. Why do any group of people dislike any other group?"

"Beliefs?"

He nods, "You are smarter than you look."

"Who are you?"

He laughs, "Who am I? Does it matter? I asked you here to help me and you brought death to all my people. I am a fool."

I shake my head, "I never knew he was my father."

"You chose not to listen to your heart, and as a result, all of these people died."

I wince, "What can I do?"

He shrugs, "What can you do?"

I feel like I am at the tea party in *Alice in Wonderland*. I sit back on the throne, "I will do anything I can to fix them."

He smiles, "Then I suggest you call the witches."

I nod.

He looks around, "Good luck, Rayne." He turns and walks away and slowly becomes a huge white stag. His hooves click on the stone floor as he walks away from me.

I get up and walk to the window, and jump. I fly back to the castle. I use the front door but it doesn't matter. Constantine gives me a hateful look from the book he is reading, "Windows are not easy to come by now, Rayne. The factories are all gone."

I can't fight the smile. Seeing him angry is funny. I'm not even sure why that is.

Stella gives me a hard stare, "Where were you?"

"The fae castle. I have to get the witches and ask them to bring back the fae."

Stella gives her brother a look. He shakes his head, "That seems like a bad idea. Why not leave them where they are? They can't hurt anything or anyone there."

"They are a pile of flowers. I won't leave them that way. The white-eyed man who turned into the white stag asked me to do it. I'm doing it. So far, he's the only person who has just been honest with me from the get go, besides Mona."

Constantine's eye twitches, "Your cheap shots are still more venomous than a snake bite."

Stella pauses, "Did you talk to the man who turned into the white stag?"

I nod.

Her jaw drops and Michelle's head snaps around to me, "Oh snap. Seriously? The white-stag guy talked to you?"

I frown, "Yeah? He's been talking to me since I arrived in the garden. Why?"

Michelle looks giddy. She gives Stella a look, "That means you are the true leader of the world, and you will birth the child who will save us. You're like modern-day Mary." Constantine coughs and Michelle laughs, "Minus the whole virgin thingy, clearly."

I cock an eyebrow, "What?"

Stella nods, "The white stag will show himself to the woman who will save the world. She will give birth to the child who will unite the masses."

Michelle nods, "That's like Jesus, dude."

I sigh, "Can we focus on the important stuff like saving the fae and killing the antichrist? I wanna sleep for real one day. I wanna sleep when I'm tired, not just when the dead take me. I have a feeling that killing the antichrist means I get to chose my form and sleep regularly."

Constantine sighs, "So back to Boston then?"

I glare, "No witches in London?"

He laughs, "No. Remember the European witch trials? We ran them out. They fled for the New World."

"Great. Just great." I stomp down the hall to Mona's room. She is wrapped in blankets and Gill is sleeping on the bed next to her.

She smiles, and I can see her period must have ended. Her virginity is gone. She is beaming and glowing. She smiles, "Hi." She puts her hands on her face, "Is it that obvious?"

I laugh, "Yeah."

She looks down, "He is so amazing."

"He probably would say the same thing about you. Anyway, the reason I came here is I am going to ask the witches to bring back his people. Did the witches who brought him back do anything special?"

She nods, "Yeah, they were dressed all fancy, like old Victorian clothes. They did a circle of thirteen, and I couldn't see in the circle, but when they were done, he and Constantine were back."

"Earth witches, interesting."

She shrugs, "I guess. So you think that's a good idea? Bringing them all back?"

"Yeah. My dad killed them all. I owe them."

She gives me a look, "You want me to come?"

I want to nod. I want to ask her to come, but I don't. She is in love and married, and she deserves happiness. She is the last living thing I love that could die. I would keep her locked away in a tower if I could. "That's okay. It won't be fun. Cold trip across the puddle with the nixie."

She wrinkles her nose at me, "Maybe shower first. You look nasty homeless."

I laugh, "Okay."

She looks around, "So Maria says there is a place under the stables where Constantine and Stella have been making vampires."

I scowl, "Why would she tell you that?"

She smiles and nods at sleeping beauty. Gill is stunning, there is no doubt. “She has a huge crush on someone. Anyway, they’re making a LOT of vampires. It’s like an army. It’s why me and Michelle aren’t allowed outside.”

I sigh, “I’m putting it on the back burner, but we have to deal with that when I get back from saving the fae.”

“Be safe and hurry.” She blows me a kiss and I nod. I turn and walk to my room. I look at myself in the mirror, and I don’t know that girl at all anymore. She is filthy and exhausted and thin, rail thin. She is tired and weak. She is not me. She is the one who has to save everything and everyone, and she is going to fail. I can see it in her grey eyes.

I pull my shirt off, shocked by the tattoo that has appeared on my right breast, over my heart.

I look down at it. It’s a single heart with an arrow’s head inside of it. The lines of the heart are red and the arrowhead is green.

“The mark of the warrior.”

I look up, instantly covering my breasts.

Wyatt smirks, “Pretty sure you don’t need to cover them.”

I scowl, “I’m sorry she died, but it wasn’t my fault. I’m done taking the blame for him. I never made him and I never knew him, not that well. I will take the responsibility for the people I have killed. I know there are many, but I didn’t kill your mother or Sarah.”

He nods, “I know. I’m sorry for what I said.”

He pulls his shirt off too. I stare at the new tattoo on his chest, “What’s that?”

He shrugs, “I don’t know.”

It is a white feather over his heart.

I reach for it, running my fingers down it, “Who is marking us?”

He tilts my chin, “I think we are.” His eyes roam my filthy face, “Let’s take a shower. It’s your turn to get soapy.”

I smile, "Okay." I can't fight the empathetic look on my face, "I am sorry for your losses."

He shakes his head, "They've been the same as your losses. That's what we do, we lose. We lose people and love and faith."

I pull him into the huge walk-in shower, "No, we don't. We can't lose people we can always remember. You can't take a memory or a feeling away. We can't lose faith, because that is what is keeping us alive. We can't lose love, because once you have it, it's there for life. It can change shape but it's always there."

I turn on the water and stand under it.

He passes me the soap, "You are a mess."

I nod at him, "Let me see your back."

He turns and I gag. His skin has healed but the scars spell something. I drop the soap.

He looks back, "What?"

I reach for it, tracing the letters, "R-A-Y-N-E."

"What?"

"Your scars spell my name."

He looks at me, "Seriously?"

I nod.

"Wow, he's a sick bastard." He smiles at me, "At least it doesn't say anything else."

I shake my head, "That doesn't make me feel better."

He turns, "It will fade. It's just taking longer, because he put his blood on the whip before he hit me with it. Lucifer's blood was toxic."

"You remember?"

He nods, "I do. He tortured me in a cell and gave me to the priest. Said I had the devil in me and needed to be held on hollowed ground. The devil would die inside of my body, never able to leave the safety of my skin and touch the hollowed ground with his own feet. The priests took me through a tunnel; it was underground. I was bleeding everywhere. They tied me up and left me there to die."

I wrap my soapy arms around him, "I am so sorry."

He shakes his head, "Baby, it's not your fault." He looks down on me, I can see the intensity in his eyes. I can taste his desire in the air.

Something happens, a switch is hit or turned. But something changes there in the water and the steam, and maybe it's the realization that we have made it part of the way and are both still standing. I am grateful for him. Even with the aches and pains of my own body, I find strength enough to want him.

His face lowers to mine, hovering above me so close that I can see it—his want and desire and love. He moves the last inch, delicately brushing his wet lips against mine. The warmth of his tongue moving in my parted lips makes me moan into him. The speed of the kiss doesn't pick up; it stays soft like he is paying homage to me. He drops to his knees, kissing my chest and pulling me into his lap. I wrap around him, as his hands roam my back, massaging with the hot water.

"I want you, Rayne."

I kiss his neck and his cheek, bushing my face against the stubble on his. It scratches and tickles, making me smile. I love the things I can feel. I don't have all the love, heartbreak, joy, and all the pain, because I share them five ways. But I have all of his face rubbing against mine. I have all of his hands brushing my body. I have all of the hot water mixing with our kiss.

And it is enough. I moan, closing my eyes and tilting my head back as my body arches into his massaging hands.

When I look at him again, I can feel the desire in my stare. I run my hands down his soaked, strong body. I touch each muscle and tattoo. I nod, slowly as my body grinds against his, "I want you too."

The water blurred the lines of our bodies as we made love. I made love. For the first time in my human life, I felt my love grow inside of me with the waves of emotion and pleasure.

It becomes more than enough.

I can feel the separation of my love from theirs. I think, in some way, I can feel them love him too, through me.

As my hand slides down the shower stall, desperate to cling to the tiles, to cling to anything that isn't moving in the dizzying spin I am in with him, I can feel his love for me.

When it's over, I don't want it to be, and yet, all I want is to have him hold me so tightly it will feel like we are one. We stand under the shower, I think both in shock. I know I am.

He looks down on me, "Are you okay?"

I nod, "Yeah."

His cheeks are red and his eyes are clearer than normal, more alive. He looks the way he did standing on the path at school, waiting for me, like I was a forgone conclusion for his bed the moment we met.

I feel the blush and the smile creeping across my face. I was. Who am I kidding? The moment I saw him and used my best Willow feminist lines on him, I was his.

I knew it, I just didn't want to admit it.

He cups my face and I feel like a piece of china. The way he touches me is unlike any touch I have ever had. It is soft and sweet, yet worshipping and intense. His fingers gripped deep into my thighs as his lips planted the softest kisses along my neck.

I can still feel the motion of our lovemaking and the heavy breath on my cheek.

He smiles again, "I know what you mean."

I frown, "I never said anything."

"You don't have to, I know what you mean." He kisses my lips again, "I didn't know it could ever be like that."

The smile on my face is goofy, and I am afraid I will never be rid of it. I smile harder, "We're officially married."

He returns my smile, "We always were to me, in my heart. Even when you weren't sure if it was him or me, I was. Even if you never picked me, it would have always been you for me."

I wince, "I'm sorry it took me so long."

He shakes his head, "I suspect the story of when we were kids is true. I suspect this has taken a lot longer than either of us even knows."

I look deep into the crystal-blue of his eyes, "I forgive you, and I hope you can forgive me. For all of it. All the bad."

He nods, "There is nothing to forgive." He kisses the tip of my wet nose, "Thank you for forgiving me."

I shake my head. We change and walk down the hall to the living room. He grips my hand, like he's making a statement. The drafty hall is colder, I swear. But I think it is the warm glow that I am leaving behind in our room.

Everyone is in the living room, reading and talking quietly. Gill sees us first. He smiles wide. I think he knows. Mona looks at our hands and smiles too. I feel awkward. I try to pull my hand away, but he holds it tight. I can see the set in Constantine's jaw even though he doesn't look up. He just knows what has happened. He has lost me, and I hate hurting him, but I have chosen my heart's love and I think he knows that.

Stella gives me a heartbroken look but Michelle winks at me. "So what's the plan?" she asks.

I shrug, "Go to Boston, unless you know of a way to call the witches."

Stella shakes her head, "No. We sent the nixie for the earth witches. I nod, "I'll fly us over."

“You and Wyatt?” Constantine asks from the book.

“Yeah, me and her. The earth witches like me better than you.”

Constantine smiles but continues to read, “Apparently, all women prefer you to me.”

Wyatt grins, “It’s my boyish good looks.”

Constantine gives him a look, “I always thought you resembled your mother.”

Wyatt laughs. Stella winks at him. Of course I get another shitty look from her though. Gill laughs, even if he doesn’t get the jokes. I smile at him, “Do you think this is the right choice, bringing back the fae?”

He nods, “The white stag spoke to you. That is everything we fae have waited for. We know of the prophecy of the white stag, only the savior may see him though.”

Wyatt wraps his arm around my shoulders and kisses the side of my face. I almost pinch myself to see if it’s real.

I look up at him, “We have to go see Willow.”

Mona looks excited, “I almost forgot—Gill can paint the painting you need. He can make a magic painting.”

I look at Gill. He nods happily. I think he only plays one station, content.

“You can paint a panting like the one I broke, and it will go to the same place?”

He nods again, “I can mend the one you have.”

I almost squeal. I rush over and grab his hand, dragging him down the hall. My wings shoot out of my back as we’re running. He starts to laugh. I wince and blush, “Sorry. Sometimes when I get excited…”

He shakes his head, “It’s fine. It could be worse.”

I give him a look. He shrugs, “There is a man cursed in the

garden. He turns into a donkey when he gets excited."

"Creepy."

We get to the room and dig the slashed painting out. He touches the slash in the canvas, "I need a couple hours, but I'll have it as good as new."

Wyatt is standing in the doorway, grinning when Gill leaves. He cocks an eyebrow, "I have an idea on how to waste a couple hours."

I look down blushing, as he closes the door.

Life

We touch the star, holding hands and hoping it works. I close my eyes and instantly we are there, on the hillside. Willow comes running as soon as she sees me. She tackles me in the grass, "NENE!"

I hug her. She stops and smells me, "Oh my God. What did I say about sex?"

I grimace. She turns and looks at Wyatt, "It drains her. She has to feed more often if she does it."

Wyatt gives her his cocky grin, "Well, she must be starving then."

Fitz walks up, giving Wyatt a disturbed look. Wyatt clears his throat and I look back at Willow, "He's kidding."

She sighs, "I told you no."

"Mom, stop. We're married."

She narrows her gaze, "Fire witch ceremonies don't count, and being married doesn't make you less of a sin eater. You are what you are."

"Popeye?"

She scowls. I smile, "Okay, sorry. I won't do it again until I have everything fixed."

She sighs, "That isn't the point I'm making. You have to eat more when you use energy."

Wyatt gives me a look, "We're doing it again."

Willow gives him the bad look. It's close to the one she used on him when she stabbed him with the knitting needles. I see him flinch a little. I'm sure he recalls it. She points, "You will get sick if she eats often."

I make duck lips, "Mom, he's an angel."

She looks at Fitz who nods, "John, the archangel."

Willow's mouth opens and then closes.

She looks at him and nods, "Oddest combination ever."

I smile, "We have another issue."

She gives me a look, "The antichrist?"

I shake my head, "Gretel and Constantine took memories from us, from when we were young. It was when I was one of the other girls but Wyatt was a boy. We want them back."

Fitz looks nervous.

Wyatt turns to him, "What do you know?"

I point at him, "That's why you let them put the evil in me. You didn't want me with him. That's why you looked like you crapped yourself the first time you saw me. You knew all this time."

He loosens his collar, "We never imagined you would find yourselves again. The curse was perfect. You could be in the same room and not even see each other."

Willow looks at him, "What did you do?"

He shakes his head, "They were so young and she was the… well, you know. We had already poisoned her. She was dying and he was a child. His heart would break and you know what happens to us when our hearts really break. We never recover. Look at Gretel, she's still evil."

Willow gets off of me and looks at him with hatred in her eyes,

"What did you do to them?"

He looks down, "We got the fire witches to curse them and then we let Constantine take her."

I wince. My memories of him saving me are not real. Maggie feels sick inside of me and Ellie feels betrayed. She's a savage, so it's not good. She wants blood.

"We knew she was dying. We had poisoned her already. It didn't matter if Constantine took her. He wanted her. He thought she might help bring back his sister, Stella. She was devastated at the loss of their family members to us. He and Gretel made a deal; Constantine would wipe their memories and recreate new ones after the witches separated their souls."

Willow's hand draws up to her lips, "You separated soul mates?"

He looks ashamed, "I'm sorry, Willow."

She shakes her head. Instantly, they are gone from the painting and only Wyatt and I are there. The lady who was there the first time I had been, walks out of the cottage. She looks modern and cleaned up. She gives me an odd look, "Are they all right?"

I shake my head, "I don't know. May we leave through your portal?"

She nods, "Of course. Careful, it's awful out there."

I take Wyatt's hand and touch the star. We are instantly in her little house. He looks at me, "We are soul mates?"

I nod, "I know."

He smiles, "I can't even be mad. I don't know why, but I can't. I have you, so I don't care."

I stand on my tiptoes and kiss his lips, "I love you."

He holds me to him, kissing me back and then my forehead, "I love you too."

"Do you think Willow will forgive Fitz?"

He shakes his head, “I don’t know. Would you forgive me?”

I don’t answer. I want to say yes, but if he tried to separate two people I loved more than life, I don’t know if I would.

He nods, “I know. I don’t know either. That’s pretty intense.”

“But we found each other again.”

He bends and kisses my face, “I will always find you.” I lean into the kiss, “I know. I tried running before, remember?”

He laughs, “You can try again it you want, but I’ll find you.” He looks down on me, “Seriously though, we need to find this witch who cast the spell. Only the one who casts it, can remove it.”

“What if she’s dead?”

He shrugs, “We’re going to the Van Helsing house and we’re not stopping until we find the answer.”

We leave the small house, clutching our jackets and sweaters. We are both dressed in Stella and Constantine’s clothes. Her boots feel weird on my feet, but I’m grateful to have the warm clothes and somewhere I can call home, besides Wyatt.

He pulls me along the street. I don’t like the fact that I don’t have any weapons.

We run like we are evading someone, looking around us and trying not to make a sound.

When we get to a car that is parked in an alley, he runs over to it. There is a dead man on the street next to the car. Wyatt doesn’t even think twice; he reaches into his pockets and pulls out keys. He presses the fob. The back lights light up. He gives me a grin. We both climb in. He backs up and drives like the psycho he actually is. I forgot how bad it is to drive with him when he is on a mission.

He looks at me, “My dad… uh… yeah. My dad might know the way to the witch.” His face flushes. I realize how he must be feeling, learning his parents are not who he thought they were. I put my hand on his, “I know.”

He looks at me, "That you do."

We drive to his parents' house on the ocean. I shudder when I see it. The memories are not only painful to remember, but I can feel the pain all over again.

He gets the door for me and takes my hand. The hateful little brat opens the door with a crossbow in her hands. She points it at me, "Why is she here?"

He shoves her out of the way, "We need to see Dad."

"He isn't here. Hasn't been in five days."

Wyatt looks at her, "You've been alone for five days?"

She scoffs, "I'm two hundred years old, Wyatt, not seven. Why is she here?" She keeps the crossbow on me.

He looks at me, "She is my wife and she is the savior of our people, so she can go wherever the hell she likes. Put the bow down."

She shakes her head. He grabs for it but she pulls the trigger. I wince as the nearly-silent arrow lodges in my stomach. My wings rip out of my shirt. She drops the bow, "Oh shit." She looks at me, "Oh snap, sorry."

I look down at the arrow. Wyatt grabs me, kisses me, and pulls the arrow at the exact same time. I almost suck from him, but he does the wind tunnel thing. I'm getting hungry. He gives me a look, "We need to get you to some bad people." I look at his little brat sister and nod.

She shakes her head, "There is no way. You're actually good?"

I sigh, "Who was the witch who cast the soul separation spell on me and Wyatt when we were young?"

Her eyes bug out. Wyatt shakes his head, not looking at her guilty face. "She wouldn't know that. Mom wouldn't have told her."

She swallows. I fold my arms, "Spill or I eat you."

She jumps, "I don't know what you're talking about."

I glance behind her, seeing something that just can't be. I narrow my gaze, shaking my head. But it is. Fitz comes towards me, "Rayne, she knows. Ask her again and tell her that her dearly-departed uncle also knows who ratted him out for being with the witch."

I glare at the evil face of the ten-year old, "Your Uncle Fitz is standing behind you. He says he knows it was you who sold him down the river for being with Willow, and he says you know who the witch was."

She takes a quick look behind her. She doesn't see him, but I do. He reaches for her, making her shudder as his hands reach her. She looks at me, "The name of the witch was Glory. She was an earth witch."

I look at Fitz, "I can't talk about it. Part of the spell was that it couldn't be talked about. Gretel must have found a away around it and told her."

I scowl, "Constantine talked about it." I get a crazy look from Wyatt and Maggie. The same crazy look with their similar dark hair and blue eyes.

Fitz nods, "He's a soulless devil. Of course he could talk about it. It was never him they were worried about."

"They thought you might spill the beans?"

He nods.

Wyatt looks around, "You can see Fitz, now?"

I point, "He's there." I look at Wyatt, "The beautiful earth witch who was friends with Willow, Glory. The redhead who loved you…"

He nods.

"She is the one who cast the spell."

His jaw sets, "Nasty bitch. Guess we're going for a boat ride."

We walk down the stairs in the secret passage and to the far side of the room. The weapon walls are empty. "What happened here?"

He looks, "They must have been fighting things, and gone to war against the darkness of the world."

We get into the elevator. He rolls his eyes when he sees my face, "It takes nothing to impress you, you realize that, right? I could show you a sparkler and you'd moan in delight."

I stick my tongue out at him.

He leans forward and kisses me, "I love that about you."

I wrap my arms around him, "Is it wrong that I want to go upstairs and let the dead take me and have a long sleep with you wrapped around me?"

He shakes his head against mine, "No. I feel the same. I'm beat. This is insane. I can't believe we are gong in circles. Glory should have told us when she saw us together."

I sigh, "I know. All their shocked faces and weird behavior is making sense now though."

He looks at me, "I know, right? Everyone. I can't believe my own family lied."

I feel the hurt look on my face, "Try the guy you thought loved you and you loved back."

He sneers, "Well, I'm not sorry that happened. I like you having reasons not to love Basarab."

"My heart broke still, it hurt."

He gets into the boat and helps me in. I look at him, "Can you drive slowly?"

He shakes his head. I wince, "Fine, but please try. I don't want to barf again. I'm clean for the first time in weeks."

He laughs as he backs the boat up.

When we get part way across the bay, the mist comes again. Such a creepy place. He docks the boat, and I stare up at the house of the witches. It's still dark and creepy. I crawl from the boat to the dock and lay there for a minute.

He lifts me up but I shake my head, pushing him away. "No." I heave and gag over the edge of the dock. I feel worse than last time I think. "I hate boats. Why didn't the horsemen destroy boats?"

"Come on, marshmallow." He wraps an arm around me as I dry heave again and stagger up to the door. He knocks hard. Glory answers after a second. She gives me a look, "You're still with us?"

It finally hits. I bend over and throw up into a potted plant next to the front door. She jumps back as Wyatt rubs my back. "It's okay, baby. Get it out."

I stand up and lean against the doorframe, "Fuck you, Glory."

Willow is there behind her, "RAYNE WILLOW WHYNDE PHILLIPS, YOU WATCH YOUR MOUTH, MISSY!"

I jump when I see Willow. She is next to Glory. I point, "Willow, it was Glory. She put the curse on me and Wyatt. She is the witch who separated our souls."

I hear gasps from inside of the house. Glory's face is beat red. She steps back, "How? They could never speak of it, that was the curse. How do you know?"

Willow's ghost is gone instantly. I look at Glory but Wyatt steps into her face, "Break it now."

She shakes her head, "I cannot."

Willow is back again, "Glory, you break that curse. You now that was wrong. You interfered with human karma. How could you?"

Her red face gets brighter, "I didn't know who they were at the time. She was a sick girl and he was a boy. How could I know who he was?"

I look at Wyatt. He scowls, "Who am I?"

She gulps, “I can try to break it. Don’t make me tell you anything else.”

Wyatt nods, “Fine.”

I scowl, “No. Who is he?”

Glory gives Wyatt a pleading look. I look past her at Willow. She shakes her head, “Trust me, Nene. You need to learn everything when it’s the right time. You can’t rush these things.”

I give her a look, “Rush what? You witches have been messing with us since day one. Giving us tiny tidbits of info. I’m done. I want the story.”

Glory lowers her head, “I can try to break the curse, that’s all.”

Wyatt grabs my hand, “She’s hangry, she gets like this. Just break the curse.”

I look at him, “Did you just call me hangry?”

He smiles, “Yeah, anger caused by hunger. You get it a lot. Impatient, mean, and bossy. Then you eat and you’re all lovey and sweet again.”

Glory gives me a sarcastic smile. I cock an eyebrow and sigh. Glory takes my hand and Wyatt’s and pulls us into the house. We walk down the hallway that we walked down last time. She opens a door I never went into before. We go down a flight of stairs, and as we get lower and lower, I start to shake. There is something in the basement that is making me shiver and vibrate. When we get to the bottom, she pulls us down a shimmering tunnel. It’s carved of rock and has torches every now and then, lighting the way.

She pulls us to a huge room. I can see the torch light from the hallway sparkling in the room. The vibration in my jaw is making my teeth rattle.

The witches form a circle around us. Glory is in the middle with us. She takes our hands and places something cold in them. I can’t see in the faint light, but it feels like glass or crystal. Like the kind of crystals Willow always had.

She holds our hands and starts to chant. Lights fill the room around us as the crystals start to glow bright red. The dark shapes of the witches around us chant louder and the crystals' light changes to pink, blue, and green. It's like watching fireworks almost. The rock in my hand starts to heat up. I wince as it burns me. I feel something pulling in my arm, like someone is taking out one of my veins. I cry out but it is lost in the chanting and swaying of the witches. Wyatt makes a face; I can barely see it in the light show. I know something inside of my heart snaps. I scream as I feel a burning I have never felt before. I look down, and hot, molten silver pours from my chest. It trails down my stomach, burning its path. It makes a puddle on the ground below. I am screaming and my knees are almost buckling. Tears have blinded me and made a kaleidoscope in my eyes with the colors.

I don't know how long it takes, or if I even stay awake for it all. I know when it stops, it's sudden. It's a sudden, jolting stop. One minute my heart and soul are on fire, and then the next, I am fine. I am standing there with a pile of dust in my burnt hand. Glory takes it and blows the dust away. She does the same to Wyatt. She clasps our hands together and looks at me, "Forgive me." She drops into an instant puddle of daisies. I start to cry.

Not just because another witch has died but that there is so much. My heart is bursting, and I can't hear the cries or moans or feelings of my sisters. I look at Wyatt and he is all I see. He is bigger than any emotion or description.

He is everything.

He smiles at me. "I remember you."

Fallen

His hand intertwines with mine as we walk through the garden gate. The earth witches look stunned.

"It's broken?"

I look at the dark-haired witch, "I killed the queen."

She looks sickened by it, "You murdered the queen of the fae? The most harmless of creatures in the world?"

I nod.

She raises her eyebrows, "Wow. That's harsh, sin eater."

Wyatt looks down on me, "Doesn't change the fact the white stag spoke to her."

I scowl, "He wasn't a stag when he talked to me."

The witch sighs, "So they are all flowers?"

I nod, "Just like you all, they turn to flowers when they die."

The witch looks around the field at the other witches. They form a circle, holding hands in the field. The sun shines down on them. It looks like *Shakespeare in the Park*. The dresses are so old fashioned. Wyatt and I step back.

They look to the sky. As they chant, everything grows brighter and lusher. The garden, which I already felt was lovely, is incredible. Flowers bloom everywhere and trees stand taller and straighter. The whole place comes to life. Birds chirp, and insects buzz about. It's like summer arrives in a matter of seconds and we get to watch it.

I see a cloud moving quickly towards us. It's white and massive. When it gets closer, I gasp. It's the flowers of the fallen.

The witches, holding hands still, walk to the gate. They leave and stand on the shores of the river and the ocean. They chant, and the most amazing thing I have ever seen occurs. Each flower joins a small group. They form a person and then the person fills in with sparkles, and then they are standing there as if nothing ever changed.

The queen of the fae, with her cake hair and creepy white eyes, looks for me the moment she is alive again. She points at me, "You are a betrayer of your own kind."

I shake my head, still in the gates of the garden.

She walks past the chanting witches but something happens. The gate slams shut, keeping her out. She grabs the bars and screams at me, "WHAT HAVE YOU DONE?"

I jump, seeing her white eyes turn evil.

Wyatt grimaces, "The garden just locked out the queen of the fae."

I smile, "Her heart is not pure. It's probably why she never left—she knew there was a risk she might not ever get back in."

He smirks at her, "Funny how the garden accepts you and not her."

She is raging and screaming, but the gate is made of something stronger than any magic she has. It is made of belief.

When the gate opens, I am a bit scared, but it's not her that comes through. It is all the other fae. She stands there weeping as they file past her, leaving her outside of the gates. I imagine they felt the way Gill did, grateful she was dead.

She looks weak and defeated but angry, in a way I know I will pay for later, when she turns and walks from the gate. The nixie snub her, not even looking at her when they walk up the shores to the gate in their jerky way of moving. When they cross through the gate, they walk normally. They don't jerk or float and their dresses lie limp like normal dresses.

The redhead comes to me, "Thank you, sin eater."

I shake my head, "What did I do?"

She smiles brightly, "You saved them. You saved our people."

The earth witches walk through the gates too. The nixie and earth witches speak, as if it is a normal occurrence. The redhead kisses my cheek and walks past me to the forest path.

Wyatt pulls me through the gate. I spread my wings and fly us back to the castle.

When we land, he looks at me, "That was crazy."

I laugh, "So crazy."

Constantine comes to the door as we walk up to it. He looks at Wyatt, "You will remember everything you have been asked to forget and forget everything you were made to believe."

Wyatt drops to his knee, taking a sharp inhale.

Constantine gives me a defeated smile, "You will remember everything you have ever been asked to forget and forget everything you have been made to remember."

My eyes close as stabbing pain fills my head. I drop to my knees too, but I cry out. I grab my head as the images of five lives fill me. I cannot hear them any more, and I cannot feel them, but I remember my soul sisters. I remember each of their lives. I remember every second I spent being tortured and murdered. The pain is there, searing my flesh as even the tiniest details fill my head.

It is a horrible flash of agony, and then as if it was a cloud passing over, it is gone. My eyes open and I am me again. I am Rayne. I am not any of them. My feelings are my own and my heart is empty of the heavy weight it has lugged around. I look at Wyatt, smiling at him. He is the boy, leaning against the light post, giving me that shitty grin. He makes my stomach flip and flop and flutter.

Everything else is gone.

I remember being a child with Willow. I remember every act I have committed as myself and no other.

I look at Constantine and smile. My attraction to him is undeniable, but my heart doesn't have him in it at all, except as a friend.

I know he sees it. He winces and turns and walks away.

"Thank you."

He waves a hand and vanishes.

My heart doesn't break. I turn and smile at Wyatt, "Hi."

He looks lost for a second, "Maggie, Ellie, and Rayne."

I smile wider. He shakes his head, "There is so much." He lifts my hand and kisses the back of it.

Gill walks up to me, "I wish you to take me and Mona home." I scowl, "What?"

He nods, "I have to go to my people. I am the ruler now. Mona will be my queen."

I look at Mona. She nods, "We have to. He felt the moment you fixed the gate. He knew he had to go home. This way, we can be together forever. I will be immortal in the gates."

I swallow hard, "But, what if I can't come in?"

She shakes her head, "You will always be welcome."

Gill looks at me and he knows what I mean. He gives me a desperate look. I offer them my hands, "I don't know if I can fly two people."

Mona pulls her hand back, "Take him first and then come back for me."

I nod. I fly him to the gate. It's a long, hard journey. There is no joy in my choice.

When I land him on the riverbank, he hugs me. I moan when I smell him. He chuckles, "I will take care of her."

I look up at him, “I know you will. You have to protect her at all costs. She is all I have left that’s real, besides Wyatt.”

He runs a hand down my face, “If I can aid you, sin eater, I will do whatever I can. But keeping her safe within the gates is my main focus.”

I smile, “Good. If I fail, never open them again.”

He nods and turns to the gate that appears. It opens and when he walks through, I feel myself lose a small piece of my heart.

I jump up and fly back to the castle. Tears slip down my cheeks as I land in the courtyard. Stella’s eyes dart from Mona in the courtyard to the stables where hundreds of her finest are kept. They would eat Mona in a heartbeat.

Mona looks excited. My heart is crumbling and she is excited.

She takes my hand and hugs me tightly. I jump into the air, “Did you say goodbye to everyone?”

She sighs, “I did. Constantine cried I think. It was weird. Michelle was a complete bitch. Wyatt acted like he couldn’t give a shit, and Stella made me promise to find a way to get her inside. Maria cried and Tom nodded at me.”

I laugh and the flying becomes a little easier. “I am going to miss you.” I mutter.

She squeezes tighter, “Me too.”

I can’t look down so I have to wait until we have landed on the riverbank before I can look at her. “If you need me, tell the dead. They will come for me, and I will come for you. Just whisper it. My sisters feel like you are their sister. It is the only thing we agree on. Tell the dead in a whisper on the wind, and I will be at the gate as fast as I can fly here.”

Her eyes fill with tears, “Rayne…”

I shake my head, “Never trust them all. Just because they’re in the gates, doesn’t mean they would get back in if they ever left. I watched as the gates closed on the queen. She is alive again.

She may have those who are loyal to her in those gates. Trust me and Gill. And even Gill has to think of his people. He may have to put you second to them."

Her eyes widen, "Why are you trying to scare me? Why can't you just be happy?"

Tears fill my eyes, "I am so happy for you. But I'm scared for you the way I'm scared for me. I trust you—in this whole world of people, I trust you and the dead. That's it."

Her lower lip quivers, "I trust you too."

"I love you."

She wraps her arms around me, "I love you too." She pushes off and takes off for the gates. They open and she vanishes. My heart crumbles. I jump into the air and just flying myself back to England is hard. There is no joy in me at all. When my feet touch down on the cobblestone, I have to drag my weepy self into the castle. Stella meets me at the door. She wraps her arms around me, "I know we will never be true sisters, but you will always be like one to me."

I cry for no reason into her shirt.

She pats me on the back, "Mona will be safe, be grateful for that."

I sniff, "I know. I wish you could go there and be safe too."

She nods against my cheek, "Me too." She pulls me back, "Constantine told me what he did, to your memory."

I flinch, "It wasn't mine. It was Ellie's and Maggie's."

She shakes her head, "I didn't know. I'm sorry I judged you."

I kiss her cheek, "You didn't. The memories are not mine and the transgression wasn't done to me."

She laughs, "You still talk like them sometimes."

I laugh, "It's like a habit. It's for the best though, I sound like an idiot when I talk like me. Rayne, the hippie's kid."

She wraps an arm around my neck, "Come on, I like it when you act like a sunflower."

I laugh, "It's flower child."

Michelle is sulking on the couch. I stand with my back to the fire and toast my buns. She gives me a look, "Why does she get to be a fairy princess?"

I laugh and look at Stella who rolls her eyes.

Wyatt comes in and sits down on the couch. He pats the seat next to him. I shake my head.

Michelle scowls, "I'm serious, it's so not fair. I didn't know I could trade my soul for stuff like that."

I laugh harder, "Stop being a baby. Mona fell in love with him and he fell in love with her. They never planned it or used magic or schemed."

Wyatt points at her, "Your problem is that you think you're entitled to things you don't work for."

Michelle gets up and runs from the room. I sigh but it's Stella who goes after her.

Wyatt walks to me, wrapping himself around me. I take a deep breath of him and savor it.

"You're weak, you need to eat."

I nod, "I know. I just don't want it to get to you."

He pulls back, "Rayne, if you don't eat, you won't be strong enough to fight the antichrist. That's the important thing, saving the world."

"I know."

Maria comes into the room with a tray of drinks. I take one, "Thank you."

She shakes her head, "I only wish it were your real food."

I give her a look, "Want me to cleanse you of your evil?"

She nods and hands Wyatt the tray. Gently, I take her face in my hands and press my lips against hers. Nothing but love and kindness and goodness comes out. It has no flavor. I would starve if I had to eat off of her. I push her back, "You are sin free, Maria."

She shakes her head, "No. I think bad thoughts about Constantine regularly."

He walks into the living room as she says it. He scowls, "Why is it always the one you love the most, who betrays you the worst."

Maria gasps, "You no meant to hear that." Her accent seems thicker whenever she gets upset.

He laughs, "I deserve every bad thought you have, fair Maria."

She is flushed and upset when she snatches the tray and leaves the room.

I smile at him, "I bet that stung."

He shakes his head, "My heart hasn't been the kind that damages easily for centuries." He sits, always looking regal. "How are the fae?"

"Good. The king and queen are likely to be seated at their throne now, the vile thing Gill called a mother is in exile. The nixie and earth witches were hanging out beyond the gate like old cronies."

His eyes narrow, "The vile thing he called mother is likely to be joining forces behind your back."

Wyatt nods, "I agree. She has probably gone to the antichrist."

He winces, "The nixie and the earth witches, friends again in celebration, huh?"

"Yup."

He shakes his head, "That's not good. That's what caused the last witch wars, sides being taken."

I give him a look, "What?"

He nods and Wyatt looks like he is deep in thought, "Maybe the air and fire witches won't know."

Constantine starts to laugh, it's his bitter laugh. Wyatt joins him. I missed the joke apparently, 'cause I am confused.

"The world is ruined and a huge chunk of the population is dead. The rest are displaced and dying. Who cares what the witches do? What power do they have now?"

Wyatt slaps his hand across my lips. It hurts the way he presses his hand. Constantine looks around the room.

I am super lost.

Constantine gives Wyatt a nod after a minute. Wyatt looks at me, "The air witches have been watching us. They think you are loyal to them, the angel faction."

I scowl, but before I can say anything, Wyatt puts his fingers to my lips, "Let's not have thoughts or feelings about anything that doesn't involve us."

"Will the angels come back?" I ask through his fingers.

He nods, "Michael will lead an army of angels with the savior against the antichrist who will also have his followers."

"Michael?"

He sighs, "I liked it better when you at least had some of the memories of the other girls—Michael, the archangel."

I give Constantine a look, "So he will fight with us?"

Constantine's eyes sparkle, "If we fight for the right side. Otherwise, we could end up with a three-way war. Or a witch war that will weaken us."

"Who will be on the antichrist's side?"

Constantine's eyes sparkle even more, like he is laughing inwardly. "Lucifer, of course. He and the other fallen."

I scowl, "But Lucifer is dead."

Wyatt gives me a look, "The angel Lucifer is dead, now Lucifer the devil will rise. He will build an army and fight alongside his antichrist, and try to kill you."

"WHAT? WHY DOESN'T ANYONE TELL ME THIS SHIT?"

"Everyone knows that Lucifer the devil breeds the antichrist."

Constantine points at Wyatt, "Everyone! It's common knowledge. Think of all the Hollywood productions."

I scowl, "I thought when we killed him, he died."

Wyatt gives me a comical look, "He's an angel. He may choose his form when he dies."

Something about that makes sense. I remember a conversation somewhere, somehow about that. I lift a hand to my face, "He may choose to be a devil? So killing him was really actually freeing him to try to kill me again?"

Wyatt nods and looks at Constantine who smiles, "Yes. However, if you had not killed him, you would be dead by your birthday. Now you may live as long as you wish. If you don't kill the antichrist, if he kills you, obviously you won't live."

He and Wyatt chuckle.

I swallow hard, look at them both, and turn and walk from the room.

"Screw that!" I storm to the bedroom and touch the star.

The lady is there, not Willow or Fitz. I sigh and sit on the hillside. She comes and sits next to me, "What's wrong?"

I shake my head, "Nothing. Just having one of those days, weeks, years, lives. You know?"

She laughs, "I do not. I have had a wonderful life." I glance at her funky style, "How come you have modern clothes now?"

She smiles, "I went out into the world and saw what is there. I am able to make myself appear how I wish."

I sigh, "You are able to choose your form."

She nods happily.

I reach up for the star to Fitz's painting, "Tell Willow I said hi, if you see her." I touch the painting and end up back in my room, alone.

The Dead

I wake with a jolt, sitting up and looking around the dark room. My eyes do their thing. I can feel something calling me. I slip from the bed and tiptoe down the long corridor in the castle.

I see light under a door. I open it, peeking inside. Liana, Ezara, Maggie and Ellie are there. They hold their fingers to their lips, "Come and see, sister."

Ellie takes my hand, pulling me down the stairs to a room I didn't know existed.

I can hear voices and smell evil when I get to the bottom of the stairs. We walk along a dark hallway, all of us hidden by the shadows except for our glowing silver eyes. We pass a mirror and I stop, looking at the five of us. We are like a horror movie. Ellie pulls me to a huge wooden door. Ezara turns the long handle and pushes the door open. No one turns to face us. They don't see us, I am with the dead. It makes me invisible.

She looks back at us, "Look."

I see hundreds of people milling about the basement. It looks like a huge tavern from a movie. It looks that way until I look harder. Then I see it.

The evil is coming off of the bleeding people lying on the bar. The men and women who are standing and talking all have black eyes and fangs. Some bend over, sipping from the dying people on the bar.

A woman laughs as dark-red blood drips from her fangs onto her pale skin. She points at the man next to her and shouts something. I can't understand it, it's not in English.

A man looks at me, but through me. I feel a shiver as suddenly the back of Constantine's head is right in front of my face. He turns and looks behind him skeptically. The people stop moving and speaking when they see he is there. They drop to their knees, in respect of him as their leader, their maker. He holds his hands out and speaks in a language I do not know.

Ellie whispers the words in my ear as he says them, "Our time is coming brothers and sisters. We will have our rightful seat at the hand of the ruler; we just have to wait a bit longer. When he calls for us, we will go to him and this will end. We will no longer be ashamed of who or what we are. We will no longer conform to their ways, to HIS ways!"

The crowd cheers for him.

He looks back and shivers again. Several of the most beautiful people I have ever seen are pushed through the doorway and through me. They are men and women, all stunning and completely naked.

Constantine waves a hand, "Have your fun and your fill." He turns and walks from the room, again through me. He pauses and looks down on at the five of us huddled there, as if he can see us. He waves a hand in the air, frowning.

The crowd goes nuts and drags the men and women into the room. Blood starts to flow as they are pushed to the tables and bar top. They join the other people as hungry fangs bite down on them.

I turn my face away, "I can't watch this."

Ellie lifts my face to hers, "Remember this, Rayne. Remember this, this time. You must try to."

I nod, "I will."

Tears pour from Ellie's face. I know her heart is broken. She loved him more than the rest of us.

They blow on my face and suddenly I am sitting up in my bed. I gasp for air. Wyatt grabs my hand, “Go back to sleep.”

Something is nagging at me. I run for the picture, wondering if that was where my dream was. I look back at Wyatt and have a bad feeling I should bring him. I carry the picture to him, hold his hand, and touch the star.

As we are suddenly standing on the hillside, Wyatt looks down. He’s completely naked. He covers himself, “What the hell, Rayne?”

I shake my head, “Something is wrong. I don’t know what.”

He looks around the garden as the lady runs from the cottage, “HURRY! THIS WAY!” She screams at us. I pull my pajama pants off and drag my tee shirt down to cover my underwear. Wyatt pulls on my pink fleece pajamas I stole from Stella. He sighs as we run to the cottage. The lady grabs my hand, “The picture has been destroyed. You have to flee to the other side and never come back. If they trap you in here, you will never fulfill your duty.”

I grab Wyatt’s hand and touch the other star. Instantly, we are inside of the lady’s house.

He looks at me in the dark, “What happened?”

I shake my head, “I don’t know. It was a dream. I never remember them.”

“Where are we? I can’t see.”

I smile, “I can. Let’s go. We need to find clothes and shit, all over again.”

He kisses the side of my face as we walk to the door. I turn and see the way my eyes glow in the mirror. It all flashes back. I stop and stare at the silver eyes and suddenly I see.

The words leave my mouth in a whisper, “I was in the basement at Constantine’s castle. I was with my sisters. We walked down a hallway and saw a mirror like this one. Our eyes glowed like mine do. We walked to a room where hundreds of vampires fed on people. No, fae. They fed on fae. Constantine is not on my side. Taking the sword from my heart and his has made him a vampire again. He no longer has his humanity."

Wyatt holds me tight to him, "What do we do?"

I shake my head, "Go to your parents' house?"

He shakes his head, "No. The other families will have gone there. They may still believe they have to sacrifice you."

I look down at the ring on my hand, "We need to go to the garden. We need to hide there until we know what to do."

He kisses my head again, "We need an army."

I open the door to the house and step out onto the sidewalk. The cold air hits instantly.

He wraps around me as I shiver, "We will find our army."

I shake my head, "I don't know if that's possible. The antichrist has people doing it for him. I have no one."

He spins me to face him, "You have me. You will always have me."

I smirk, "Not that I'm not grateful, but babe, you are one man."

He shakes his head, "I am more than that and so are you." He nods behind me.

I turn and there is the blonde from the Air Angel Nazi party. She smirks at me, "Is he going to sprout his own wings this time, or will you be carrying him again."

I scowl, "He's only half, he doesn't have wings."

She winks at him, "He's a Van Helsing. They're angels. So he's more than half and he has wings. He just needs to pop them the first time."

I laugh and look at Wyatt. He shakes his head. The angel jumps at him, grabs him, and flies up into the air fast. I look up when he screams. She drops him and as he's falling to the ground and screaming like a girl, huge white wings burst from his back. They catch a breeze and he shoots off to the right, still screaming. I gasp and then laugh. He lands on the road a hundred yards away. He looks back at the wings and then at me. A huge smile creeps across his lips. He jumps into the air, and of course, he is a natural instantly. He lands in front of me, "This is awesome."

I roll my eyes, "Yeah, so are your extra-tight, pink fleece pants."

The blonde angel lands next to him. He shoves her. She laughs, "That's how you learn."

His chest is rising and falling as he nods, "Okay." He is out of breath and still a bit pale, but I can see he is excited. She looks at us, "Ready?"

She jumps into the air without waiting for our answer. Wyatt smiles at me and jumps into the air too.

I follow his pink pants to the palace of the air witches. I don't look down when we get there. I hate the whole cloud walkways thingy. I hate heights. I hate flying and I hate that they don't have a regular house on regular ground.

The air witch looks at me, "Your thoughts are so harsh for an angel."

I cock an eyebrow, "Stay out of my head."

She bows, "As you wish, sin eater." She looks cocky. Wyatt looks back at me. I am as always, stunned at the vision of his broad chest, muscles and tats. But adding the wings to the already beautiful man, is devastatingly sexy.

He gives me that grin that makes my stomach tighten, "You like them?"

I nod once. He laughs and struts over to me, "You having the same thought I am?"

I shrug, "Probably."

His blue eyes light up, "You wanna have sex while we're flying?"

I make a face, “We are not having the same thought. What is wrong with you? That’s disgusting.” I walk past him, forcing myself to pay attention to the pink pants, and not what I can clearly see outlined beneath them.

He’s worse than the Hamm-aconda.

The white priestess gives me a warm welcome, “Sin eater, we understand you are worried about your army?”

I look at her and smile, “I am.”

She takes my hand and walks me to the edge of the cloud floor. She points below at a hillside. There is a castle made of white on it. I don’t even understand how it isn’t something everyone has seen. It’s huge and obvious. She holds her hand there, “The reinforcements have been awaiting this moment for hundreds of years. Let Lucifer and his little minions gather, they will not touch you!”

She jumps, bursting wings from her back and pulling me with her. We float—well she floats, I dangle until we reach the ground. I drop to the grassy hillside in a heap. She lands like she rode a pillow down. Wyatt does the same. The white priestess gives me a grin, “I hope this is more to your liking.”

I nod, “Thank you.” I point upward, “Sorry about being a judgy whore about the cloud castle. It’s lovely, really.”

She scowls, mouthing the words judgy whore and walks to the castle.

“It is stunning. I wish Mona could see it. It is worthy of a *Lord of the Rings* reference and beyond what I am capable of retelling.

Wyatt picks me up off of the ground, “You suck at flying.”

I pull my arm from him, “I hate flying. I don’t suck. I just wasn’t prepared for that.” I look down, “You’re wearing girls’ pants, don’t make fun of me until you’re wearing something a little more appropriate.”

He laughs and pulls me along the grassy hillside.

When we get inside of the huge white walls, I am shocked and in awe. I stare like a fool in every direction. Thousands of angels, witches, and other things I'm not even sure I can categorize, walk the small city. The castle is the heart and around it is a land like I have never seen before.

"It's like Narnia."

Wyatt sighs, "Just don't say anything that makes you sound stupid, okay? These ones are going to have a hard enough time with the fact you're actually only a girl from Vermont."

I fold my arms across my chest and walk after the priestess. The people who see her drop to their knee and wait for her to pass.

She climbs the stairs to the castle with us following along.

When we get inside, I am desperate not to moan in awe at everything I see. It is incredible. The castle is like ivory or something. It glistens and shines at every angle. It's so clean. It's weird. Earth witches are not that clean. Air witches are the OCD witches of the world.

She brings us to the main court. A man turns and faces Wyatt and me. He smiles at us like he's expecting us. He turns to Wyatt, "Hello, Nephew." He nods at me, "Niece."

Wyatt beams, "Michael?"

He nods, "At your service."

Wyatt gives me a look, "This is…"

Michael walks to me, taking my hand in his, "I am your Uncle Michael. Your parents were archangels with me, long before they fell." He squeezes my hand, and I have a feeling he is rifling around in my head, like the nixie queen did but without the biting.

I smile, "Nice to meet you."

He laughs, "You are a strange little thing."

I scowl and he laughs harder. He looks at the priestess, "Our father has a sense of humor, I will give him that."

The priestess nods, almost bowing. "I couldn't agree more, my lord. She is unique, even to her former selves."

He smiles, "Very." He nods to several people lining the white wall, blending in with their blonde whiteness. "Show them to their rooms and speak aloud. They are not used to mind talking."

The men and women curtsey and bow. Michael points, "They will show you to your room and get you clothed in something less, interesting." He looks at the priestess. She snickers. I hate it when people snicker. The priestess gives me a look and I point at her, "Stay out of my head."

She laughs harder.

Wyatt takes my hand, gripping it almost painfully and drags me from the room. "Stop, you are so rude. These are the people who want to help you. That's a friggin' archangel in there."

I jerk my hand free, "You stop. Don't get moody with me, Wyatt. I don't like the whole mind-reading crap. If I want to think a bad thought, I want to be left alone to do it."

He sighs and climbs the stairs. The ladies open the doors, and the men fetch clothing for us and lay it on the bed.

They leave instantly except for a lady and a man. I look at Wyatt, "You have to tip them."

He laughs, "They are our dressers."

"They hold the clothes?"

He covers his eyes with his hands and takes a deep breath, "They change our clothes for us, undress, and dress."

I make a face, "Oh, uhm. None for me, thanks. I'm good."

The lady looks confused. Wyatt smiles, "We can dress each other. It's a custom where we are from."

She backs out of the room with the man. They both look lost.

Wyatt cocks an eyebrow, "Are you being horrid on purpose or is it something else?"

I give him a look, "You don't think it's funny we have an army, instantly, as we need it? Constantine betrays us after all this time helping us?"

He gives me a look, "It was your dream."

I nod, "I just think it's meant to look—what is that word. Serendipitous. But to me it seems too coincidental."

He smiles sweetly, "My pet. You are just used to being betrayed at every turn. It's nothing."

I can see the way he is speaking exactly the way Constantine does and I nod. He wants us to play the part until he can get to the bottom of it.

He walks to me, kissing me on the top of my head, "Let's take a hot shower and then curl up in the crisp sheets. That bed looks divine. I'm exhausted, you're exhausted, and we are both dirty. Let's relax a little and know we are safe here. The air witches and the angels are made of love, they want us to win."

I nod, letting him pull me to the shower. I can see the look in his eyes. He is being on his best behavior. He is being fake as hell. He pulls my shirt off and kisses my collarbone. I reach for the shower and turn it on. The white room is so clean, I swear every inch squeaks. The shower is a round tube-like area with a huge nozzle above our heads. It rains down on us when we step in. Wyatt wraps his arms around me and kisses the top of my head, "I love you. That's what matters. I've always loved you."

I close my eyes and let it all wash off of me.

The whole thing is too big to sit in my brain. There has been a betrayal at every turn and an injury or death directly behind it. In my heart I know that dream was off. Something isn't right about the dream. Something isn't right about Constantine betraying me.

I close my eyes and let the water wash me clean. I have to have faith; that is the thing I need to get through the rest. Faith that God will show me the answers when I am ready. I need to let go of the things in the past and move forward, and trust that God has my back in this. He wants me to win, he believes in me. That makes me believe it too.

Epilogue

I lay my head against the pillow but my eyes won't close. I know I'm tired, but I have never gone to sleep on my own before. I lay there, wondering if I should count sheep.

I get up and sip the tea the ladies have brought me. It's weird, smells like mint, but it tastes like oranges. So bizarre. I finish the cup and walk to the tall thin windows. I can see the moon and the stars, and I wonder if Constantine is looking at them too.

I hear something and move closer to the window as I hear it again, "RAYNE!"

I hear him scream my name but it's far away. I open the window, but when he screams again it is quieter. I turn and leave the room. In the hallway it is loud again. I run down the hall, my bare feet slapping against the cold white floor. I run to the voice. There is a door made of glass and a white tree in a garden behind it. I open the door. My breath becomes frosty mist. I shiver as I walk into the cold garden. The ground crunches under my feet.

The white tree is beautiful, shimmering in the moonlight above. The garden is like an open spot in the middle of the castle. The tree is the only thing there. I touch a leaf on it.

"RAYNE!" I hear him like he is next to me.

"WHAT?" I whisper harshly.

"TURN AROUND!"

I spin quickly, seeing him in the reflection of the glass door. I scowl, "What are you doing in there?"

"You are in danger."

I nod, "I know."

He scowls. I can barely make out his face. "How?"

I take a step closer to the glass door, "I figured as much when I got here and saw the army. The angels and witches here are intense and it's creepy the way they all look the same."

He nods, "Michael made the air witches. He mated with the fae that he stole and made children. When they matured, he mated with them again. He is the father, grandfather, and great-grandfather of them all."

I make a face.

He laughs, "I know. Very creepy."

I narrow my gaze, "Why did the dead show me your basement full of vampires?"

He sighs, "The dead lie, like I told you before. You never listen to me. You always think the worst of me."

I scoff, "You are always the worst."

His eyes look pained, "I deserved that."

I laugh softly, "Stop changing the subject. Are there vampires in your basement?"

He nods, "It's full. But I didn't put them there."

"Stella?"

He nods, "She and Michelle have been team bad guy for a while now. They faked research, manipulating this to end the way Lucifer wanted. He wanted the fae queen all along."

"Why?"

"She is a strong ally, not to mention, she still has some who are loyal to her in the gates. This is a mess. You have to get away from the angels."

I give him a puzzled look, "Where are you?"

He chuckles, "Boston, with the fire witches. I had to flee my castle. They came in the night to get you—beasts. Something startled you, and as I entered your room to warn you to fly away, you and Wyatt vanished into the painting. I cut it and disappeared. Maria and Tom had fled already. I had a sensation earlier. I was walking in a garden alone, it was cold, and there was a single tree, and I was talking to you through a mirror. I came to the fire witches to get answers. They said you had to be with the angels at the castle where the tree of knowledge was preserved."

I look back at the tree, "That is the tree of knowledge?"

He sighs, "Don't cheat, Rayne. If God wanted you to eat from the tree, he'd grow a piece of fruit for you. Just leave the damned thing alone. It's better not to know."

"How can I get away?"

He smiles at me, "Look into my eyes."

I laugh, "No, creepy Uncle Dracula."

"Do it and I'll make it so you can't let them into your head."

I look at him, leaning foreword. He stares at me harshly, "You will not let anyone read your mind without your permission. You will be a steel trap and no thoughts will be shared without words, unless you say so. No one may enter your mind without permission." He sighs, "Go wake Wyatt and let me do the same thing."

I shake my head, "No. If they can't read either of our minds, we may get into trouble. I told them to stay out of my mind, maybe they will think I am all powerful."

He nods, "Okay, that works. Now I will send a message somehow, and you will flee the moment I tell you to. You will not share this with Wyatt, you will just bring him and make him trust you." He scowls, "And don't be rude to them. They are archangels for God's sake, and we all know how you get."

I make a sound like I am offended, but we do all know how I get.

He points, "Don't be stubborn. Lila says hello and hope you have had a chance to consummate your marriage." He turns his face to look at someone, "What? I don't want to know that." I assume he is speaking directly to Lila. I smile, "Tell her I said hello and indeed, I am a fully-married woman."

Constantine sneers, "Goodbye and goodnight."

And he is gone.

I stand there, freezing and excited. My instincts about him were correct.

I turn and face the tree. Something about it calls to me. I walk three steps towards it. I can feel my hand wanting to reach out and touch it, but I don't. Suddenly, there are several pear-like pieces of fruit on it, but I still don't think I should eat any of it. Knowledge of the future is bad. Willow always says 'the unknown future is like fluid, it can change at any time and your destiny can become something greater.' But if you knew what your future was, you would manifest that exact thing and freeze it there. You would be stuck with the limits of it. I look up at the sky, "That's tempting. Why on earth would you have ever made one?"

I look at it once more and then turn to walk away. Michael is standing on the other side of the glass door, staring at me.

He gives me a weird look and opens the door, "You have found the tree of knowledge. Did you eat from it?"

I shake my head, "I don't trust fruit that knows more than I do."

He laughs, "But the fruit is there for you. You could see your victory."

I nod, "I could also see my defeat, and then that is all I would ever see."

He narrows his gaze, "You were raised by witches, weren't you?"

I nod again.

He sighs, "Such a fate to be the sin eater."

I shake my head, "I don't know any other fate. This is it."

"Do you not wish you had known from the beginning?" he steps back so I can come into the warmth of the castle.

I shake my head, "No. I think it would have been harder waiting for that to start and take over. It would have sucked to have known I had a certain amount of free time. Plus, I'm terrible with secrets. I would have told someone the world was ending." I look back at the glass door and it is gone.

"How did you know it was there?"

I shake my head, "I just had a feeling, like I should go there."

"Did you see anything else?"

"No. Just the fruit instantly appearing for me. Well, and God of course."

He gives me a look. I smile, "I'm kidding."

He smiles back, "You are a strange girl."

"I guess so. Of course I am walking back to my room in the ivory castle with an archangel. So maybe I'm just strange enough."

He laughs, "Touché, that is true."

I get to my room, but he leans against the doorframe and runs his hand down my cheek, "You are so pretty."

I feel instantly sickened. The whole uncle, grandpa, daddy thing is still whirling around in there.

He opens the door for me, "Your lover is a lucky man."

I hold my hand up, "Married."

He scowls, "Not in the eyes of God." He turns and leaves me there, feeling very vulnerable.

I slip into the room and close the door. I lean my back against it and take a deep breath. He never asked me why he couldn't read my mind. Had it worked or not?

I climb back into the bed, curling into Wyatt. He wraps around me and I lie there, unsure of how to fall asleep.

When he wakes the next morning, I am exhausted. He yawns and stretches and looks at me, "Have you slept?"

I shake my head.

He groans, "Rayne, you have to sleep. We're safe."

I close my eyes, "I don't know how. My whole life, the dead took me to sleep."

He sighs and pulls me in, "Once upon a time, there was a girl who lived at the edge of the forest in a little cabin. She had six brothers, all older than her..."

I could see the picture of the little cabin, and before I know it, I am waking up. The room is filled with light, and the last thing I recall is Wyatt telling me a story.

He smiles at me from the chair in the corner. "You slept."

I smile, "Did you tell me the whole story?"

He nods, "I did."

"I missed it. I remember her having brothers and that is all. The cabin by the edge of the forest. How long did I sleep?"

He laughs, "Seven hours. Rayne, you were exhausted." He gets up and climbs into the bed with me, kissing my neck. He pulls his shirt off.

I close my eyes and let him start something we probably shouldn't finish in a castle full of very religious angels who don't see us as married.

But when he pulls my nightgown off, I know we are going to finish.

We walk down the hall an hour later, grinning at each other like idiots. We get into the dining hall, and I am starved for every kind of food.

A lady comes and brings us a tray of food each. We sit at a corner of one of the massive tables. I look around at the lavish life these people live. "It's weird the whole world is destroyed, and they are up here living the life."

Wyatt scowls at me and mutters, "Inside voice."

I smile and eat a grape, closing my eyes and moaning. "Oh my God, this is good."

He smiles at me, "I want to take this back to our room."

"So you can finish telling me that story and I can sleep some more?"

He shakes his head and eats a grape, getting juice from the sweet grape all over his lips. I lean forward, sucking his bottom lip. He kisses me back, grabbing the back of my head and running his hands up into my hair. The kiss is interrupted by a man's voice.

"Good afternoon."

We stop and turn to see Michael strolling towards us. He holds his hands out, "You both look lovely. Outfits suiting you more than the pink pajamas maybe?"

Wyatt blushes and looks down at his white dress shirt and khaki dress pants, "These are awesome, thank you."

I feel less grateful for my dress. I tried to steal some of his pants, but he made me wear the dress, customs being what they are and all.

Michael motions his hands forward, "We have something for you."

I scowl as a man is brought to me. He has on the same clothes as Wyatt and looks like he belongs in the Nazi herd. But something is different about him. His eyes are not bright blue, they are black. He has done something bad. I can smell it on him.

"He has committed a terrible crime against another of our kind.

We figured you could go for a bite to eat, so to speak. God did send you here to be the executioner."

I open my mouth to thank him but decline the offer, when Wyatt nods, "She would love to." He looks at me. I scowl but he doesn't budge on it. I stand, smoothing the pale-blue dress that looks like I stole it from a heritage museum, turning to face the handsome man.

He trembles when I step closer. I look around the room at the people about to watch.

"Just do it." Wyatt says.

I look at the man, "I'm sorry."

He shakes his head but doesn't speak. I put my hands on either side of his face and pull him down to my height. I press my lips against his. The kiss is delicious. He tastes like something I have never had before. I moan as I pull it from him, my hands gripping into his hair. He kisses back, his hands sliding across my back. He lifts me into the air, and I suck, like I have never before.

It is cut short and I am ripped away from him. The man's eyes are blue again. He smiles at me, "Thanks."

I am breathless and looking back at Wyatt who looks like he might kill everyone in the room. I look at Michel, "What was that?"

The man winks at Wyatt and me and walks away. Michael puts a hand up, "That was a fallen angel. You can save them. Suck them clean of the sins they have committed."

I step back into Wyatt, "They can also ask God for forgiveness."

Wyatt steps in front of me, holding me back with his hands like I've done something wrong. "You can find another way."

Michael meets his gaze, "You have no right to speak for her."

"I am her husband. I have every right." I would argue that point but I agree. He can talk, Michael scares me.

Michael gives him a look, "Not in God's eyes. A witch ceremony hardly counts. You, of all people, should know that."

Wyatt grips me harder, "I know she is my soul mate. I know I will kill everything I touch if she is harmed. I know I can kill everything in this room. That's what I was sent here for, isn't it?"

Michael steps back, putting a hand up, "Easy, Nephew. We are among friends and family. If you say no, then no it is." He smiles, but I can see his ruffled feathers, so to speak. He gives Wyatt a look, "No need to think such harsh things."

The other angels and witches look shocked. He must have been plotting their death. Wyatt doesn't let go of me. His grip doesn't lessen at all. He grabs harder even and pulls me from the room. I almost trip, trying to keep up to him. I pull back when we are alone in the hallway. I am strong again. Whatever was in the angel was the good stuff. I couldn't even get a sense of what it was.

Wyatt looks at me, breathing heavily like he is desperately trying to get control of his anger. "I am sorry. I am sorry I was a psycho. I shouldn't have grabbed you like that." The words are forced and painful for him.

I laugh nervously, "Let's just say that if anyone ever kissed you like that, I would gut them like a fish."

He nods, "Okay. We're good?"

I nod, "Just don't grab me like that. It wasn't my fault. I didn't know."

He sighs, "Me either. I thought you could eat him alive."

"You and me both."

He looks back at the hallway and opens his mouth. I plant a kiss on his cheek, "Don't say it. Just trust me."

I grab his hand and walk back to our room. I close the door and go brush my teeth. The paste is actually paste, made from mints. I look up into the mirror, jumping back when I see Willow.

I scowl, "What's with you guys and the mirrors?"

She whispers, “Who else came by mirror?”

“Constantine.”

She nods, “The mirrors in the white towers are magical. Always have been. The glass is made by the witches. They use it to spy. So Constantine’s in Boston with the fire witches? The earth witches are furious.”

I nod, “I don’t care. The fire witches have helped me loads.”

She looks at me in the dress and starts to laugh. I tilt my head, “Not even a little funny.”

She laughs harder, “It so is.”

“Whatever.”

She stops laughing and gives me a look, “You need to get away. I can’t believe I’m going to say this, but go to the fire witches. They use ancestral magic, it’s intense and a little bit evil.”

I look in the mirror, “Is this thing being used to spy on me?”

She shakes her head, “No. I spelled it. I’m a ghost; it’s not the same thing as a regular witch trying to see you.”

I wince, “Constantine made me go to the glass door with the tree of life. They must have heard him talking to me.”

She shakes her head, “That’s a special spot. Can’t be used that way. Only dark magic can use it as a portal. Air witches are snooty, they don’t do dark magic. You have to run, Rayne. You aren’t safe there.”

I nod, “I know. I just figured that out when Michael made me cleanse a fallen angel.”

She looks stunned, “FUCK! HE CAN DO THAT?”

My jaw is on the floor. She snaps her fingers, “Rayne, he can do that?”

I nod, “You swore.”

She rolls her eyes, “I’m not a saint.”

I shrug, "Pretty close."

"Focus, Nene. He can cleanse the fallen angels with you? Angels who have no conscience and are able to do the darkest of things?"

I nod. She presses her lips together, "Get to the fae. Forget the fire witches, he is going for the gate. I guarantee it. Get to the fae and warn them.

I look at her, "About what? What can they do?"

"Seal the gate forever."

I step back. She sees my look, "Hurry. Get out of there and go for the gate. I'll get the earth witches to warn the nixie. Leave now."

I shake my head, "How?"

She sighs, "Fly as fast as you can for the ocean. The nixie will catch you and bring you to the gate."

"Can the nixie just warn Gill?"

She shakes her head, "He will need to see. To read what you and Wyatt have seen. It will take that for him to make this decision."

I turn and run into the room. Wyatt gives me a look, "What?" I hold my hand out for him, "Do not think a single thing. Sing a song in your head and trust me."

He nods.

I take his hand and we leave the room. We slip to the room with the tree. It is the only place I can think of with access to the roof. When we get inside of the small room, he looks at me, "Are you kidding?"

I snarl, "Shut up and hum." I jump into the air, dragging him until he too starts to fly. We fly up to the highest point on the roof. I look at the ocean and take a deep breath. I grab his hand and point. He hums and nods. We dive off the roof at the exact same moment. I can hear the guards behind us when we are halfway. I hold my body tighter, like a bullet. We are flying for the ocean. At the last second, we both pull out our wings and float to the surface of the ocean. I wince as my wings almost rip off from the force. As we enter the water, we are snatched and dragged down. The nixie swim like I have never seen them do before. It is a rough, horrid, short trip across the ocean. They literally fling us from the water to the shore. The gate appears as I land, with no desire but to save my friends.

"Think of saving our friends inside of the gate."

Wyatt and I step inside, wings still out.

I fly for the castle, sailing over the village. When I get to the window ledge where I had leapt from, I see the fae giving me a dirty look. I pull my wings in, almost gagging from the last couple of hours of my life and step inside. Mona runs to me but Gill frowns, "What is happening?"

I am out of breath and still gagging when I reach him, "You may read my mind, I give you permission."

He places his hands on me and gasps, "Abomination and betrayal." He gives me a look, "Is that true about Michael?"

I shudder, "I think so."

Wyatt is still heaving his breath, "What the hell is going on?"

Gill gives me a look. He holds my hand tightly, "You must leave the gates now." He looks at Mona, "Say goodbye, fast."

Mona looks at me. Tears stream my face, "I love you." I want to ask her to come with me. I want to ask her to be my friend more than she loves him. But I cannot.

I step to her, hugging her tightly to me. "Be safe, Mona. Please don't ever forget me. I think very soon the only place I will live is in your memories, so please don't forget me."

She sobs, "What's going on?"

I look back at Gill but he points and shouts, "RUN!" I grab Wyatt's hand. I can see the protest on his face. I shake my head, "Trust me."

He grabs me and jumps out the window. We fly for the gates. When we cross over to the riverbed, he tries to land but I fly higher. We pause for a moment and watch as the gates crumble onto the earth, turn to dust, and blow away.

Wyatt looks at me, “What happened?”

I tremble with the sobs ripping from me, “Michael was coming for the fae. He made me cleanse the fallen so they may enter the gates and kill the fae. We had to get Gill to seal the gates forever. Constantine came to me, so did Willow. Michael is a bad man.”

Wyatt hugs me to him, “Where do we go now?”

I sniff, “Boston. The fire witches.”

He sighs, “Flying or swimming?”

I make a face, “Neither.”

He laughs, “Has to be one.”

I lean into him, “Swim. Nothing can reach us in the water.”

He kisses my cheek. “I’m sorry about Mona.”

I nod, “Me too. It hasn’t hit yet. When it does, I know it’s going to be bad.”

“Where is Michelle?”

“The whole Constantine and the vampire army is Michelle and Stella’s doing.”

He sighs, “Wow, rough friend week.”

I nod, “Rough friend week.”

We drop into the water, letting the nixie comfort us as they drag us across the Atlantic Ocean for the hundredth time. I wonder why they never get tired of it all? Why they never say no? Why they don’t just sink into the dark shadows of the water and never surface again. I would if I could. I look up at the light of the sky high above us and know it isn’t the truth.

I wouldn’t even if I could.

God believes I can save the world, so I have to try.

Maybe that's why they do it too.

Maybe we are all doing our little part, and one day it will make sense, and it will be worth it.

Today is not that day, and I doubt it will be tomorrow. But today I have friends and I have Wyatt, and in my heart, I have Willow and Mona. My heart is full and I am safe, and for today that has to be enough.

The End

Stay tuned for the final novel in the Light Trilogy due in 2014

Here is a teaser of Tara Brown's newest book

First Kiss

There is a house at the end of an empty road,
where many a men have lost their soul.
Sweetest love's first kiss is enough to guarantee the payment to the dead.
It was there in the mist and the warmth of her embrace, I met my end.
I shall never rest again.
Nor shall any man who gives his heart to a lady of The Loch.

Chapter One

The leaves scuttle along the road, scratching in protest as the wind forces their destination.

The cool spring breeze that comes off the lake is worse than any I recall this late into spring. It's nearly the middle of June, and I am still clinging to my sweater. I wish I had put on an undershirt. Maine isn't a warm state but this is ridiculous.

I try not to see the way the leaves fall from the trees, long before they're due, as I walk under them. I work hard at not noticing the way the breeze seems to follow me, cooling everything around me. I have to try to ignore it all. It really is the only way.

In my family, ignorance is almost like believing none of it is there. It's been this way for five hundred years.

I walk through the back door, clinging to my guitar and taking deep breaths. I try not to think about the crowd or the eyes that will be upon me, judging me as I always imagine them to be.

I stand in the back, in the dark little room and wait. It's there in the dark that I can't help but feel like maybe something has changed in the air. Change is good; different is like a miracle for a girl like me, but this change doesn't feel like an improvement. It feels like danger.

Whatever it is, I can't worry about it now. I have to perform. I need the money. At least the wind hasn't followed me inside, this time. That is one of the harder things about me to ignore or explain—the indoor breeze that always seems to be there.

I look around and wait for Mike to announce me. My fingers tremble a little, but I know once I'm up there, it will be better. Somehow and someway, it always is. Like exposing myself to the evil townsfolk makes me relax.

In a twisted way.

They all hate me or at the very least, fear me, and yet, I want nothing like I want to show them how normal I am. I can't stop caring about the way they see me.

"You're up, I'll announce you now."

I lift my face and grin at the man standing in the sliver of light of the open door. "Thanks, Mike."

"Yup." He is always cool toward me.

Most men are. Most men fear the curse.

I blush and try not to think about it. If I ignore it, it isn't real.

I take a deep breath and open the guitar case, pulling the six-string from it. My palms sweat and my heart beats like mad as I walk to the stage door. I'm shivering but I'm excited.

Again, in a twisted way.

"Next up, we have the talented Erralynn Lake performing for you. This is her last summer here in Lakeland, so let's help her out by leaving tips at the bar. College ain't cheap people. Please, give her a round of applause."

As I walk on stage the room cheers, it isn't their best effort. I'm not like the other performers this stage sees. I have to earn their applause. I have no family or friends in the crowd.

A trickle of guilt hits me when I think about the fact they'll be leaving tips for college. I'm not going to college. I never went last year and I have no intention of going this year. Even though I don't plan on going to college, the tips will help me move. Because, like the man said, this is my last summer in Lakeland—it has to be. I have to get away from here before I turn nineteen. I just have to. I can't explain it. I hate this town and I hate who I am here. We moved here when I was ten, and it has never gotten better, not even a tiny bit.

The bar goes silent. Creepy quiet. I can hear my heartbeat

and exhales, as if I were alone in the dark closet Mary used to lock me in when my mom first died. The heat from the lamps blinds me and makes me sweat.

The applause comes softly as my fingers lightly grace the guitar strings, just testing the sound. The clapping starts slow but builds up into wild gratitude and excitement as my lips turn up into a grin. I stand in front of them all and look into the lights.

My nerves vanish as I let the warmth of the room wrap around me. I close my eyes and lean into the mike. "Good evening. Thanks for coming out tonight." My voice cracks. The talking, for me, is worse than anything.

I clear my throat and let it all go.

It takes a second for my body to relax into it. I pick at the strings softly, dragging my callused fingers in a fluid motion. My flawless sound is honestly made. It is from the pure love I feel for the music. My lips part and the song trickles out, lazily at first. I always imagine it is like making out. Slow and flirtatious initially, then the kisses become desperate and the fingers knead with hopeless passion. Eventually, the two bodies move against each other in opposite directions, and yet toward the same goal.

This is how I feel about music. Mostly, because all I can do is imagine making out. I have never kissed a boy. I may never kiss a boy.

My guitar and my voice battle to a climax that makes beads of sweat drizzle down my throat and into my shirt. I am part of it all, yet feel completely detached from it. Like I'm watching myself perform.

I don't notice them, the people.

I don't notice the way they shout and cheer.

I ignore it all. I rock and sway with the music and my guitar.

I don't notice how long I am there or how many songs I sing. I just sing until I feel done.

The music stops like it's turned off. I pause and I look up, noticing the lights again. When I see them again, I know I'm finished.

I tremble and take a bow, wishing Sarah were here to take my guitar, but she had studying to do for end of the year. Silence fills the room, just as it always does. It's like the crowd needs a second too, before they erupt into violent cheers.

I turn and leave the stage, waving at them all.

"Erralynn Lake, people. Give it up for Lakeland's very own." Mike's deep voice calls out to the crowd.

It always takes me about fifteen minutes to come back down afterward. The high I get is intense.

I sit on my barstool in the back and take a deep breath. I watch a trickle of sweat slither down my arm; it's familiar to me somehow. Not much is ever familiar. My memories have been pushed away to make room for the horrible things Mary does to me. I have flashes of memories, of mom and dad. That's all that's left of them, flashes. Rosie is the only one I really remember.

Mike comes backstage as I'm doing my case up and slaps a wad of cash into my hand, "See ya next week, kid."

I nod, "Thanks, Mike."

"Yup." He waves and walks away. My fingers twitch as I finish putting the guitar away and walk out the back door, to where the wind has waited for me. I shiver when my sweat and the cool breeze meet on my exposed throat as I stuff the majority of the money into my back pocket, so I only have the fifty to give Mary. She doesn't know about the tips; she doesn't need to.

"Ready?" a voice asks from the alley as I get outside.

I look sharply to where a group of girls wait for me with smiles. I nod, "Can I stash the guitar in the back of your car?"

My bestie Lune, short for Luanne, laughs and nods, "Yeah. Let's go before all the hotties are taken and we end up either alone or with the bottom feeders."

I roll my eyes and link arms with her, "I never end up with a hottie anyway."

Sarah, my other friend, giggles, "Maybe tonight is the night."

I stick my tongue out at her. She smiles, "How was it? Sorry I had to study."

"It was a good one, I think."

"Let's go get Lynnie some man meat!" Lune does a kissy face at me and moans.

"Lune, you're a weirdo." I say in the most loving way. She really is but that is the thing I adore about her. When I got here as a new kid at school she was the first one brave enough to befriend the Lake girl.

The blonde's face splits into a grin, "Yet, you love me. What fun is it to be a wanker, if you're all alone? You, my friend, are in good company."

I laugh and shake my head, "Sometimes, I think you need a support group."

She winks a blue eye, "Oh, I got one. Don't you worry about me. Now, I need some hot-boy loving, so let's go."

A brunette named Maggie, getting into the car on the other side, laughs, "Dirty ho."

Lune puts her hands up innocently and gives us a mischievous grin, "You know it. Best friends with the one and only Erralynn Lake. You have to be weird to keep up."

The brunette nods, "Agreed."

I frown, trying to make a joke out of it all, "I'm not a dirty ho. When did being dirty amount to being weird? And how is it I'm the bar for what's weird in this town?" I speak before I really think it through. My face flushes crimson when they all stop talking and climb into the car.

Of course, I am the bar for what is weird. In this town and every town. I don't remember what my town was like before we moved here, but I bet I was weird there too.

I look down and carry my guitar to the trunk. I slam it and climb into the front seat. I look down at my jeans and scowl, trying not to let it get to me.

Lune turns around to look at the girls in the back seat but points at me. "This girl is the most normal person you all know. Just for the record."

They laugh. Maggie crosses her arms and gives me a smirk, "Your family makes you guilty by association, Lynnie." She winks at me but I know it is the truth, I am guilty because of my last name.

I cock an eyebrow at her, "Guilty by relation, and I choose not to believe in any of it." And that is the truth. It is a choice to be cursed and I choose no. No curse, no bad juju, no family problems. Well, except for insanity and being horribly gullible, that we are famously guilty of. The rest, I force myself to believe is a lie, a con, and a joke. I am guilty of being a Lake but that is all.

Jenny, the raven-haired girl in the back left corner, puts her knuckles forward, "I don't believe it either."

I pound my knuckles against hers.

Lune points a finger at the other two, "You morons are easily fooled. A couple freak accidents and the whole town starts screaming witch and you whores jump on the bandwagon. Lynnie never even grew up here, she's from Maryland."

Maggie laughs, "Few accidents… dude. How do we know there isn't a Maryland chapter of evil Lakes?"

I turn around in a fake huff, "It isn't a club. You guys suck." I don't mean it and I hope they don't either. I can't even help but be glad they're all home from college for the summer. It's been a hard year. Mary has been worse than usual and Sarah is busy a lot with guys. She dates and I sit at home until she gets home and calls to fill me in. I close my eyes and listen to the details and wish they were mine. Lune, Maggie, and Jenny do the same from school. They don't know silent tears roll down my cheeks as they tell me about their wonderful nights, the boy and the kisses, the sex, and butterflies in their tummies. The horrid feeling the next day, when they realize he wasn't as hot as their beer goggles told them he was, or he's married. I wish it were me. I wish for once I could regret everything. I wish I could just be reckless. But it isn't my life I'm gambling with. No, the Lake women always live through it. The men are the unlucky ones.

Lune smiles and nudges me, "Let's get trashed and see if any suckers try to hit on you."

I scoff, "You know they don't mess with the Loch monsters."

Jenny whacks me on the top of the head softly, "You're a dork."

We laugh. They laugh at me and I try to laugh with them.

"I can't believe school is finally over and we are all home! This is going to be the best summer ever." They all scream and shout. Lune presses the stereo on and cranks the newest Kesha song. "You see the video?" she screams over top of the blasting song.

I shake my head, "No."

"Dude, it's like porn."

I frown, "Thanks for the warning." I know I will have to Google it when I get home. If I can get on the computer. If Mary doesn't feel like smacking me around.

Lune laughs and pulls into the driveway of the packed mansion. Every light is on inside making the driveway feel darker. Sam Collins is rich, very rich. His parents' house is massive and they don't care if we party here. They never have cared.

When I get out of the car, the wind rushes me, as if grateful it has caught up to me. I ignore it. Lune has parked against the curb of the long driveway, under a huge tree. The leaves dump, as I take my first few steps towards the house, and flit across the grass. I ignore them; leaves shouldn't fall in the spring and they shouldn't chase me down the road like they're my children.

"We bringing the guitar, Lynnie?" Sarah asks as she rounds the back of the car.

I look at their faces and sigh, "Fine, but only one song."

Lune squeals and pops the trunk.

Sarah grabs it and runs for the front door before I can change my mind.

I glance at Maggie and frown, "You gotta sing back up, k?"

Maggie nods, "Fine. Let's get drunk first though, huh? I hate it when they make you sing."

I grin, "Yup." I don't actually get drunk, but I too hate it when they make me sing. I don't mind the stage but an intimate gathering makes me feel funny, too close to them all maybe, considering they all fear me or hate me, or both.

We walk up to the door Maggie looks up, "You ever notice the way the leaves fall, even in the spring, around yo…."

I turn my face sharply and stick my finger to her lips, "Shhhhhh. Don't say it. Don't acknowledge it."

Her eyes grow wide as she nods and walks through the door. "You get weird sometimes," she mutters.

I whisper and close the door, "I'm normal. It's you all that are crazy—and no—the leaves do not fall when I'm around." The wind hits the door, making it rattle. I ignore it. She turns and notices the way the door is rattling, like a horror movie. When she sees the desperate look on my face, she turns, "Yup, totally normal." She leaves, as if she doesn't see it, and walks into the house.

The party is in full force with dancing going on in the living room and drinking everywhere else. Shots are at the dining room table, so I saunter that way. It looks like Fort

Lauderdale, but it's the sweater version. Coldest June on record, I swear.

"Well, well, look what the devil dragged in. Did you miss me all year, Lynnie?"

I grin at the boy taunting me. "Be nice, Sam." He is always nice, from a distance. I can't help but stare and wish he could be nicer.

He smiles, flashing the dimple in his cheek, "I missed you. It's been a hard year not seeing your face every day. We need to get you a cell phone, for real."

I sigh and wish for a second that things could be different. He runs a hand through his dark-blond hair, giving me a look that makes my stomach instantly ache. Everything about him is taunting me with the one thing I can never have, love. His sparkly blue eyes stare at my lips for the briefest of moments as he points to the shots. "You want one?" He seems so serious and weird.

I sigh and realize I too am staring at his mouth. He is so tanned and stunning. Golden skin, dark-blond hair, bright-blue eyes, and strong nose and jaw line. His football player's body is rock hard. I've seen him in his swimsuit, it's good. He looks like a Calvin model. College has only improved him. His body is even more taut and hard than last year.

I almost moan as I pry my eyes from his chest and sigh again. I drop into the oversized dining room chair and nod, "I can do one shot."

He looks cocky as he sets up seven shot glasses in front of me. He gives me a sideways glance as he pours seven different shots from the bottles in front of him. "How about one round instead? We do need to catch up. Everyone else has had seven." His eyes sparkle with mischief. I want to read more into it than I should, but I remember who he is and who I am. A year hasn't changed anything. He will never be reckless enough to kiss me, let alone date me.

I lick my lips and lift the first glass, "To catching up!"

Everyone in the dining room is watching me, watching the freak. I just want to be one of the normal girls for once. I still feel like the little girl standing in front of the class, listening to the whispers as the teacher introduces me as the new girl. She says my name, Lake, like it's poison. It is, but I was only ten; she didn't have to say it so harsh.

Someone interrupts as I put the glass to my lips, "You shouldn't drink that many shots. It's too many for a small girl."

I don't recognize the voice; it's deep and different and makes the wind rattle the glass in the dining room next to me. His accent is something I have never heard before, except on TV. Maybe West Coast or even European but really faint.

His eyes are the first things I notice when I turn around. They're weird, gray. Gray like the weather in Maine. Stormy maybe. He's tall and lean in a way that makes me think he plays preppy sports like tennis or swimming. He isn't solid and bulky like a football player, like the boys in Maine. They fish, log, and hunt and are brawny. He is posh and trim. My eyes roam his face, noticing the chiseled jaw and soft-looking lips. He's sexy, stuck up maybe, but sexy. The way he leans against the wall, with a cocky grin and his grey eyes challenging me from under his shaggy, light-brown hair, is smug. Smug is the word for everything about him. It's like he hates me even before meeting me. It's not something new for me though.

"Who are you?" I ask.

He ignores my question and continues, "You weigh what, a buck five, maybe ten? You drink those shots and we'll be taking you to the hospital. This is a pretty sad little town, not the place I would want to spend a night in a hospital." He sounds mean the way he speaks, like I am nothing or a child.

Brandon, a huge football player I graduated with, slaps the tall guy on the back. "This is my cuz, Briton. He's here to hang with us for the summer, get to know the family and all.

His parents are away in Africa. Doctors Without Borders. We just met, never even knew about each other."

Briton cocks an eyebrow, "Super excited about it too."

I offer a smug grin back, “You have to stay with your cousin while your parents are away? Aren’t you also nineteen? You can't stay on your own?”

He nods, “I’m in my twenties, and yes,, I can.” He isn’t bothered by the fact I’m mocking him or offers an excuse. I like that, I just don’t know why.

I meet Briton's stare as I lift the first shot to my lips, accepting the challenge in his eyes. I lift it like I’m saying cheers to him and shoot it back. I shiver and swallow, "Yuck. Nice to meet you, Briton."

He shakes his head like he’s unimpressed. I slam back the next shot and smile at the face he’s making.

"Where you from, Briton…not Britain is it? You sound like you have an accent." Lune asks, sitting on the table next to my shot glasses. She drinks one, all the while watching him, "Briton from Britain would be funny."

His eyes narrow, "Hilarious. I'm from, er…Oregon."

She crosses her legs, flashing her bare skin. He glances at her legs, running his eyes down to her silver platforms. His lip twitches. I watch him, feeling a cheeky grin crossing my lips. No one can resist Lune.

She drinks a second shot from my line up and puts a hand out, "Lune."

He frowns, taking her hand, "Lune?"

She grins, "Luanne, but nobody calls me that. This is my girl, Lynnie."

When his gaze meets mine, it doesn’t stray from my eyes. His gaze doesn’t travel beyond mine. "Lynnie and Lune?" His tone is mocking. I don’t think he has any other tone.

I slam back the next shot and let the shiver warm me as I

continue staring at him. The tension is thick but fleeting. It's broken by warm hands touching down on my shoulders. I can feel the heat of them through my sweater, but they are nothing compared to the whispered breath that hits my ears next, "Lune keeps stealing your shots, Lynnie. I'll have to pour you two more." Sam starts to massage my shoulders. The contact is making Briton and me uncomfortable, though why he is bothered is beyond me. His eyes watch Sam's hands with emotion, anger maybe or disgust. It makes me feel dirty either way, like he knows about the curse. Or he just hates me.

Sam never touches me. Guys don't ever touch me, beyond a slap on the shoulder or a light shove.

Ever.

I wonder how pathetic I would look if I closed my eyes and let myself savor the moment, because I know it's innocently done. If I closed my eyes, I could pretend we were somewhere else, and I was someone else. I almost hate that it's Sam touching me. I have missed him more than anyone. I've missed staring at him and being his friend.

Glancing back, I realize I haven't missed setting him up with other girls. That was always the worst—watching him be with girls he could actually touch.

Instead of savoring it, I nod at the glasses Lune just drank from, "Just reuse them. We share everything else." I look back at Briton and grin, "I weigh a buck twenty-five, for the record."

He laughs, "Not a chance."

I shrug.

Sam leans over me and pours more drinks. Lune gets up from the table and brushes past Brandon and Briton, as if it is nonchalantly done, but she has a plan. She looks up through her lashes and smiles as she slides between the two large guys. Her chest presses against Briton's abdomen. He looks lost for a moment. It bugs me she's flirting with him. It bugs me that she can. I don't even know him, nor like him, but I wish I could torture him that way. He looks like he deserves to be tortured, like he's stuffy and smug. I almost wish she would do to him what she does to all boys—love and leave them in a public display that rips their hearts out. I almost wish it, but something about him guts me. I hate that his eyes wander her body and his lip fights a twitching grin.

My agony is interrupted by a voice, "You gonna sing, Lynnie?"

I glance over at Brandon and shrug, "I guess."

He smiles wide, slapping his 'cuz' again, "You're in for a treat. She's our very own star. She sings every Friday, Saturday, and Sunday night at the local bar. She packs the house. Been singing there since we were kids."

"Down boy!" I blush.

He laughs, "I'm surprised you never went to LA or Nashville, or somewhere with a wicked music scene."

I shrug, "I had to work for the year to save up money before I could leave. I don't have parents paying for everything like you guys." I frown at the over share and suck back a shot. It makes me shiver as I breathe through the fumes, glancing back at Sam, "Ouzo? Really?" I can barely talk through the twitching.

He laughs, "Just thought I'd mix it up."

I gag, "Don't do that again. Sick." I shoot the next shot to rid my mouth of the taste.

Briton's gray eyes sparkle like stars, "You really that good?"

I shake my head, "I don't know. It's not exactly like Nashville's music scene here. We don't have a lot going on." I shiver from the drinks.

"You want to drink all of those before you sing?" He sounds like he could be my dad, if I had one.

Sam grips my shoulder, "You seem pretty bothered by her

drinking, dude. You got a problem with her having some fun? Poor Lynnie's been here all year waiting for us to get back." He is touching me again.

Briton's eyes gleam, "I just think drinking to the point of passing out is pretty immature. We aren't high school kids."

I snort, "I don't get drunk, Briton." It's true. I don't. They blame the curse, I blame the practice—we used to drink every weekend.

"She's a beast. She can drink all night. She can out drink every linebacker on the team, including Miles over there who weighs in at 285 pounds." Sam slaps me on the back, like a friend. Because we are friends and never will be anything but, regardless of his touching my shoulders.

Briton folds his arms and watches me. I slam back the last shot in front of me and cough a little. It tastes like death in a glass. My right eye won't open from the shudder that rips through me. I wince when I'm finally able to, "What was in that one?" The group around me laughs. I see Miles make a face from the corner, "He conned me into that one too. Damn dude."

Sam rubs my arms, "That was a rocky mountain bear fucker. It would fuck up a bear."

I shake my head, "So bad."

Sam bends my head back and plants his lips against my forehead, "You are now my hero."

I feel a shiver of heat rush through me. I glance over at him and frown, "How many of those have you had?" He has pressed his lips against my face; he must be more drunk than he seems.

He shakes his head, "I don't do tequila and sambuca together. Yuck."

I swat at him, "That's what you put in there?" When my stomach gurgles, I rub it and frown, "What did you do? My stomach sounds like I've been eating spicy food."

Miles laughs, "I almost threw up, Lynnie."

Sam laughs again.

"You are all kinds of reckless, aren't you?" Briton asks and shoves himself off the wall. He turns away from me and walks into the crowd of people in the living room.

"What?" I shake my head and look at Brandon and speak quietly, "Dude, what's with your cousin? Why does he hate me?" I brace myself for the obvious answer—500 years of killing men left, right and center.

Brandon shakes his head, "He's pissed about being here. Hell, we didn't even know we were family. My dad's brother met some lady and he's her son. They decided to go do Doctors Without Borders and left him with nowhere to live. He just showed up yesterday with a letter for my dad from his brother explaining he was coming. We didn't even know he existed or that my uncle had remarried. The guy's always hated being from Podunk Maine, always been a bit snooty. My dad said he was always like that. So poor Briton's being forced to stay with my family for the summer because he was in residence at Yale and couldn't find a rental in time for the summer. He thought he was going home for the summer to Seattle to work at the hospital with his mom. Nope! They booked Africa or some crap, and then even let one of the doctors from their hospital stay at their house. So then he had nowhere to stay. They kinda just dropped this bomb on him and us. Needless to say, he's not pumped about being here. Dad's excited though, cheap labor for the summer." He winks at me.

I laugh, "He's going to work at the store?"

He nods, "Yeah, not exactly a hospital in Seattle. Dad said maybe he could also work at the school. Ya know, help people with upgrading. Dude's a genius."

I roll my eyes, "Great." I am doing upgrading at the school, in case the music thing doesn't work out.

Brandon shrugs, "He's gonna be a surgeon or something.

He seems pretty straight-laced. He spent the whole morning reading old classic books from the library. You should have seen how excited he got about it. It was a little weird. I think watching you drink alcohol like a drunk is making him leery of us all. He probably thinks we're all drunks now. Thanks, Lynnie." He winks at me again and leaves the dining room.

A giggling brunette comes bouncing into the room and lays across the table, "Pour it in my mouth, Sam."

He flirts with her the same way he did me, rubbing her shoulders. I hate myself for liking him more than I should. I don't look back at him as I leave the room through the opposite door that Briton left through. Sam is a daydream, nothing more. I need to be real about the things in my life.

I weave and snake my way through the crowd. I see Sarah, Maggie, Jenny, and Lune sitting on the couches in the huge living room. I walk through the dancing kids and find a seat with my girls. My eyes never leave Sam. He kisses a girl in the hallway on the lips. She shoves him back playfully. I don't hate her for kissing him. I wish I were her. I wish it were my lips placed against his, pressing into them. Letting him suck my bottom lip the way he did hers.

"Okay yum. Brandon's cuz is hot. Like H.A.W.T," Lune shouts loud enough for him to hear it.

I roll my eyes, "Not my type. He's stuck up. He knows he's hot. Yuck."

She nudges me, "That is a sexy boy. Plus, he goes to Yale. If he isn't your type then no one is your type."

I nod, although it's not true. Sam is my type. He is my secret type. Hard to have a type publicly, when the threat of them dying is lingering over them at all times.

I leave my seat after a few songs, in search of a bathroom. A huge hand grabs mine. I'm pulled into a closet.

"Lynnie, you look really hot today," Sam whispers down on my mouth.

My heart aches. He's so drunk. I have always wished for him to say that very thing to me, but not drunk. His warm face brushes against mine.

"Sam, don't," I push at him.

"Just one kiss. I've missed you so bad," he whispers. His hands roam my back and butt.

I shake my head against his hard chest, "I can't—we can't." I close my eyes and let it feel good for the moment I can afford to give it. I push him off of me and walk from the closet. My hand is grabbed again, "Come on. Time to sing."

Sarah hands me my guitar, beaming. She can't see my aching heart or the pain in my throat where the lump is sitting. Something has changed in my world. My unrequited love might not have always been so unrequited. That was something I let myself have. Sam likes me back, even if it is just a little, and even if he only really shows it when he's drunk. That has to be enough.

I walk with the guitar, more nervous about playing for the intimate gathering of sixty kids in a house, than I was in the rowdy bar. I close my eyes and lower my face. No one talks, in anticipation. It feels weird.

I have a storm of things brewing inside of me.

My fingers start it, they usually do. They stroke the strings a few times. I open my mouth and start to sing. Nothing else matters once I start. My voice scratches through the ballad. Maggie and Sarah sing back up for me. They know I hate singing alone in a house full of people. I don't mind the stage where everything is impersonal.

The song is mine. I wrote it when I was fourteen. I wrote it for the boy who nearly kissed me. Who nearly died to kiss me, if the curse is true? If it's not, he's still more brave than I am.

We sing and I strum until the end of the song. I finish, feeling my cheeks burning. I glance up and catch the stormy eyes of Briton. He glares at me. I can't help but notice his handsome face, even with the evil glare. It isn't something I have seen before. My singing has never made someone glare at me before.

My staring is interrupted by someone shouting at me, "Sing Baylor next."

I clench inside, about to shake my head, but the room starts to chant it, “BAYLOR, BAYLOR!”

They don’t understand that’s the song that makes me sad. I wrote it one night when I was feeling something I couldn’t understand. I wrote the song and my heart hurt, but I didn’t know why. I still don’t. I don’t know a Baylor. I didn’t even know it's a name.

I open my mouth and let the haunting words slip from my lips. It sounds depressing. It’s supposed to. After the haunting solo intro, I start picking at the guitar. The song can bring tears to my eyes, but I won't let it.

I finish and hand Sarah my guitar. She knows I need her to take it.

Everyone claps. The house music starts back up, but it feels small, compared to me singing, like my voice is still ringing off of the walls. I fidget with my fingers and bite my lip. I hate the attention singing gains me, but I love that it's something that makes them all happy. I am one of them.

I slip through the room and let the back pats and gratitude wash over me.

I grab a glass of water in the kitchen, leaning against the counter, staring out the back window. The feel of Sam’s breath on my face is still there. I’m a coward. I should have let him kiss me there in the dark. No one would have known. If he had died, no one would have suspected me. I close my eyes, pushing my horrid desire to take liberties with someone else’s life.

"You are good."

I try not to freeze completely after hearing Briton’s voice. I spin, wiping my mouth, "Thanks."

I put the glass on the counter and walk out of the kitchen. He grabs my arm. It feels weird having someone touch me. The fact it's been happening all night with Sam is odd enough, but Briton is a stranger. I look down at his huge hand wrapped around my arm and frown, "What are you doing?"

"I didn't mean to offend you and call you a drunk or anything." His gray eyes catch my stare again. They hold me hostage.

I watch them and forget what we were talking about. "What?"

He blushes and looks down. His thick lashes cover his eyes, "Before. I wasn't implying you're some kind of small-town drunk or something."

I shake my head. His fingers are burning into my arm, "I'm not." I sputter, "O-o-offended. I'm not."

He grips my arm and his words become a whisper, "I just wouldn't be able to handle something bad happening to you." He speaks like he's in a daze. I don't know why, but I believe him. It doesn't make sense he should care about me, but I can tell he does. It's intense and sincere and creepy, in a way I apparently enjoy. Of course I do. The girl who kills boys with a single kiss would also be a sucker for weird insta-love.

I have no idea what's just happened, but I wonder if the alcohol has gotten to me.

Sam bursts into the kitchen and grabs my other arm. He pulls me. Briton holds on tight for a moment and then lets me go.

"I want to dance with you." Sam kisses the top of my head, pressing his lips into my hair. I look back at Briton and notice the way his jaw is clenched.

Sam grips my hips and rubs his body against mine, making me move with him.

I look up at him, "You're acting weird."

He grins. His smile makes me smile back, "I'm just done,

Lynnie. I'm done with all the nonsense of this small town. I went to Harvard this year and it opened my eyes in a lot of ways. I know what I want now." He's always been the most popular boy in school, and by far, the best looking. I've liked him forever. We have always been friends. I'd even helped fix him up with Lune and Sarah, convincing them how awesome he was. Mostly so I could date him vicariously through them. He's dated everyone but me, and Maggie. I can't help but be suspicious, "What's different? What did you learn?"

He shrugs, "I just have wanted to do this for a long time and I'm done letting this small town tell me I can't."

"Dance?"

He shakes his head, "Be with you. You're almost nineteen, Lynnie. Surely you have to be allowed to live at some point."

My stomach flips and I can't help but beam and work out possibilities in my head, "Why now? In October I'm going to New York, and you're going back to school in Boston. What do you want—a summer fling, Sam? I don't think I'm up for that."

He kisses my cheek, "I don't know. I just want this. I don't want to think about anything else." His lips press their warmth so close to my lips. When he pulls back, his deep-blue eyes search my face. He's beautiful. He smiles, flashing his dimples at me. I could sigh and stare, but I have an odd feeling in my stomach. It's the other side of the possibilities. The things I am known for. The things my family is known for.

I glance over to the darkest corner of the room. A pair of gray eyes watch me. They look torn.

I swallow and look at Lune. She's mouthing things at me like, 'what the hell' and 'OMG'. I'm not great at reading lips but her wide mouth makes it easy. I shake my head subtly, and continue dancing. I can't shake the unsettling conflict inside of me.

I think he can feel me cooling off. He smiles like we are friends again, "You still thinking New York then?" he asks over the music.

I nod, "Yeah. I saved up enough for this year, and when I turn twenty, I'll get the money from my dad. So that should get me through next year. Two years should be long enough to not worry about starving. Plus, I'll work full-time wherever I end up. So the savings will be my in-case money."

He pulls me in close and kisses alongside my mouth again. I know he isn't actually kissing my lips, but it's close. No one has ever been that brave before.

No matter how badly I want to tell him he shouldn't, I don't. I close my eyes and let his skin against mine feel like everything I have been missing. I like the touching and the way he feels all over me. It's different, and after eighteen years, different is exceptional.

I run my hands up into his hair. It's softer than I thought it would be. He cups my ass. My skin is on fire. It feels like when I'm singing, like we're alone and everything is electrically charged.

I look up and smile. He smiles down on my lips, "Can I just kiss you?"

I shake my head, "Aren't you at least a little scared?"

He shakes his head, "I'm more scared of never doing this." His eyes are lit up with passion, staring down on my mouth. It almost feels like he's kissing me. I feel vulnerable and scared just as the wind arrives. It's cold.

It's always cold.

It blows through the room and chills us all. We stop dancing and look over at the two girls struggling with the front door. The wind is trying to get to me. It wants me safe. I take the warning to heart. The reality of it all crashes in on me. I blush and pull away, giving Lune a look. She's at my side in an instant, "We should get going. See ya 'round, Sam." She says it in a singsong voice and drags me away.

I look back at him. He looks confused. He's doing the math in his head. No doubt coming to the obvious conclusion, that I caused the wind.

As Lune drags me out of the party, I catch a glimpse of the gray eyes from the corner. He gives me a look I will never forget. It breaks my heart and makes my stomach cringe all at once, and I don't even know why.

Once we're outside, the wind dies down after about a minute. Lune straightens her hair and glances around, "Spooky, Lynnie."

I give her a grave look, "I didn't make it windy. The door came open."

She laughs, "I know that." She drags me to the car. Sarah and Maggie come running out after us. Sarah has my guitar.

"Where's Jenny?"

Maggie laughs, "She isn't coming."

Lune opens the door, "Slut."

We laugh and try to let it all be nothing.

I look out the window at the dark night as we drive to my place and know it was something.

Maggie mutters, "Briton was hot, huh? But kind of sleazy, I think." I glance back to see her wagging her eyebrows.

I make a face, "What?"

She nods, "You guys must have noticed the way he was eyeing all the girls up."

"I don't know about that. I never saw him doing that." I want to say "to anyone else" but I leave that part out.

Lune nudges me, "What was up with you and Sam?"

I shake my head, "I don't know."

Sarah leans forward, "Did he kiss you as the wind started?"

I roll my eyes, "No. That's stupid."

She shrugs and looks out the window, "You know that's what they're gonna say."

I can't fight the pained expression as it hits my face. "I know."

Lune squeezes my leg, "Don't listen to them, Lynnie. You did nothing wrong."

I turn back around and watch the dark night roll past us.

Maggie squeezes my shoulders through the gap in the door and the seat, "She's right." Her hand on me almost makes me believe it.

It doesn't matter though. It doesn't matter how much I ignore it or how much I pretend it isn't true, I'm a Lake. Everyone knows what that means.

Lune drops me off and I run up the old vine-covered path quickly. I walk through the door quietly and sit my guitar next to the stairs. I put the fifty bucks, I get every week for singing, on the desk.

"What you been at, girl?" The haggard, mean, old voice slips through the dark hallway. "Huh? Where you been?"

I flinch and wait for the pain. I'm tight everywhere. I never know where she'll hit first. The hallway it too dark to see her. I shake my head with a twitch and whisper, "Nowhere. Out with Lune after I made the money."

"You little slut. You're just like your momma." It's like she's stuck on repeat. She only ever says about seven sentences and she's just said five of them. She thinks my mom was evil; she doesn't factor in that her son was the Lake family member and not my mother at all.

Pain hits in my belly first. I double over and heave as her fist hits. I turtle and let her kick me. I close my eyes and wrap my fingers around my head with my chin tucked. Her old boots stomp and kick until she's tired. It never lasts long. I taste my own blood in my mouth. My cheek stings where she's managed to get a boot in. My teeth hurt.

She spits at me. I tremble and let her. I always let her. I deserve every strike. Her and I both know it. That and I have nowhere else to go. My father's will demanded I stay with her until my nineteenth birthday or I wouldn't get my inheritance on my twentieth birthday. That is freedom.

Chapter Two

The dark night has a magical feeling. Even if I don't believe in magic, my face is swollen, and I'm exhausted, the night still feels like magic to me. Once she kicks my ass, my grandmother always goes to bed. She watches TV, infomercials and smokes. I have always wished long and hard for her to fall asleep with the smoke in her mouth and burn the house down. Then I could be free. Even if I were dead, I would be free.

She hated my mother. Mary blamed her for the death of her son. She never thought about the fact that her family was the Lakes and not my mother's at all. The curse doesn't care about who has the Lake blood, only that there is love in a heart. The man always dies, always. Even when he is the Lake.

I sit in the window and wait for the only thing that matters. Nothing matters—not the Lakes or the curses or the pain—just her. I wait for the moment I can sense Rosie. I don't always feel her, but when I do, it's like the noise and pain in the world stands still for her. For us.

The wide window seat is the only place in the world I can still feel her. It isn't like her ghost is there, but maybe a stain. She died in the house and I always prayed she would haunt it—me. She never did though, not properly, but I will take her anyway I can get her. A whisper in the wind on a window seat is better than nothing at all. The whisper happened the first night after she died. I had sat in the window crying for 24 hours straight, when suddenly it was there. A whisper on the wind. The wind that had taunted and provoked me, brought me something amazing. I could smell her in the wind. It only ever happens at night and only when I am my saddest and most desperate.

I gaze at my reflection in the window and notice something, movement down on the street. I frown and squint, willing my eyes to focus that far. A figure stands under a lamppost across the road. It doesn't move, not at first. It stands there, leaning against the lamppost, as if daring me to look out at it or pretending to be part of the lamppost. But I have sat in that window a long time, I know what the shape of the lamppost is.

My heart is racing as I open my window more and lean out into the cool air. The wind is there, but it doesn't smell like Rosie. It's something else.

I almost slam the window shut when the figure walks toward me but, when I recognize him, I'm more worried about hiding my fleece pajamas. When I see the handsome face of Brandon's cousin, I lean forward, still hiding my pajamas. "What are you doing?" I whisper harshly.

He shakes his head and whispers back, "I had a bad feeling. I was falling asleep and then suddenly I saw you. You were crying and hurting, and I had to see you."

I cock an eyebrow, "You're psychic?" I regret asking it right away.

"No, were you screaming and hurting?" He looks confused.

How do I answer that? I shake my head, "I'm fine, so you can go." My stomach's freaking out. Does he have visions, like a preacher? Did he see me getting my ass kicked by the mean old lady who I have four months, three days, and eleven hours left with?

He hops over my fence and stumbles into the yard through the weeds. I accidentally giggle, watching him trip and cuss about the state of the yard. He is making an awful racket. I glance back at the door to my room. If Mary comes in, she'll beat the hell out of me… in front of him. I wave my hands, "Please go."

He jumps onto the porch and climbs with ease to the roof, to where my window is. I gasp and notice how cold the air is suddenly.

I should scream and push him off, I don't even know him. Hell, Brandon doesn't even know him. But something about him makes me feel something new. New is always good.

He climbs right to my window. He grabs the frame of the window and smiles at me. He is forceful and in my space, but I'm not afraid of him. It is like my sanity flew right out the window.

"Hi," he whispers, like he has done something he does every night—like it's no big deal. He looks around, "This is a nice house you have here." His sarcasm is duly noted.

I laugh and cover my face to muffle the noise. I turn and tiptoe to the door and lock it. I slide my chair up against it and under the knob, just in case, and creep back to him.

"You're limping," he notices.

My eyes widen as I struggle with my exhausted brain for an answer, "I twisted my ankle on the way up the stairs." I whisper my lie. I've done it for so long, I don't even know how to tell anyone the truth.

He reaches in the window and grabs my hand, "Your face." He brushes a warm hand against my cheek. I don't even have a response for that. I stand there, frozen. His warm hand against my cheek is the most amazing feeling.

When the shock leaves, I shake my head. My eyes must look dreadful because he shakes his head, "I won't say anything to anyone. Just tell me who."

I glance back at the door nervously, "She doesn't mean it. She's old and scared."

He frowns, "Of what? You're a small girl. Do you fight back?"

I bite my lip and sit on the window seat, “I don’t want to talk about it. Why are you here?”

He’s so close, I can almost taste him in the air. His smell is refreshing and makes my heart swirl and flutter about in my chest. Those stormy grey eyes have me in their clutches. “Do you fight back?”

I sigh, shaking my head and whisper, "I deserve it." I've never told anyone that before.

He looks pained, like he had earlier. He brushes his warm hand across my cheek again, "Never say that again. No one deserves to be hurt by the person who is supposed to protect them." He looks like he regrets saying it instantly. I don’t know what to do or say.

I look down, "She's old and confused. She doesn’t mean it the way you think she does. I don’t really want to talk about it. You shouldn’t be here." My words are hoarse. He’s killing me inside. I can feel too many things all at once.

He tilts my chin. His gray eyes take me hostage again. "I had to see you again. I knew I couldn’t wait until morning."

Heat fills my face, “You don’t even know me.” He gives me a smile like he might say something, but he doesn’t. I swoon almost but then common sense comes rushing in. I cock an eyebrow and pull back.

He tilts his head, "What was that? That face you just made?" He is mocking me, I think.

I cross my arms over my red and white striped fleece pajamas, "What face?"

He points, "The one where you were looking all sweet and then you changed and pulled back, like you were shutting me off. What happened? What were you thinking?"

"That you think because I'm poor white trash that I'm easy. You think I'll let you in the window and make your trip to visit your new cousin exciting."

Amusement crosses his face in a wave starting at his eyes,

"What?" He grins.

"You city boys are all the same." I wave a finger at him.

He crosses his arms too and balances on the roof perfectly, "So that makes you country girls all the same? Pregnant at fifteen and barefoot at home with youngsters?" I laugh at the way he slurs his speech to make an accent. He grabs the window again and shakes his head, "I'm not like that. I would at least buy you dinner first."

I gasp and smack his hand, "Ass." We are flirting and it feels like the most natural thing in the world.

He chuckles. His laugh makes me relax but his words make the butterflies in my stomach dance. “Why do you live with her if she’s mean to you?”

I shake my head, “I have to. She's old, she needs the help. Plus I have to save up money. She doesn’t charge me rent, I live here for free. My father's will says I have to stay with her until the year I am turning nineteen too, or I get nothing."

He grimaces, “Doesn’t sound free to me.”

I want to tell him it’s the only place I can feel Rosie, but I don’t. I just shrug, “I’ll be gone soon enough.” And I will never be back.

“This is weird. Don’t you think it’s weird?” He watches me, speaking after a minute, "You aren’t how I imagined you would be. Normally, I like confident girls who know what they want in the world and care about their instruction. Not artsy girls who like to sing. But there is something about you."

I grin teasingly, "I don’t know what instruction means, but my not being your type is probably a good thing, ‘cause I seriously think Sam just asked me out."

He watches me, waiting for something. "You’re joking, right? The big dumb jock?"

I smile, "Yup and nope. He isn’t dumb. He had a very high GPA. He goes to Harvard."

He looks down and sighs, "You country girls are so predictable. Always going for the big jocks."

I look at his hand, gripping the sill of the window and nod. "I guess we are." It's weird he says that, ‘cause he's big himself, just more lean.

He looks up like he’s trying to attack me with his gray eyes. I frown, "Why are you here, for real?"

He shakes his head, "I don’t know." He says it like he truly doesn’t know. He stands up as if coming out of a daze, "See you tomorrow, Erralynn Lake." He climbs off the roof and jumps onto the grass.

I watch him until I can't see him, and even then, I don’t want to leave the windowsill, terrified I might miss a glimpse of him. I forget about Rosie and just watch the road where he walked away.

I feel like I've been wafted over by fairy dust, like it's all fake. I can’t be this lucky, not now. Not after so many years of unlucky.

The next day as I get ready for work and school, I forget about the many things that usually plague me. I pull out my cutest brown mini skirt, knee-high dark-brown riding boots, and a pale-yellow three-quarter sleeve shirt and a teal scarf. Clothes I bought with the singing tips I hide from Mary.

I step back and look at myself. More dressed up than normal, less small town hopefully. I look hipster and cute. My red hair is smoothed but still wavy. My blue eyes are bluer against the scarf and my skin looks peaches and cream pink, instead of pale. My few freckles that are spattered across my nose don’t look so obvious. They’re always faded in the spring. My summer glow is long gone by winter and I stay pale until summer. I look like her and I know that is what Mary hates the most about me.

I look at the chair against the door and gulp. My makeup is heavier to cover the bruises from the night before. I just hope the one on my cheek isn’t too noticeable.

I try to feel brave but I'm anxious. I want so badly to see him; I have a feeling I would let her do anything to me, just to get to school. Not like the other days when I've hid in my room and wished I'd died that night too. It hardly seems fair Rosie got out and I never. She escaped and I am still trapped. I look at my calendar and nod. Four months, ten days, and twenty-three hours. It isn't so long. I've lived through years. I can do months. Especially with Briton in town and Sam home from school. They are both excellent distractions. I glance back at the window where he had sat and take a deep breath as I pull the chair away. I turn the knob and brace for it. She isn't there. My nerves are on edge.

I peek a head out into the dark hall. I don't smell her smoke. I tremble as I turn the lock on my door before I close it and take my first steps down the hall.

I wait for it.

The suspense is enough to kill me. I gulp as I reach the stairs. Sometimes she likes to surprise me, keep me on my toes. I look behind me. She isn't there. I slip down the stairs and bolt for the door.

My fingers grip the lock.

I almost scream as I rip the door open and fly down the front stairs to the path.

"Have a good day at work, honey," she speaks sweetly. I look over at her watering the weeds in her nightgown. I freeze and wait for a knife to be thrown or for her to turn the hose on me, or instead of water, she douses me in gas and lights a match.

She smiles and waters and I don't know what to do.

"Bye, Mary," I speak softly. I turn and sprint up the road. My feet ache. My boots aren't really running shoes, but I am terrified. I get a block before I can comprehend that she was pretending to be nice to add a little twist for the morning. I nod and add that to the list of things that she is capable of. I assumed she was too old for guile, but I guess not.

It scares me more.

She has shown me who the boss is and who is in control, and it will never be me.

"You look like you've seen a ghost."

I smile, looking up. His voice makes me smile.

Briton is dressed in a light-blue, long-sleeve polo and a thick, navy down vest. I can't help but enjoy the cut of his dark-navy jeans. He's yummy, and somehow even though we aren't each other's type, we're grinning at each other like fools.

"How do you know where I live?" I ask. "I forgot to ask last night."

He leans against the fence he's in front of, "You have no secrets in a town this size, Erralynn." He bites his lip and I imagine it between my teeth. It's an odd image for someone who has never been kissed, but I read a lot. *Black Dagger Brotherhood* is my favorite by far. There is a decent amount of biting in those books.

I realize what he has said and clench my jaw as I walk up to him. He wipes the peeling white flakes of paint from his hand and holds it out, making me frown.

He pulls his hand back when I don't take it. He frowns back, "We just never really got properly introduced."

"I'm cool with it. You know, since you saw me in fleece and all."

He chuckles. "So what's the news on you and jock?"

I shake my head, "No news yet, I haven't seen him since last night."

"He didn't text you?"

I shake my head, I don't want to tell him I have no cell phone. It always makes the people of my generation uncomfortable. Like I am some kind of freak.

"I have a pretty bad feeling about his intentions."

I flash him a grin, "Me too." Excitement is everywhere. I pretend it's all for Sam but it's not.

He watches me like he was searching for something in my face. "Have you ever met someone and wondered everything about them all at once?"

I laugh and am about to lie but I don't. I nod and look down. I can't be forward and look at him.

He turns me around to face him, "You are bewitching me. I am starting to think the rumors are true."

I freeze in my steps and literally wait for the sound of my heart smashing on the cold cement. That had been the thing I liked the most about him. Until the moment we are frozen in, he had seen me and only me. No rumors or stupid curses.

I like being the girl with the guitar, the voice, and the red hair. I hate being the Lake girl who is from the Lake family and suffers from the Lake curse.

He cocks his head, "I was joking."

I shake my head and pull free of him. I take a step back and look down at the broken sidewalk, "It's cool."

"I'm beginning to see that it was a bad joke. I was honestly kidding."

I shrug and try to laugh it off but my eyes are close to welling. I hate that he sees me the way they all do.

He grabs my hands and holds them. "I don't know what happens in small towns, but I know the minute I watched you enter that house, I have thought of nothing but you. I want to touch your red hair, I imagine it feels like copper silk. You have me acting like a stalker, freak show, and I can't help myself. I don't think it's magic or curses. I don't believe in them." He lifts a hand and tilts my face, "It was a bad joke. Brandon told me about the Lake curse. He was making jokes up about it. I didn't know it was something you have actually suffered from. You seemed popular at the party. I assumed no one but the elderly believed it."

My eyes dart, avoiding his. The pity on his face stings in my heart. I pull my hands away and walk past him, "It's no big deal." My voice is soft.

"Please, don't do whatever you're doing."

I shake my head and smile at him, "I'm not doing anything. Really, it's fine."

He frowns, "Your smile hasn't reached your eyes and I can almost feel you pushing me away."

His warmth against me gives me chills but everything feels different. He knows the truth. I should have assumed he would.

Four months and no one will know about it.

"So can we just talk about the whole curse thing for like a minute longer?"

I laugh bitterly and wrap my arms around myself. I have to hold myself together.

"I don't get it."

I look straight ahead and try to let it all be nothing. I speak with a hollow voice and avoid his eyes completely. "What did Brandon tell you?" I ask flatly.

"That your great-grandmother angered her husband and he killed himself and offered his soul up to the devil so he could haunt your family. Every woman in your family who marries or loves a man is cursed and the men all die from some sort of accident."

I nod, "That's about it. She was my great-great-great-grandmother though. She settled here with my great-great-great-grandfather. They were the Lachlan family then. They were given the hundreds of acres surrounding the lake and named it after the family, Lakeland. The story goes something like that."

He whistles, "Sounds spooky." I can hear him mocking me. "So that's it? Every man who loved your grandma would die?"

I nod.

"That's the dumbest thing I have ever heard."

I snort, "Okay. Well, the story has more details than that. When they settled here my grandpa went away to do business and when he came home, my grandma was pregnant. He'd been gone too long for it to be his baby, or so he thought. He couldn't bring himself to murder her or abandon her. Instead, he went to the South and found a woman who did hoodoo—a slave from Africa. He bought her and brought her back to the farm. Grandma had had the baby boy. He couldn't prove it wasn't his kid and Grandma swore it was his baby, so he had to raise it. But he knew it was his best friend's. The man who had stayed on the farm with her while he was away. Grandpa forced the slave to perform a ritual and curse my grandmother's loins, but she was pregnant again already with his child, and no one knew. The curse was so that any man who loved her or slept with her would die tragically. It was his way of guaranteeing that she would be his. She didn't know he did it. The best friend was dead within the year, dropped dead in the field. Heart attack we think."

"Okay, I'll admit it sounds interesting. But coincidence, I would say. No other man died? How can you all be cursed?"

I nod, "Grandpa was dead two years later. My grandmother gave birth to the third child, just after my grandfather died. The slave had made the curse so powerful that when my grandmother's second child, a daughter, got older and she fell in love, her husband was dead within the year. My grandmother and the slave lived out their years on the farm until the next generation took over. Every one of them lost the person they loved. Most were after they gave birth to several children, but some were young when the person they loved most in the world died after just one kiss."

He chuckles, "Okay, adding that to it makes it heavy. Has it happened to recent generations?"

I shrug, "I don't know, I guess. My grandfather had a massive heart attack just after he lost the mansion, leaving Mary alone with her kids. Her son—my father, died in a car accident and my mother killed herself out of desperation."

He nudges me again, "Well, small towns are sad little places where people need to find something to gossip about. They'll find something else."

I glance at him and fight the smirk eating away at my face, "It's been hundreds of years and they haven't, so I'm going to say no. No, they won't. My sad little family will always be the gossip of this crap hole. But it dies with me. I am the last of the Lakes and I will never have a child."

His eyes twinkle and then he laughs and nods exaggeratedly, "I guess so, huh? I am sorry." He leaps in front of me again and grabs my arms, "I swear from this moment on, I won't bring it up or talk about it."

I look into his eyes and watch for his smile to reach them. Apparently, he is serious. I nod, "Okay."

He looks into my eyes with such intensity, I have to look away. He shakes his head like he's coming out of a daydream. "Weird. I just find myself getting so lost when I'm with you," he mutters.

I bite my lip and push past him again, "I can't talk, I have to go to the school. I work in the library and do upgrading in the community college classroom."

He nods, "I know, Brandon told me you were. That's why I'm here. I'm working there too this summer. When school's out I'll be the summer school instructor."

I sigh, "So you're going there now?"

He nods.

"Fine, but I need to hurry. I don't like being late. It isn't like regular school. It's upgrading and they expect us to be on time."

He grabs my hand and makes my skin light on fire where he touches. He walks toward the school, almost dragging me.

He looks back and grins, "You don't think it's weird we feel so close, so suddenly?"

I pull my hand away, leery of him. "I think it's weird."

He reaches over and pulls my backpack off my shoulder, "Let me carry this for you."

I let him. It's heavy and I like being with him. Even if I'm terrified of him.

Heads turn, like they're witnessing a car accident, as we cross the grounds to the school. Everyone knows who I am, from the eighth graders to the seniors and the teachers. He's oblivious to it all.

My hand rubs against the back of his, we are so close. I want him to touch me and hold me, and maybe even kiss me. I think he might be strong enough to live through kissing me and loving me.

Then again, maybe not kiss me, just in case.

I like him too much.

Tara Brown is a Canadian author who writes Fantasy, Science Fiction, Paranormal Romance and Contemporary Romance in New Adult, Young Adult and Adult fiction. She lives in Eastern Canada with her husband, two daughters and pets.

Other Books by Tara Brown

The Devil's Roses

Cursed
Bane
Witch
Hyde
Death

The Born Trilogy

Born
Born to Fight
Reborn

The Light Series

The Light of the World
The Four Horsemen

Imaginations

Imaginations

The Blood Trail Chronicles

Vengeance

Blackwater Witches

Blackwater

The Single Lady Spy Series

The End of Me
The End of Games

Her standalone novels

My Side
The Long Way Home
The Lonely
LOST BOY